*Maggie squeezed ~~her~~ eyes shut
as the horrible truth dawned.*

"Oh, no." She swallowed once, twice, then
opened her eyes and struggled to find her voice.
"Don't tell me you're… You can't possibly
be—" her voice lowered to the merest whisper
"—the other brother? The one who's out of the
country?"

Even as the question tumbled out, she knew. The
same penetrating eyes and thick, dark hair. The
same firm, jutting jaw. And though the face was
twisted into a furious scowl, she could see the
similarity between this man and the two who
had hired her last night.

Those dark eyes were staring daggers through
hers. "I already know who I am and why I'm
here. But what business do you have in my
kitchen, woman?"

The terror evaporated as quickly as it had
begun, leaving in its wake a terrible feeling of
weakness. Maggie was almost giddy with relief.
She hadn't been followed. He wasn't here to see
that she didn't leave here alive.…

Dear Reader,

It's time to go wild with Intimate Moments. First, welcome historical star Ruth Langan back to contemporary times as she begins her new family-oriented trilogy. *The Wildes of Wyoming—Chance* is a slam-bang beginning that will leave you eager for the rest of the books in the miniseries. Then look for *Wild Ways*, the latest in Naomi Horton's WILD HEARTS miniseries. The first book, *Wild Blood*, won a Romance Writers of America RITA Award for this talented author, and this book is every bit as terrific.

Stick around for the rest of our fabulous lineup, too. Merline Lovelace continues MEN OF THE BAR H with *Mistaken Identity*, full of suspense mixed with passion in that special recipe only Merline seems to know. Margaret Watson returns with *Family on the Run*, the story of a sham marriage that awakens surprisingly real emotions. Maggie Price's *On Dangerous Ground* is a MEN IN BLUE title, and this book has a twist that will leave you breathless. Finally, welcome new author Nina Bruhns, whose dream of becoming a writer comes true this month with the publication of her first book, *Catch Me If You Can*.

You won't want to miss a single page of excitement as only Intimate Moments can create it. And, of course, be sure to come back next month, when the passion and adventure continue in Silhouette Intimate Moments, where excitement and romance go hand in hand.

Enjoy!

Leslie J. Wainger
Executive Senior Editor

Please address questions and book requests to:
Silhouette Reader Service
U.S.: 3010 Walden Ave., P.O. Box 1325, Buffalo, NY 14269
Canadian: P.O. Box 609, Fort Erie, Ont. L2A 5X3

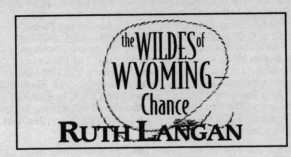

the WILDES of
WYOMING —
Chance
RUTH LANGAN

Silhouette®

INTIMATE™ MOMENTS®

Published by Silhouette Books

America's Publisher of Contemporary Romance

For my own Wild Bunch.
Tom, Jr., this one's for you. With love.

And, of course, for Tom. Always.

 SILHOUETTE BOOKS

ISBN 0-373-07985-0

THE WILDES OF WYOMING—CHANCE

Copyright © 2000 by Ruth Ryan Langan

This edition published by arrangement with Harlequin Books S.A.

® and TM are trademarks of Harlequin Books S.A., used under license. Trademarks indicated with ® are registered in the United States Patent and Trademark Office, the Canadian Trade Marks Office and in other countries.

Visit us at www.romance.net

Printed in U.S.A.

RUTH LANGAN

Award-winning and bestselling author Ruth Langan creates characters that *Affaire de Coeur* has called "so incredibly human, the reader will expect them to come over for tea." Four of Ruth's books have been finalists for the Romance Writers of America's (RWA) RITA Award. Over the years, she has given dozens of print, radio and TV interviews, including *Good Morning America* and *CNN News,* and has been quoted in such diverse publications as *The Wall Street Journal, Cosmopolitan* and *The Detroit Free Press.* Married to her childhood sweetheart, she has raised five children and lives in Michigan, the state where she was born and raised.

IT'S OUR 20th ANNIVERSARY!
We'll be celebrating all year,
continuing with these fabulous titles,
on sale in February 2000.

Special Edition

#1303 Man...Mercenary... Monarch
Joan Elliott Pickart

#1304 Dr. Mom and the Millionaire
Christine Flynn

#1305 Who's That Baby?
Diana Whitney

#1306 Cattleman's Courtship
Lois Faye Dyer

#1307 The Marriage Basket
Sharon De Vita

#1308 Falling for an Older Man
Trisha Alexander

Intimate Moments

#985 The Wildes of Wyoming—Chance
Ruth Langan

#986 Wild Ways
Naomi Horton

#987 Mistaken Identity
Merline Lovelace

#988 Family on the Run
Margaret Watson

#989 On Dangerous Ground
Maggie Price

#990 Catch Me If You Can
Nina Bruhns

Romance

#1426 Waiting for the Wedding
Carla Cassidy

#1427 Bringing Up Babies
Susan Meier

#1428 The Family Diamond
Moyra Tarling

#1429 Simon Says...Marry Me!
Myrna Mackenzie

#1430 The Double Heart Ranch
Leanna Wilson

#1431 If the Ring Fits...
Melissa McClone

Desire

#1273 A Bride for Jackson Powers
Dixie Browning

#1274 Sheikh's Temptation
Alexandra Sellers

#1275 The Daddy Salute
Maureen Child

#1276 Husband for Keeps
Kate Little

#1277 The Magnificent M.D.
Carol Grace

#1278 Jesse Hawk: Brave Father
Sheri WhiteFeather

Prologue

The sweeping grazing lands of Wyoming were ringed by towering mountain ranges already white with snow. The calendar said October, but the razor-sharp bite to the wind made it feel more like the dead of winter. The crowd that had gathered around the open grave huddled inside coats and parkas, hoping Reverend Young would spare them his usual long-winded eulogy and string of prayers, always offered in a monotone. Though their hearts went out to Wes Wilde's three sons, they were eager to return to the warmth of their trucks. Besides, though Wes had made many friends in these parts since his arrival, he'd been a wild man. An outsider. Some said a crazy gambler. And his sons were just like him. The bad boys of Prosperous, Wyoming.

When the last prayer ended, the casket was lowered. The people watched in silence as each of the Wilde boys picked up a handful of dirt and tossed it on the lid of the casket. Then, though a few of the mourners

stayed to whisper a word of comfort or to press a hand
to the boys' shoulders, the others drifted away, leaving
the three to their grief.

Chance, at seventeen, was the oldest. He'd been
working this land with his father since he was big
enough to mend fences and ride herd. He'd learned to
drive heavy equipment as soon as he was tall enough
to see over the steering wheel. Though he was only a
senior in high school, he was already as muscular as
most men.

He was the most like his father. Tough. Hot-
tempered. Some would say bullheaded. A pure gambler.
Willing to risk whatever it took to get what he wanted.
And a fierce competitor. He'd been playing varsity football for his high school since he was a freshman. He
was a natural. Not only because of his size, but because
he enjoyed the brutal physical punishment. There was
nothing he liked better than a good head-banging, bone-
jarring fight.

He'd carried little Prosperous High's football team to
all-state victory, three years in a row. There was talk of
recruiters coming to watch his final year with the hope
of luring him to their colleges.

"Come on." He turned away from the grave, knowing his brothers would follow his lead.

"Where're we going, Chance?" Hazard, at fifteen,
was as tall as his older brother and nearly as muscular.
And though he played on the football team, he didn't
have the same hard-driving, competitive edge. He
wanted to win, but not at any cost. There were some
who thought he'd inherited more of his mother's traits.
Soft-spoken. Gentlemanly. Slow to anger. But he would
only be pushed so far. When his temper exploded, he
was even more dangerous than Chance.

"Home." Chance yanked open the door to the truck and slipped behind the wheel. In almost the same motion he tugged at his tie and unbuttoned the first two buttons of his shirt.

It was the first time he and his brothers had ever worn suits and stiff, new shoes. He'd done so out of respect for his father. Now he couldn't wait to get back into the comfort of jeans and boots.

"What about the ranch? Are we going to be able to keep it?" Ace, the youngest at twelve, crowded between his two brothers in the cab of the truck. Tall and rangy, with arms and legs that seemed too long for his body, he had a quick, easy grin and a reputation as a free spirit. He had once, on a dare from a friend, leaped from the roof of the barn into a moving hay wagon, just to prove that he wasn't afraid.

"What do you mean?" Chance's voice was almost a snarl.

Ace shrugged. "With Dad gone, will it still be our home?"

"You listen to me." Chance's fingers curled around his brother's arm; he was surprised to feel the beginnings of muscle. "Nobody's taking the land away from us. Nobody. You hear me?"

"Yeah. I hear you." Ace pried his brother's fingers loose and gave him a hard punch for good measure. "I just hope the bankers hear you, too."

For that he was forced to endure two quick fists to the shoulder in retaliation.

He got in a couple more licks before Hazard physically moved him over and placed himself between his two ornery brothers until they could cool off.

Ace turned to stare out the window and fought back a trickle of fear. He had caught sight of the ferocious look in his oldest brother's eyes. Like a wolf he'd seen once, cornered by a pack of dogs. Backed into a corner. Fighting for his life.

They drove in silence until they reached the main street of Prosperous. Chance parked in front of the E.Z. Diner and turned off the ignition.

"We'd better stop here and fill up on some of Thelma's chili before we head home." He turned to his brothers. "How much money you got?"

Hazard dug into his pocket and pulled out some bills and change. "Three dollars and seventy-six cents." He handed it over.

Ace counted out a handful of quarters, dimes and nickles. "A buck twenty-five."

"I've got…" Chance reached into his pocket, then froze as his fingers encountered his father's money-clip. He'd forgotten all about it. He pulled the clip from his pocket and stared at it for long silent seconds, feeling an almost overwhelming sense of loss. Then he forced himself to count the money that had been on their father's dresser until two days ago. "Twenty-seven dollars." He shoved it back into his pocket and opened the door. "Come on. We'll eat, then pick up some groceries before heading home."

As the three walked into the diner, every person there turned to watch them. If the girls stared a little too hard and sighed just a bit, the Wilde brothers took no notice as they walked in that loose-limbed, sauntering way to the counter.

"Hey, boys." Thelma Banks set down three glasses of soda before they even settled themselves on the stools. "Sorry about your pa. He was a good man." Thelma was stick-thin, with short, blunt hair dyed the most peculiar shade of purple. She had penciled in half-moon eyebrows, giving her a wide-eyed, questioning look. Her voice, scratchy, tobacco-roughened, sounded like a duck with laryngitis.

"Yeah. Thanks, Thel." The lump that settled in Chance's throat caught him by surprise. He'd have to be more careful. At least for the next few weeks. It wouldn't do to have his brothers see him make a spectacle of himself by allowing his grief to show. "We'll have three bowls of your chili. And some fries."

"Comin' right up, honey." Thelma turned and shouted their order to Slocum, her sometime-cook, who had just returned from his latest stay in the county jail for drunk and disorderly.

"Here you go, boys." Within minutes she set down steaming bowls of chili and a plate of fries before refilling their sodas.

As they wolfed down the food, Chance realized he hadn't eaten in more than two days. Not since he'd found his father slumped over a bale of hay in the barn, fighting for every breath.

The memory slammed into him and he shoved aside the half-emptied bowl.

"What's the matter, honey?" Thelma leaned a hip against the counter. "Too spicy?"

"No. It's fine, Thel. I guess I'm just not as hungry as I thought." Chance watched as Hazard reached over and grabbed the bowl, dumping it into his own, before adding a mountain of crackers.

Ace polished off the last of the fries and downed his drink in one long, noisy swallow.

The high-school football coach ambled over to offer his condolences. Chance kept his features stiff and frozen as he absorbed another round of pain.

"I heard some news that might take the sting out of

this day, Chance.'' The coach turned to include Hazard and Ace. ''A friend of mine covers sports for UPI, and says you're a cinch to win high-school player of the year.'' He slapped Chance on the back. ''You'll have your pick of ivy-league colleges, boy.''

''Thanks, coach.'' Chance avoided his brothers' eyes as he cleared his throat. ''I was going to phone you later. I won't be able to stay on the team. In fact, I won't even make this Friday's game.''

''What?'' The coach blinked, then shook his head. ''I don't think you understand, Chance. This is what every high-school football player dreams of. We're unbeaten this season. A couple more games and you'll be able to call the shots. Every college with an eye on winning a bowl game will be chasing you.''

Chance stood a little taller, meeting the older man's eyes. ''I have a ranch to run now. I won't have time for football.''

''Won't have time for…? What about school?''

Chance shrugged. ''I'm going to try to finish. But I made a promise to my old man. And I mean to keep it.''

The coach seemed about to argue until he caught the fierce look in this young man's eyes.

He nodded. ''I'm sorry, Chance. But I guess I'll just have to understand.''

As he turned away it occurred to him that if he were a gambling man, he'd bet all the money he had on Chance Wilde succeeding at whatever he set his mind on.

Thelma, who'd been listening, paused beside the counter. ''Where're you boys staying tonight?''

Chance's chin came up. ''We're heading home.''

"You got a grandmother or aunt or something, honey?"

Chance shook his head. "Dad didn't have anybody. Just us."

"You planning to stay at the ranch alone?"

"Yeah." His eyes challenged. "We don't need anybody. We'll be fine."

"I know you will. It's just a lot to take on." When he reached into his pocket and withdrew the money, she placed a hand over his to still his movements. "You're not buying, honey. This one's on me."

"I can afford…"

"I know you can. But let me do this. For your pa." Her tone softened. "You boys may not know this, but when I arrived in Prosperous nearly ten years ago, I was alone and scared, and running from a guy who'd been using me for a punching bag. It was your pa who loaned me the money to get a room. He talked old Oscar Stern, who owned this place, into hiring me. And it was your pa who loaned me the money to buy it when Oscar got sick and wanted to go live with his sister." She patted Chance's hand. "Your daddy was the finest man I've ever known. He never asked anything in return for his kindness. That's not something you find every day." She smiled. "And I have no doubt that his sons will grow up to be just like him." She leaned over and kissed his cheek, then did the same to each of his brothers. "Now go on home and take care of each other. And if you ever need anything…anything," she said with a catch in her voice, "you better call old Thelma, or I'll skin you alive. You hear?"

Chance nodded, then turned and stormed out of the diner, with his brothers nearly running to keep up. The minute all three were settled in the truck he took off, the wheels spewing gravel.

"I thought we were stopping for groceries," Ace said as they barrelled out of town.

"I changed my mind."

The grief had caught him by surprise. He'd been doing fine until Thelma had reminded him of just how much they'd lost.

And then, as the truck ate up the miles that separated their ranch from the rest of civilization, Chance Wilde felt another, newer emotion. Fear. In his entire life, he'd never before been afraid. But how was one seventeen-year-old supposed to hold it all together? The ranch. The land. And most of all, the family.

He didn't know. Right now, he was out of answers. But this much he knew. He'd give it all he had.

Hadn't he promised his father?

Chapter 1

"**S**immons." Chance Wilde held the cell phone to his ear as he pushed away from the leather recliner that served as a seat in his private jet. With an economy of movement he strode toward the bedroom in the rear of the plane, shedding his jacket and tie as he did. After two weeks of non-stop negotiations with clients in Saudi Arabia, he'd had his fill of suits and ties. And razors. A quick glance in the mirror showed the stubble of a beard already beginning to darken his chin and cheeks. The years of hard work and struggle had etched craggy lines into his handsome face, giving him a rugged, dangerous appearance.

"How'd it go, Chance?" Avery Simmons was head of the financial department at WildeChem, a division of WildeOil. As always, his voice had a hollow sound because he insisted on using his speakerphone. "Did you clinch the deal?"

"Yeah." Chance tossed his clothes on the king-size

bed and rummaged through the closet for his favorite jeans and shirt. "Most of it."

"So." Simmons paused, and Chance knew he was pouring himself another cup of coffee. The man could run for hours on pure caffeine. "Would you like us to plan a little celebration for your homecoming?"

"Sorry to mislead you." Chance's tone chilled by degrees. "I'm not calling with good news."

At once the voice at the other end sharpened perceptibly. "What's wrong, Chance?"

"I've found a discrepancy in the Miller deal. We won't be signing tomorrow, after all."

"We won't be…?" The silence on the line was ominous. Simmons cleared his throat. "You know I spent months drawing up those documents."

"That's why I'm calling you about this before I notify the others."

"You approved every word of that contract, Chance, after I had it cleared by our legal department."

"That's right. But since then, some of the provisions have been changed."

"Changed? That's impossible."

"Is it? Check page seventeen. And forty-two. You'll find a clause on each page that wasn't there when I approved this deal."

He could hear the rustle of paper and the muttered oath as Simmons found the first error. "I want you to know I didn't approve this, Chance."

"Really? Then who did? Who else handled the Miller account?"

"It was my baby. There may have been a few others who had input, but the final decisions were mine."

"Then the solution is simple. You find the source of the problem, and you have it cleaned up." Chance paused for just a beat. "Or your head will be the one to roll."

Without waiting for a response, he disconnected and tossed the phone on the bed while he changed clothes. Minutes later the pilot's voice came over the intercom.

"We're on our glide path, Mr. Wilde. We should touch down in twenty-five minutes."

"Thanks, Alex." Chance picked up the phone and headed for the main cabin, where he strapped himself into the recliner, then turned to stare broodingly at the land shrouded in darkness far below.

How his father would have loved this. Wes Wilde had known, of course, that the land would one day prove to be valuable. Hadn't he poured his life into it? Hadn't he risked everything to hold on to it? But he'd never dreamed of the hidden riches it would yield. Oil. Natural gas. Coal. Uranium. In the years since his death, the name *Wilde* had become a legend. Not just among ranchers, who considered the Double W to be some of the finest grazing lands in all of Wyoming. There was so much more to the Wilde empire than cattle. They now had corporate offices in Cheyenne, with representatives in Dallas and New York. Overseas, their representatives had offices in London, Paris and Rome.

As their holdings grew and diversified, each of the brothers had taken charge of that part of the company that most interested him.

The youngest, Ace, now a charming ladies' man, liked nothing better than a game of cards, a roll of the dice and a tumble with a pretty woman. It was only natural that he was especially suited to be head of WildeMining. He considered speculating for gas, coal and uranium nothing more than a toss of the dice, only for bigger stakes.

Hazard was now a veterinarian, whose love, as always, was the land. Since he was more at home with animals than people, it was only natural that his brothers had left the operation of the vast ranch, its lands and herds and cattle empire, to his capable care.

Chance was still the toughest. The leader of the pack. He had mellowed enough to parlay his father's legacy into one of the area's most successful conglomerates. Like his brothers, he had an interest in all areas of the Wilde dynasty. But it was the oil company, WildeOil, that owned his heart. And he ran it with an iron fist.

Chance's next call was to his secretary in Cheyenne.

"Carol Ann?" He paused. "Thanks. Yeah. It's good to be heading home. I won't be coming in tomorrow morning. The Miller signing is postponed. Let everyone involved know about the change in plans." He listened. Nodded. "Yeah. I plan to take the copter in tomorrow afternoon. Fax me those documents. I'll look them over on the flight in."

He rang off, then, on a whim, punched in a series of numbers. When he heard a voice on the other end he said, "Cody, bring my truck out to the landing strip. And throw in my rifle and parka. Oh, and have Martin follow you out with the limousine. He can bring you and the pilot and crew back to the ranch."

As soon as the jet landed and the door was opened, Chance stepped from the plane. A short distance away a truck and a limousine sat idling alongside the runway.

When the drivers spotted Chance, they both stepped out to greet him.

The driver of the limousine touched a hand to his cap. "Welcome home, Mr. Wilde."

"Thanks, Martin."

A leather-skinned cowboy with a thatch of white hair

stood beside the truck. ''Your old parka and rifle are right behind the seat.''

''Thanks, Cody.''

The two men shook hands. Chance slid behind the wheel and drove off, making a wide arc, before heading into the hills.

''Must have something big on his mind,'' the cowboy remarked to the formally dressed limousine driver. ''Anytime Chance Wilde has a problem, he does one of two things. He either solves it immediately, in which case there're just a small amount of casualties. Say, the size of a Texas massacre. Or he drives up into the hills to ponder, just like his daddy used to. And believe me, by the time he comes down from those hills, he'll be meaner'n a wounded grizzly. And the fallout could be more like World War Three.''

Chance sat on the big, flat rock, leaning back on his elbows so he could see the stars, high above the peaks of the Bighorn Mountains. He never tired of looking at them. Especially here. This had been his special place, where he'd often come to spend the night with his father. Even after all these years he could see his father's face so clearly, and hear his voice sharing his philosophy with his first-born.

I've been a gambler all my life, son. It wasn't so much the winning or losing. It was just the thrill of the game. Until I won this. And I just knew this was different. Special. Take a look at this land, son. It's all ours. As far as the eye can see. If we treat it with respect, it'll give us everything we've ever dreamed of.

But I've learned from experience that there are a million ways a man can lose everything. The simplest way is still the one that catches most men by surprise. It's greed and jealousy. Don't ever want more than you're willing to work for. And don't ever forget that other men will covet your treasure. They'll try to steal it, by whatever means possible. So look over your shoulder. Mistrust any deal that sounds too good. Read every paper twice. Dot the i's and cross the t's. And then do it again. I know I didn't always live by the rules. I risked everything for this land, so I could live the life I'd always wanted. This is your legacy, Chance. Yours and your brothers'. Take good care of it, son.

Chance leaned his back against the rough stone and stretched out his legs. The rifle rested on the rock beside him. In his mind he went over the words in the Miller contract that had snagged his attention. The addition of those few words had changed the meaning entirely. It was possible, of course, that both the legal and financial departments had slipped up on the contract. But not very likely. What seemed more logical was that someone had included those words after the contract had been approved.

But who?

Simmons gave final approval. He was the last to read the documents before they went to signature. It would be a foolish mistake on his part to make such a blatant error, for he stood to lose everything when it came to light.

Avery Simmons had been with them for ten years. In that time there had never been a single blot on his record. All the more reason why Avery was now suspect. If anyone wanted to do damage to WildeOil, the man to get to would be Simmons.

Did he have a weakness that an enemy could use against him? A dirty little secret in his past? Or maybe just a fondness for money? How much would it take to buy his cooperation?

The changes had almost slipped through without detection. With so much on his mind, Chance had almost let it get past him, trusting that his people had taken the necessary care of the document.

Read every paper twice. Dot the i's and cross the t's.

Chance realized that it was his father's admonition that had saved them. If he hadn't decided to read the documents once more on his flight home, the contract would have been signed in the morning. And WildeOil would have been bound by its terms. The mistake would have cost them millions.

Chance closed his eyes and listened to the sound of the wind whispering among the pines. Though he looked for all the world like a man at rest, in truth, his mind was mulling over every possible solution to the problem. And just below the calm surface, his temper was simmering.

Maggie Fuller awoke with a start and struggled to sit up. Passing a hand over her face she waited for the feeling of panic to pass.

She'd had the nightmare again. She'd been back home in Chicago. A shadowy figure was chasing her between buildings, down an alley. Suddenly she found herself trapped. No way to escape. And the figure kept coming closer, closer. In his hand was a gun. He lifted it, took aim, fired. And then, as always, before the bullet could reach her, she awoke. Cold. Trembling. Her heart racing. Her breathing ragged. And the beginning of another headache just behind her eyes. The headaches were something new. Just one more thing to deal with, in a life that had once been as normal as apple pie. A life that had suddenly begun a long, frightening slide out of control.

She glanced at the bedside clock. Nearly four. Not a civilized time to be up, but she couldn't face going back to sleep and dealing with the night terror.

She took a long shower, letting the spray of hot water soothe her. She toweled her hair dry, then rummaged through her duffel until she located clean clothes. She dressed quickly in a pair of jeans and a knit T-shirt before leaving the suite of rooms to explore the kitchen of the Double W.

Oh, this was even better than she'd expected, she thought as she snapped on lights. There hadn't been time last night to really see it. She'd been so exhausted, both mentally and physically, she'd nearly collapsed into bed. But now she stared around with a sigh of appreciation.

The house, from what Ace and Hazard Wilde had told her the night before, was a sprawling, three-story building, with separate suites of offices to accommodate the three brothers who occupied it. Those rooms and the men who lived here held no interest for Maggie. But this kitchen was to be her domain. If anything could get her mind off her troubles, it was working in the kitchen. Especially one as well-equipped as this.

There were two ovens and a microwave, four ceramic stovetop burners, plus a grill and a rotisserie. The re-frigerator and freezer stood side-by-side and were fully stocked. Many restaurants couldn't boast the food and equipment she was discovering as she opened doors and cupboards.

She squeezed orange juice and used it to wash down two aspirin, before lining up several glasses of juice on the countertop. Then she filled an automatic coffee-

maker with water and began to grind the beans. Soon
the air was rich with the aroma of freshly made coffee.

"So. You're the new cook. I thought I heard somebody moving around in here."

At the soft, little-girl voice, Maggie whirled. In the
doorway stood a woman in a shapeless gray dress. She
was barely five feet tall and nearly as wide. Two fat
braids fell across her shoulders. Her face bore the wrin-
kles of age, but her eyes were as sharp, as alert, as any
child's.

"Hi. My name's Maggie Fuller. You must be Agnes.
I'm told you're the housekeeper here."

"That's right. Agnes Tallfeather." The old woman
looked her up and down. "You're up early."

"I couldn't sleep." Maggie tried a smile, hoping the
woman would return it. "I guess I'm excited about the
new job."

"Where'd they find you?"

"I was working at the E.Z.Diner."

"Huh. Another one." It was obvious that Agnes had
already dismissed her. She sniffed the air. "I see you
made coffee. No need to waste your time. I make an
individual pot in each of their offices. As for the juice,
don't bother. They don't drink it. The same goes for
breakfast. They're usually too busy. Got appointments,
phone calls, visitors. Big important businessmen. They
take their meals on the run."

"I see." Maggie turned away. "Well, since they
hired me to cook, that's what I intend to do. Even if
they don't want to bother eating what I fix."

The old woman shrugged. "Suit yourself." She
tucked a basket of laundry under her arm and waddled
toward the opposite doorway. "Just so you clean up

after yourself. I got all I can do cleaning up after my men.''

Maggie noted the proprietary way she'd called them "my men." She shrugged. Not her business. She didn't want Agnes Tallfeather's men. She just wanted to stay as busy as possible to keep from thinking.

While she sipped her coffee, Maggie began to whip up biscuit batter. That done, she rummaged through the freezer until she located a package marked Steaks. When she unwrapped them she realized these weren't the thin breakfast variety, but thick slabs of beef. All the better, she thought with a smile. Hadn't the Wilde brothers told her that, when they had time, they had hearty appetites?

The Wilde brothers. She paused, staring around as though she still couldn't believe her good fortune.

Two weeks ago she'd caught a bus out of Chicago with nothing but the clothes on her back. When the ride had ended in Prosperous, Wyoming, she'd taken refuge in the E.Z.Diner, not knowing where she'd even spend the night. But when she'd overheard the owner, Thelma Banks, complaining about losing her cook to a two-week jail term, Maggie had swallowed her pride and her fear and volunteered for the job. Thelma had hired her on the spot and had even allowed her to sleep in a small storage room in the back of the diner.

In the next two weeks, Maggie had repaid Thelma's kindness by turning her little diner into the most talked-about spot in town. The people of Prosperous stood in line for Maggie's stew, her pot roast and her mouth-watering biscuits. When Thelma had asked where she'd learned to cook like that, Maggie had managed to evade the question. It wouldn't do to admit that she'd once owned one of the hottest restaurants in Chicago. Right now, the less known about her, the better.

She shook her head, dispelling the little sliver of fear that inched along her spine. Right now it was enough that that little job in Prosperous had landed her a chance to cook at the Double W Ranch. Ace and Hazard Wilde had tasted her herb-and-spice-roasted beef tenderloin and, learning that Thelma's regular cook was ready to come back to work, asked if she'd like to cook for them. According to Thelma, the Wildes could never keep a cook for more than a couple of weeks. Mainly because of the isolation. The Double W was many miles from its nearest neighbor. A fact that suited Maggie perfectly. To her way of thinking, the more isolation, the better.

Another reason the Wildes couldn't keep a cook, according to Thelma, was because of the temperaments of the Wilde men. They were known around Prosperous as hot-headed, demanding cowboys, who didn't care about cost, as long as they could satisfy their appetites. Though most often they ate alone, they had been known to fly in half a dozen business executives without notice when it suited them. Then there were the ranch hands. Dozens of them, according to Thelma. Men mostly, though some had wives and children. Scattered in ranches or bunkhouses over thousands of acres of the Double W. And though they rarely left their own sections, they were sometimes called upon to visit the main ranch and report to their bosses with any questions or problems. When they arrived, they had to be fed.

None of that bothered Maggie. She didn't care how many people she had to feed, or how plain or exotic their tastes, as long as the job afforded her enough privacy to hide and lick her wounds. She just hoped their tastes didn't run strictly to chili and overdone burgers.

With the biscuits baking and the steaks thawing, Maggie began assembling the ingredients for an omelette. She chopped mushrooms, onions, green peppers. She grated cheese, then set aside the mixture while she diced potatoes. And while she worked she found herself mulling this latest change in her life. It had been a shock to step off that bus from Chicago. The first thing she'd noticed was the silence. No buses spewing dust and fumes. No teeming masses of people along the streets. And the *size* of everything in Wyoming. Vast stretches of open land. Highways that seemed to go on forever, without a single vehicle in either direction. Towering mountain ranges. Sweeping vistas of breathtaking countryside. And more cattle than people.

Thelma had warned her that the Double W was the largest privately owned tract of land in the state. Hundreds of thousands of acres, stretching as far as the eye could see. From what Maggie had seen so far, she was beginning to think she'd made a wise choice. For a while, at least, she had found a very peaceful haven.

She was humming while she searched the cupboards for jams and jellies. She managed to find six varieties, including wild strawberry. She gathered all six jars into her arms and was just turning toward the counter when the kitchen door was thrown open. In the shadows, the figure of a man filled the doorway—a tall, bearded man, carrying a large, deadly rifle.

For an instant Maggie froze. The only thing she could focus on was the gun in his hand. It was her nightmare revisited.

"Oh, no. No. No." As she backed away the jars fell from her grasp, crashing to the floor, spilling rivers of grape, raspberry and orange across the scarred wood floor.

For a moment she merely gaped, as did the man. Then, with a look that shifted from surprise to fury, he lunged forward.

Maggie's first thought had been to turn and race to the safety of her room. But now, having wasted precious seconds, she knew she had but one choice.

Reflexively she snatched up a knife from the counter and sprang. The man's hand holding the rifle swept in a wide arc, knocking the knife from her grasp. Both of their weapons clattered to the floor. She bent to retrieve them, but before she could make her move the man caught her and shoved her roughly against the wall. For a moment all the breath was knocked out of her. As she struggled for air, his hands grasped her shoulders, pinning her firmly against the length of him.

The hands at her shoulders were so strong she feared he would snap her bones like twigs. But instead of the physical assault she expected, he gave her a violent shake and let loose with a string of furious oaths.

For a moment panic rendered her speechless. Then, feigning courage she didn't feel, she lifted her chin and stared into those cold, dark eyes. "Go ahead," she whispered, over a throat clogged with fear. "But you'll have to kill me to keep me from telling what I know."

"What I want to know is—" his hot breath stung her cheeks, and his hands moved lower, to grasp the flesh of her upper arms "—who you are and what the hell you're doing in my kitchen."

"Your…?" Her mouth opened, then closed. "Your kitchen?" She squeezed her eyes shut as the horrible truth dawned. "Oh, no."

She swallowed once, twice, then opened her eyes and struggled to find her voice. "Don't tell me you're…you can't possibly be—" her voice lowered to the merest whisper "—the other brother? The one who's out of the country?"

Even as the question tumbled out, she knew. The same penetrating eyes and thick, dark hair. The same firm, jutting jaw. And though the face was twisted into an angry scowl, she could see the similarity between this man and the two who had hired her last night.

Those dark eyes were staring daggers through hers. "I already know who I am and why I'm here. But what business do you have in my kitchen, woman? Stealing my food? Attacking me with my own knife?"

"I wasn't stealing…I saw your gun…" The terror evaporated as quickly as it had begun, leaving in its wake a terrible feeling of weakness. Maggie was almost giddy with relief. She hadn't been followed. He wasn't here to see that she didn't leave here alive.

A trembling began in her legs. She knew if it weren't for the rough hands pinning her, she would surely sink to her knees.

"Chance." Hazard's voice came from the doorway. "What's all the commotion?"

Ace, still more asleep than awake, rushed up beside him. "Hey, bro. Looks like you've found a unique way to introduce yourself."

Ace and Hazard had barely taken time for anything as unimportant as covering their nakedness. Both men were barefoot, wearing nothing more than faded denims still unsnapped at the waist.

"I'll bet Maggie never forgets you," Ace said with a laugh.

"Maggie? What the…?" The man holding her looked from his brothers to the woman, then took a step back and lowered his hands to his sides.

At once she leaned stiffly against the wall and prayed she wouldn't embarrass herself by collapsing.

"Will somebody tell me what's going on here?" came her attacker's angry voice.

"Sorry, Chance. You weren't here last night when we got back."

"I was up on Tower Ridge. Been up there all night. Ever since the jet got back from Saudi. I just drove down at daybreak."

He bent and picked up his rifle. Out of the corner of his eye he saw the woman flinch. It gave him a perverse sense of satisfaction.

"Who is she?" He pointed the hand holding the gun and saw her flinch again. "And what's she doing here?"

"Chance, this is Maggie Fuller. Our new cook. We hired her last night."

"Is that so?" Instead of acknowledging the introduction, he turned his back on her and said to his brothers, "Well, you can fire her this morning."

Ace started forward. "Hey, you're the one who's been complaining the loudest about the swill we've been eating lately."

Hazard wisely caught his arm and held him back, knowing how easily an argument could turn into a brawl. Even after all these years, there was nothing the three Wilde brothers liked better than a good fight. Sometimes a minor discussion about favorite football teams or a suspected change in the weather, could bring on a fistfight that wouldn't end until the three were bloodied and breathless. Though it was a satisfying way to settle their disputes, and had been since they were kids, it didn't seem a good idea to initiate Maggie into that rite so early in the day. Especially since she'd already had a taste of Chance's temper.

"Your new cook," Chance said with unconcealed sarcasm, "attacked me with a butcher knife. If my reflexes were a little slower, we wouldn't be having this conversation right now. She'd have it buried in my chest and you'd be planning my funeral."

Maggie didn't know what to expect next. Most probably a united front. The three brothers demanding an apology. And then an abrupt dismissal.

Instead, after a moment's silence, there was an explosion of laughter.

Laughter?

Ace and Hazard threw their heads back and roared. They laughed so hard, they finally flung their arms around each other, slapping each other's backs as they continued chuckling. And all the while their older brother stared at them with a look of silent fury.

Finally they sauntered across the room and began punching him in the shoulder, slapping him on the back.

"Son of a..." Ace glanced at Maggie, then muttered, "Son of a gun, if that isn't the funniest thing I've heard in a year." He was actually wiping tears from his eyes.

"You should see your face, big brother." Hazard punched Chance's arm again. "Oh, I'd pay a month's salary to have a video of your reaction when Maggie came at you with that knife."

"Yeah. It was a riot." Chance was still seething with fury.

"She'll make it up to you," Ace said when he could find his voice. His lips curved in a grin. "Wait 'til you taste her cooking. You'll forget all about this first meeting."

"As a matter of fact," Hazard said, sniffing the air.

"I think she's already started cooking. Is there something in the oven, Maggie?"

"Oven?" Dazed, Maggie lifted her head. Then gave a shriek of dismay. "Oh, no! My biscuits."

She raced to the oven and opened the door. A cloud of black smoke billowed. It took her several moments to locate oven mitts. Pulling them on, she removed a pan of charcoal. The smoke continued to fill the room until she had the presence of mind to slam the oven door. By then, their eyes were burning, and Ace hurried to open the doors and windows to clear the smoke.

Maggie tossed the pan of burned biscuits in the sink and turned to see Chance stalking away, Ace trailing behind.

When his brothers were gone, Hazard said softly, "I'm really sorry, Maggie. But my brother's bark is worse than his bite. After he takes time to cool down, he'll get over this."

"You must be kidding. Would you get over being attacked in your own home?"

He merely shrugged and muttered, "I'm telling you, if you'll just be patient, it'll all blow over in a day or two."

With a muffled rumble of laughter and a shake of his head, he strolled away.

Maggie looked up to see Agnes in the doorway. On the old woman's face was a look of unconcealed disgust.

"I hope you don't think I'm cleaning up that mess." She turned on her heel and was gone.

Maggie set about picking up the shards of broken glass. But after only a few minutes she sank down on the floor. Overcome with a sense of weariness, she leaned her head back against the cool wall. Well, Maggie, you did it this time, she thought, fighting tears. It wasn't exactly the homey scene she'd envisioned when the morning had begun. This new life of yours has certainly started with a bang.

Chapter 2

"You still here?"

At the sound of Chance's voice, Maggie stiffened her spine. She'd had an hour to clean up the sticky mess. An hour to calm herself down and figure out just how she was going to deal with this angry man. She'd decided that her best course of action was to admit defeat. There was no way to salvage a working relationship after that little fiasco. She was resigned to moving on and seeking employment elsewhere.

From what Thelma had told her, the three brothers were equal partners in Wilde Enterprises. But of the three, Chance was the unspoken leader. She doubted the other two would argue with him if he wanted her gone. And from the tone of his voice, his feelings hadn't magically changed in the last hour.

She stayed where she was, stirring something on the stove. "I figure the least I can do is serve you a good meal before I leave."

She turned and had to catch herself before her jaw dropped. He'd showered and changed. The dark stubble of beard was gone, revealing a face that was almost too handsome to believe. A strong, firm jaw that only proved her earlier opinion of him. Stubborn. Mysterious eyes the color of smoke. They probably served him well in business, to hide what he was thinking. Thick dark hair still glistening with drops of water. A body that was impossibly hard and muscled, looking like a Madison Avenue ad in tight jeans and a faded shirt.

"You figure a little food will change my mind?" His smile was quick. Dangerous. Causing a ripple of unease along her spine.

"No. But it'll be payment for the room I enjoyed last night." She turned away to remove the steaks from the broiler. "I like to pay my debts."

"You could have saved yourself the trouble. I never bother with breakfast."

"That's a shame." She fiddled with the oven temperature. "You're going to miss something special."

Ace, looking incredibly boyish and rugged in worn denims and a plaid shirt, paused in the doorway of the big kitchen, breathing deeply. "Something smells terrific."

Maggie looked up. Her smile was back. It was easy to smile at this charmer. "I didn't know what you liked, so I'm fixing steak and eggs."

"I think I've just decided I have time for breakfast." Ace sauntered across the room and poured himself a cup of coffee just as Hazard let himself in on a rush of frigid air. He was trailed by a thin, wiry cowboy who whipped off his wide-brimmed hat the moment he caught sight of Maggie.

"I'll have some of that." Hazard rubbed his hands together for warmth. "And so will Cody."

He turned to the cowboy. "Cody Bridger, meet Maggie Fuller. Maggie, Cody's giving me a hand with my chores this morning. So if you don't mind, he's joining us for breakfast."

"I don't mind a bit. I'm happy to have somebody who wants to eat what I'm fixing, since your oldest brother just informed me he never takes time for breakfast. Hello, Cody."

The old man bowed in a courtly fashion. "How do, Maggie Fuller."

Ace poured another cup and handed it to the cowboy, who sipped, then sighed with pure pleasure. It was rich, freshly ground.

"Maggie Fuller, this may be the best cup of coffee I've ever tasted."

Across the room Chance frowned. It was pathetic, watching grown men making fools of themselves over a pretty face. And it was a pretty face, he decided. Small, heart-shaped, with high cheekbones and the most intriguing lips. Her eyes were dark, ringed by the thickest lashes he'd ever seen. Her hair was cut short. A simple cap of dark curls that kissed her cheeks. Despite her attempt at simplicity, there was a sophisticated look about her. A big-city look that the jeans and T-shirt couldn't camouflage. This was a woman who would look perfectly at home wearing something sleek and sexy that clung to every curve of that slender body.

"What did you do to this coffee?" Hazard asked as he took a long drink. "Do you grind your own beans?"

"Uh-huh." Maggie nudged the oven shut with her hip and balanced a platter of steaks.

From where he sat, Chance studied that hip, the way

it sloped just so in the denims, then upward, to the tiny waist, then higher still, to the swell of her breasts straining against the fabric of her shirt. There was no denying it. Maggie Fuller was a whole lot easier to look at than their last cook. Of course, Ora Mae Prinder had been a couple hundred pounds heavier than this one and about forty years older. She'd lasted all of two days when it was discovered that the only things she knew how to make were greasy burgers and burned hash browns. That was something the three Wilde brothers could make on their own. And had, for many years when times were lean.

"Will Agnes be joining you for breakfast?"

Ace shook his head. "Agnes is out in the bunkhouse. Besides keeping house for us, she cooks for our wranglers."

"Why doesn't she cook for you as well?"

When the others didn't answer, Cody cleared his throat and said diplomatically, "Cowboys are notorious for eating just about anything. Some cowboys, that is."

Maggie turned away with a smile and retrieved the platter of steaks, which she placed on the table. Then she folded omelettes onto three plates and carried them across the room.

Chance took a look at the food, and at the wolfish way his brothers were eyeing it, and cleared his throat. "I guess I may as well stick around and find out just why my brothers hired you."

Without a word Maggie filled another plate and carried it toward him. As she set it down, Chance caught a whiff of her perfume. Something light and floral, like a meadow in springtime. It suited her.

He watched as Maggie walked away to fetch a basket of toast. "How about you? Aren't you eating with us?"

"I'm not hungry." She handed the basket to Ace with a grin. "No biscuits, I'm afraid. They were so badly burned, I don't think even the birds would eat them. You'll have to make do with this."

Relieved that she was able to laugh at the morning's disaster, Ace helped himself to several pieces before passing the basket to Hazard.

Maggie retrieved the coffeepot and topped off their cups before filling one for herself. Then she sat down and watched as the four men dug into their food.

For several minutes no one said a word. Maggie glanced around, trying to read the expressions on their faces. The three brothers wore identical looks of concentration. The old cowboy merely grinned.

Finally Ace looked up. "What did you do to these steaks?"

"Just marinated them."

"In what?"

She shrugged. "Some stuff."

"Stuff?" Chance lifted his cup and drank, then realized that Hazard hadn't exaggerated. After years of drinking the mud Agnes passed off as coffee, this was incredible. The best coffee he'd ever tasted. In fact, this was the best breakfast he could ever recall. He studied her over the rim of his cup.

Cody, who was thoroughly enjoying himself, managed to pause long enough to ask, "Where'd you learn to cook like this, Maggie?"

"From my grandmother. After my mother died, she came to keep house for us. I loved cooking alongside her."

"Where'd you work before you came here?"

She stared down into her cup. "A little restaurant in Chicago."

Chance pinned her with a look. "Why'd you leave?"

She'd had all night to think about what she would say, but now that the time had come, she found herself avoiding his eyes. Lying didn't come easily. "They didn't appreciate my talent."

"And so you just turned your back on Chicago and thought you'd take a chance on someplace new. Like…oh, maybe Wyoming."

Though she resented the sarcasm, she managed to say, "Yeah. Something like that."

He kept his tone deliberately bland. "It's a long way from Chicago to Prosperous, Wyoming."

She lifted her head. Forced herself to look at him. "Maybe that's why I did it. Just to see how far I could go."

Ace and Hazard looked from Maggie to Chance. Though each of them had pleaded her case in the privacy of their brother's bedroom, they were leaving the final decision to Chance.

As for Cody, he figured, with all the fireworks about to explode around the table, he'd just watch and listen. And enjoy the show.

Chance frowned. "Did you bring references from that little restaurant in Chicago?"

"No. They weren't happy when I told them I was leaving. I figured my talent was all the reference I needed."

"No references." Chance stared holes through her. "I'll remind you that you attacked me with a butcher knife this morning. For all I know, you could be an ax murderer."

"And you walked in carrying a rifle. For all I know, you could be a mad gunman."

Across the table, Ace cleared his throat to keep from

laughing. He could see his older brother's temper beginning to simmer. But it was refreshing to find someone who could hold her own against that famous Wilde fury.

Seeing the silly grins on his brothers' faces, Chance's tone sharpened. "There's a big difference between carrying a rifle in Chicago and carrying one on a ranch in Wyoming."

"Maybe. But when a woman feels threatened, there's no difference at all. I'd put up the same kind of fight whether I was in Chicago or Prosperous."

Cody decided to put his two cents in. "Sounds like you two got off to a shaky start this morning. What'd I miss?"

"Nothing." Chance continued staring at the woman across the table as he mulled over his options. He couldn't remember the last time he'd tasted food this good. He'd hate to fire a talented cook because of a single incident. Maybe there'd be no harm in keeping her around for a little while longer. Still, he knew a woman on the run when he saw one. And this woman was definitely running scared.

Finally he muttered, "Okay. Maybe this morning wasn't the most auspicious beginning for an employee—employer relationship. I'm willing to start over if you are."

Maggie ducked her head, but not before he saw her eyes go wide with surprise. All she said was, "I don't mind if you don't."

"Good. Let's say we give it a two-week trial. Then we'll decide where we want to go from there." He stuck out his hand. "Deal?"

Her head was reeling. That was all there was to it? Is this how the Wilde brothers did business?

"Deal." She had no choice but to accept his hand-shake. But the moment his fingers closed around hers, she felt the jolt. She pulled her hand away quickly and pushed herself from the table.

"Well." Her throat had suddenly gone dry. "Who'd like seconds?"

"Not me." Hazard shoved away from the table. "Not that I didn't enjoy every bit of it. But if I ate any more, you'd have to roll me out of here. Besides, I have a herd to see to. But I'll be here for dinner."

Though the old cowboy looked as though he'd gladly stay and have seconds, he had no choice but to follow Hazard. At the door he grabbed his hat from a hook and held it to his chest.

"That was just the best, Maggie. I think I could even ride a couple of our meanest bulls after that breakfast. Thanks, ma'am."

She had to smile at his gentlemanly demeanor. "You're welcome, Cody. Anytime."

"I couldn't eat another bite either." Ace followed suit and headed toward the door. He turned. "I wasn't planning on coming home tonight. But now that I know you'll be cooking, Maggie, you can count on seeing me here, too."

Maggie was relieved when they exited the kitchen. But when she realized that Chance had remained behind, she felt a ripple of unease. He wasn't through with her yet, it appeared.

He remained at the table, sipping his coffee, watching as she moved from the stove to the sink and started running the water. There was no denying what he'd felt when their hands had met. A jolt clear to his toes. It had been a long time since he'd felt that much electricity at the mere touch of a woman. Maybe that was why he'd decided so quickly to keep her here. Or maybe it was simply that her talent in the kitchen was hard to ignore. He hadn't enjoyed a meal this much in a long time.

Still, he wasn't about to ignore the uneasy feeling he had about her. There was a lot more going on here than she let on.

"What're you hiding, Maggie Fuller?"

"I beg your pardon?" She made herself turn and face him. "What makes you think I'm hiding anything?"

He flashed that dangerous grin. "Anybody who can cook like you belongs in one of those big-city restaurants. Like the one you claim to have left back in Chicago."

"I told you. They didn't appreciate me." She turned away and squirted liquid soap into the sink, then filled it with hot water. She was shocked when she heard his voice directly behind her.

"Liar."

Her chin came up. She kept her back to him. "If you believe that, why did you agree to let me stay?"

She was startled when his shoulder brushed hers as he reached into the water and lifted her soapy hand.

So. He hadn't imagined it the first time. There it was again. That little jolt to the midsection. That quick sizzle of heat the moment their hands touched. Now why was this woman having such an effect on him?

He continued to hold her hand, running his thumb over her wet fingers while he stared into her eyes. Not dark, as he'd first thought. More gold than brown. The color of warm honey. "Maybe because I've always liked a mystery. And I'm intrigued by the mysterious Maggie Fuller."

When she started to pull back he added, "I'd better

warn you. I have a reputation for never giving up until the mystery's solved.''

With more reluctance than he cared to admit, he released her hand and walked out the door.

Maggie stood where she was, waiting for her heart to settle down to its natural rhythm. In her twenty-eight years, she'd never had a man affect her like this before.

Of all the places she could have picked to hide, she had to choose one with a guy who could turn her knees to jelly with a single touch. A guy who reminded her of a smooth, sleek panther circling its prey—just before the attack.

It was late afternoon. Maggie had just finished baking a batch of biscuits when she heard the roar of engines. She rushed to the window to stare in surprise at a helicopter hovering just above the ground, blades whirring, dust flying.

When Hazard stepped into the room a minute later, she spun around looking absolutely terrified.

''Is someone looking for...?'' She caught herself in time and amended, ''Is someone coming for a visit?''

Hazard shook his head, wondering about the wild look in her eyes. ''The copter just dropped off Chance. He had business in Cheyenne.'' He saw her relax visibly as she turned away from the window.

He cleared his throat. ''About my brother. I know you two got off to a rocky start this morning, but if you'll give him a little time, you'll find that he's really a decent guy.''

''Uh-huh.'' She rolled her eyes. ''Next you're going to tell me he's not nearly as tough as he looks.''

Hazard's grin was quick and disarming. ''That'd be a lie. Chance is even tougher than he looks. You don't ever want to cross him. But he's fair, Maggie. And as long as you're straight with him, he'll treat you the same way. Now, if you'd like a tour of the place some time, I'd be happy to oblige.''

"Thanks, Hazard. I'll need a few days to get my bearings here in the house. But I'd be happy to take you up on it later in the week.''

"Okay. Just say the word.'' He picked up his hat and strolled from the room.

When Agnes walked in minutes later, Maggie crossed to the island countertop, where the beef was marinating. ''I hope as the days go by the Wilde brothers will be willing to try some more exotic foods. I noticed the freezer was brimming with nothing but beef.''

Agnes made a cackling sound that Maggie decided must be her way of laughing. ''You're in Wyoming now, city-woman. This is cattle country. Why would they buy meat when they have all they want on the hoof?''

Maggie flinched at the sarcasm, but decided to stand her ground. ''I can understand that. And I guess I can try to come up with a thousand ways to make beef taste different. But it would be fun to try other things.''

The old woman shrugged. ''The Wilde brothers will eat just about anything, as long as they don't have to fix it. But if it's not something they like, they'll never try it a second time.''

"But as long as they have to eat, wouldn't you think they'd prefer something more…interesting than plain old steaks and roasts every day?''

"I can't say. All I've ever seen cooked around here is beef.'' Agnes poured the last of the coffee, sipped, then glanced over at Maggie with a look of surprise. It was better than she'd expected. Without a word she drained the cup. "What'd you do to this?"

"Hmmm?" Maggie glanced over. "Nothing much. I just grind the beans and start with cold water."

"You bring some special coffee with you from the city?"

Maggie shook her head. "Just what I borrowed from Thelma at the diner. She said she buys it at the local store. About the steaks…"

Agnes shrugged. "I can't say what they like or don't like. Hazard spends most of his time here on the ranch. But Chance and Ace do a lot of traveling. Big fancy planes and helicopters taking them all over the world. I guess it's given them a taste for some pretty strange food. Still, it hasn't seemed to change them all that much. Like kids everywhere, they spent their growing up years eating a lot of junk. That's what happens when you grow up alone. So I figure, if you want to try cooking other things, they'll be more than willing to eat them. If they don't like what you fix, they'll let you know."

Maggie looked up, intrigued by something Agnes had just said. "Why were they alone? What happened to their parents?"

"Their mother died when Ace was five. I guess that's why the boys have always been a little rough around the edges. Their father died a few years later."

"And they lived way out here all alone? What did they do about school?"

"Chance drove them when he could."

"But who took care of the ranch?"

Agnes shrugged. All of this was common knowledge among the citizens of Prosperous. "They did. They did most of the chores before school. The rest they did when they got home.''

She spoke in such matter-of-fact tones that it took a moment to register. Maggie stared at her in surprise. ''Three boys ran a ranch and raised themselves?''

''They were pretty much raised by then. The two older boys were teens. Between the two of them, they probably figured they could bully Ace into doing what was right.'' Agnes picked up a dust rag. ''I can't stand here gabbing. I got chores to see to.''

As she waddled away, Maggie stared after her, a million questions begging to be answered. How did Chance, Hazard and Ace go from three boys alone on a ranch to all this? From what Thelma had told her when she'd been offered this job, the Wilde brothers owned more land than anyone else in the entire state of Wyoming.

She glanced out the window at the rugged landscape, with the snow-capped mountain peaks in the distance. Last night Ace had told her that everything, for as far as the eye could see, belonged to them. Thinking back, she realized he'd said it in the same matter-of-fact way that Agnes had just spoken. Not a boast, meant to impress her, but a simple fact. Except, she thought as she began rummaging through the cupboards, there was nothing simple about these men. And especially the oldest, Chance.

As long as you're straight with him, he'll treat you the same way.

Hazard's words sent a trickle of ice along her spine as she began to stir the marinade on the stove. Of all the people in the world, Chance Wilde was the last she would trust with the truth. If he knew the real reason she was here, he'd have her removed without a second thought.

She knew his type. A tough, no-nonsense business-man who would never sit by and permit a stranger to invite danger to his very doorstep.

Could she have placed them in danger? Could she have been followed? She shook her head, denying the very thought. She'd been so careful. No credit cards that could be traced. She'd fled with just the money in her purse and the clothes on her back. She'd paid cash for the bus ticket, and had chosen a town at random. She was in the middle of nowhere. How could she be found out here?

"That must be some soup you're making."

At the sound of Chance's irritated voice she nearly bolted. She realized she'd been stirring the same thing on the stove for…how long? How long had he been standing there watching her?

Before she could form a reply Ace bounded into the room. "So? Did you and Simmons get your problem resolved?"

"No." Chance continued staring at Maggie. She'd been a million miles away. And the tight expression on her face had told him her thoughts weren't pleasant. "He has little time left before he'll be looking for a new job."

At Chance's furious tone Maggie glanced over at him and was again startled by what she saw. This wasn't the cowboy who had sat at the breakfast table in jeans and a casual shirt. Chance Wilde looked every inch the business tycoon, in a dark, perfectly tailored suit and silk tie, holding a hand-tooled leather briefcase in one hand.

"Hey, Chance," said Hazard. He and Cody strolled

in the back door and managed to catch the end of their conversation.

Seeing Maggie, Cody whipped his hat off his head and hung it on a hook by the back door.

"Still no answer, huh?" Hazard turned to his older brother. "Does Simmons suspect anyone in the company?"

"If he does, he isn't saying." Chance automatically loosened the tie and dropped the briefcase on the table. Both his brothers saw the fire in his eyes and recognized the signs. After his unsatisfying meeting with Simmons, he was spoiling for a fight.

"So you'll be flying up to Cheyenne again tomorrow?" Ace pulled out a chair and turned it around, straddling it while resting his arms along the back.

"Looks like I have no choice." Chance turned, admiring Maggie's backside as she removed a steaming tray and set it on the stove.

Hazard peered over her shoulder to the biscuits cooling on a rack. "So that's what smells so good. You actually bake your own biscuits?"

"Doesn't everyone?" She almost laughed at the look on his face. "Would you gentlemen care to try a few with some cheese while I finish cooking?"

Maggie was reminded of a pack of hungry dogs as they watched her arrange the steaming biscuits on a tray with cubes of cheddar. When she placed it on the counter, the tray was empty in minutes.

As he ate, Chance could feel his simmering anger beginning to fade as quickly as the sunlight over the mountains. Good food had always had that effect on him. There'd been so little of it in his life. "What time is the next course?"

"Dinner should be ready in an hour."

"Good. That gives me just enough time to get out of these clothes and into something comfortable." He picked up the briefcase and started out of the kitchen. At the door he turned. "I haven't tasted homemade biscuits since I was a kid."

Hazard nodded. "I was just thinking the same thing."

Ace merely looked from one brother to the other. "I don't remember."

"You wouldn't," Cody said with a laugh. "You were too little. But trust your brother. There was nothing else in the world like the smell in this house when your mama was baking biscuits or bread. She always used to save the heel of the loaf for your dad. Do you remember, Chance?"

"Yeah." Suddenly Chance's smile widened. Until this moment, he'd completely forgotten why he always preferred the crusty ends of bread. "Come on. Let's get washed up for dinner."

When Chance and his brothers were gone, Cody started toward the back door.

Maggie turned. "Aren't you staying for dinner?"

"No ma'am. Not tonight. I'm riding up to lend a hand with one of the herds."

She lowered her voice. "Agnes told me that the Wilde brothers lost their mother when Ace was five."

"Yes'm." Cody twirled his hat around and around in his gnarled fingers. "I've hung around this family since I was no more'n a pup myself. Wrangling. Mending fences. Doing odd jobs. And watching them pull together when things got rough. Their mama always worked hard to make things nice. And after she died, well, things were pretty bleak around here. I used to help out, making chili or burgers. But it's been a long time since the house smelled this good, Maggie. It sure is nice to smell good food cooking in this house again. Makes it feel like home.''

When he walked outside, Maggie stared at the closed door, lost in thought. She was glad she'd decided on the biscuits. Bread was one of the most basic of all foods. One that most people took for granted. But for three men who hadn't had a mother for most of their lives, it was more than mere food. It was a smell, a taste, a texture that would give them back, for a little while, their childhood.

Best of all, it had helped deflect that anger she'd sensed when Chance had first walked in. He'd been spoiling for a fight. It made sense that she would have been the logical target for all that anger.

If all it took to soothe the animal in him was a good, home-cooked meal, it was little enough price to pay for one more day of employment.

She set to work with a vengeance. She'd make them a meal they'd never forget.

Chapter 3

Agnes shuffled through the doorway of the kitchen and paused to wrinkle her nose. "What's that smell?"

Maggie looked up from the stove. "Garlic bread."

"Huh. Thought maybe you were roasting a skunk." She grinned at her little joke. "Better not let the wranglers smell it. They'll be hauling buckets of water to put out the fire."

As Agnes started away, Maggie called, "Mind if I tag along and see some of the house?"

Agnes sniffed. "Suit yourself."

Maggie followed the woman's shuffling gait as she started toward the main section of the ranch house.

"This is the great room. My men hardly ever seem to use it anymore."

The huge room was dominated by a four-sided open fireplace, with comfortable upholstered sofas placed around it for warmth and conversation. Floor-to-ceiling windows looked out at a sweeping vista of fields and forests, and in the distance, the soaring peaks of the Bighorn Mountains.

Agnes led her along a hallway to a suite of rooms twice the size of the great room. "This wing belongs to Chance." It was a combination bedroom-sitting room, with a second room that was obviously an office containing a multitude of phones, faxes and computers. Two walls contained floor-to-ceiling shelves of books and ledgers. A third wall was a soaring granite fireplace. The fourth wall contained more floor-to-ceiling windows overlooking the countryside.

Agnes walked to the coffeepot and switched it off. "Huh. Doesn't look like Chance even tasted it today. A waste of good coffee if you ask me." She turned. "Did he drink any of yours?"

Maggie shrugged, aware that the wrong words could hurt this old woman's tender feelings. "He may have. I didn't notice."

She walked to the huge slab of mahogany that served as a desk. Atop it was a faded photograph of a boy of about three or four on horseback, smiling down adoringly at a man who bore a striking resemblance to Chance.

"Is this...?"

Agnes nodded. "Chance and his father, Wes Wilde."

Maggie was amazed at the transformation in the older woman as she took the photo from Maggie's hands and gazed at it. There was a softness in her eyes that hadn't been there moments before.

"Did you know him, Agnes?"

"I knew him. He was a good man. The only man around these parts who would hire a Sioux. My husband, Louis Tallfeather, couldn't get a job until Wes Wilde was willing to give him a chance. After that,

Louis would have done anything for him. And did. He mended fences, fixed truck engines, went up into the high country with the herds. And when Louis died, Wes told me I'd always have a place to live. I wasn't sure I believed him. Especially after he died. But his sons saw to it that every promise he ever made has been kept.''

Agnes abruptly set the photo down and turned away. But not before Maggie caught a glimpse of her face. Was that a tear in her eye?

Over her shoulder she called, ''You want to see the rest of the place?''

''Another time. I think I'd better get back to the kitchen, Agnes. Thanks for your time.''

As Maggie walked along the hallway, she could hear the older woman shuffling along behind her.

On an impulse she called, ''What are you making for the wranglers' supper tonight, Agnes?''

The old woman paused to catch her breath. ''What I always make on Tuesdays when the weather's starting to change. Firehouse chili. Know why we call it that?''

Maggie stepped into the kitchen. ''No. Why?''

''Because the wranglers say you need a hook-and-ladder crew to put out the fire in your belly when you eat it.''

Maggie laughed. ''Sounds like the cowboys like it hot.''

''Yeah.'' Agnes nodded. ''Hot and well done. It's the only way they know how to eat anything.'' She glanced at the steaks marinating on the platter. ''I hope you're going to burn those?''

Maggie grinned. ''Maybe not burn. But I'll remember to char them a bit.''

The old woman looked pleased that her advice wasn't

being taken lightly. "I'd better get out to the bunkhouse and start serving my chili."

"Would you like to take some of this garlic bread with you?" Maggie held out a tray of the freshly baked bread. "I've got plenty to spare."

Agnes seemed about to refuse, then, after a dubious sniff, nodded. "Okay. If the wranglers won't eat it, I'll toss it out for the critters."

Maggie stood shaking her head as the old woman shuffled away. What had passed between them could hardly be called a truce. But at least they weren't at war. And Agnes had shared something personal. It was a start.

"Okay, Chance." Ace opened three beers, and handed them around as the brothers gathered in the kitchen before dinner. "Let's hear about your meeting with Simmons."

"Not much to tell." Chance, comfortable in faded jeans and plaid shirt, tipped his head back and took a long pull. "For two days now he's been poking and prodding through the company records. And he still claims nobody knows the password to access his files. He swears he read the contract just before it was printed out and faxed to me for approval."

"That still leaves time and opportunity for somebody else to make the changes before the file reached you. Who did the actual typing at the computer?" Hazard drank. Frowned. "And who did the faxing?"

"Those are the questions I asked him." Chance frowned. "How many hands touched the file before I found the errors? Maybe half a dozen." He paused a moment, watching as Maggie set a steaming platter on the table. His mouth was watering, but he couldn't be certain if it was the rich smells coming from the oven, or the sight of her as she straightened and turned toward him. The first glimpse of her face had his pulse racing.

The heat from the oven had damp curls kissing her cheeks and forehead. She brushed at them with the back of her hand. He watched the movement through narrowed eyes.

"So?" Ace prompted.

"So…" Chance pulled himself back from the distraction. "Simmons claims that by then it had all been proofed and printed. Which takes us back to him. And he denies ever seeing those changes in the contract until I pointed them out to him."

Maggie caught his eye and smiled. "Dinner is ready, gentlemen. Help yourselves."

She walked to the stove and removed a steaming bowl of Provençal sauce, pouring a little over the meat before serving it.

"Aren't you joining us?" Hazard asked.

"You're talking business. I think I'll leave you alone."

As she turned away, Chance crossed the room and caught hold of her arm. Alarmed, she froze.

"Sorry." He lowered his hand. Flexed his fingers. They were tingling from the contact with her flesh. "I was just going to remind you that this is where you're living now, Maggie. You have to eat, too."

"I can have something in my room."

"We don't have any servants here." His tone was slow, measured. "Only employees. You work here. Consider this one of the perks of the job. You get to eat with the bosses and listen to boring talk about business."

"Yeah," Ace added with a laugh. "And if you don't

like the treatment you're getting, you can slip something into our coffee.''

''Hmmm.'' She smiled then, forcing herself to relax. ''Careful. I might find that suggestion a little too tempting.''

She was disconcerted when Chance held a chair and waited until she was seated. Again she had to fight her nerves as his fingertips brushed her shoulder.

As the others took their places, Ace drained his beer and unceremoniously filled his plate. The others followed suit and soon they had once again fallen silent as they tucked into their meal.

For someone like Maggie, who loved to cook, it was very satisfying to watch these three men eat. They did so with smiles and sighs and a great deal of concentration—as though each taste contained a slice of heaven. She found herself thinking that the Wilde brothers made the act of eating a purely sensual pleasure. Almost like making love. The thought brought a touch of color to her cheeks.

''What do you call this?'' Hazard asked as he helped himself to seconds.

''Beef Maggie.'' At the blank looks on their faces, Maggie laughed before explaining. ''It's just beef sautéed in burgundy.''

''But the sauce isn't dark and sweet.''

''I made it with garlic and thyme and rosemary to lighten it up. And since it's my own creation, I thought I'd name it after myself.''

''I don't care what you call it,'' Ace muttered as he filled his plate again. ''It tastes like sin.''

''No wonder you're having such a good time,'' Hazard said with a laugh.

The others joined in the laughter.

Ace took his time enjoying the food before turning to Chance. "So, you gave Simmons more time to come up with a list of suspects."

"Wrong. I want more than suspects. I want him to find the guilty party or face dismissal."

"And what if he can't figure out who did it?" Ace asked.

"Yeah." Hazard nodded. "Or what if we're dealing with a very clever crook? Then you'll end up having fired one of your best employees, and you'll still have a crooked one in your employ."

Chance set down his fork, his appetite suddenly gone. "Don't you think I haven't asked myself those same questions? There was a time when I would have been Simmons's most ardent supporter. But this is too big and the mistake too costly. Now that I have questions about his integrity, how can I trust him again?"

Maggie sipped her tea and struggled not to fidget. But this discussion was beginning to hit a nerve. They were talking about judging a man guilty before they had all the facts. Nothing could be more unfair. Or more personal, as far as she was concerned.

Chance caught the look on her face. "What's that frown for, Maggie? Do you have an opinion as well?"

Startled, she looked up. "Sorry. This is none of my business."

"All the more reason why I'd like to hear what you're thinking."

She shook her head. "I don't think you'd care to know what I think."

Intrigued, he arched a brow. "Why? Come on. For the purpose of argument, just tell us what you're thinking."

She took a deep breath. "I don't know anything

about this man, Simmons. But I'm curious to know how long he's been working for you.''

Chance thought a moment. "Ten years. Maybe eleven.''

"Ten or eleven years? And until now, has he been a good employee?''

"The best.'' Chance nodded for emphasis.

"I see. And this error was on a contract. Was he the obvious suspect?''

Chance's tone lowered. "The only suspect. The Miller contract was his from beginning to end.''

"So, if someone wanted to plant a seed of distrust within the company, and also wanted to rob you of your most trusted employee, Simmons would be the one to go after.''

Maggie was already beginning to regret jumping into such uncharted territory. Chance was staring at her as he set down his cup of coffee with a clatter. So were his brothers.

He nodded. "That's the dilemma. Either I trust my instincts and keep Simmons on, hoping we find the culprit. Or I fire him, and hope the error doesn't happen again. Do I sense some disapproval from you?''

As the center of attention, she felt her cheeks grow hot. But now that she'd agreed to voice an opinion, she had no choice but to see this through. "How many years have you succeeded by trusting your instincts?''

Chance was still watching her. "Too many years to count.''

"I guess that says it all.'' She sipped her tea, allowing her words to speak for themselves.

In the silence that followed Chance nodded. "Okay. Maggie makes a good point. If I wanted to ruin someone, the first thing I'd do is get rid of those around him who might be too loyal. Which brings me back to the first question I asked when I discovered the errors in the contract. If Simmons was taking a kickback from the Miller people, would he have been so obvious as this?''

Ace and Hazard shook their heads.

''But if someone wanted to make it look like he was taking a kickback, that's the way to do it.''

Ace voiced the obvious question. ''But who would be out to ruin Simmons's reputation?''

Chance fixed him with a look. ''The same one who's out to ruin WildeOil. Or maybe it isn't a plot against the company. Maybe it's someone who's out to ruin me personally. Either way, I'll fall right into his plans if I start removing trusted people from my employ. Pretty soon, all I'll have left is a pack of amateurs. And before long, there will be even bigger mistakes made on future contracts.''

Hazard smiled, feeling oddly relieved. ''So you're going to keep Simmons on the payroll?''

Chance nodded. ''For now. If he's guilty, he'll make another mistake. And when he does, I'll be down his throat before he has time to swallow. But if he's innocent, it won't hurt to have him watching out for our interests within the company.''

Hazard pushed away from the table. ''I'm glad that's resolved, at least for the moment.'' He smiled at the woman who had tipped the scales in favor of Simmons. ''That was a fine meal, Maggie. Thanks.''

''Where're you headed?'' Ace asked as he got to his feet.

''Out to the south gate, little brother. Going to check the herd before turning in. How about you?''

Ace grinned. ''The night's young. I thought I'd drive

into town. Maybe find a game.'' He turned to Maggie. ''I second what Hazard said, Maggie. That was worth coming home to.''

She couldn't help laughing. ''Careful. All those compliments might turn my head. Next thing you know, I'll be asking for a raise.''

''No harm in asking. Of course, those who work for us will tell you we're not the most generous bosses in the world. But you keep feeding us like that, we'll be groveling at your feet.''

''Ah. I think I'm going to like the groveling.''

As the two brothers let themselves out, Maggie pushed away from the table and retrieved the coffeepot, topping off Chance's cup.

''Thanks.'' He sipped, deep in thought. It amazed him that Maggie had been able to put into words the very thing he'd been thinking about the errors in the Miller contract. If Simmons had been set up, it was because someone wanted to get him fired. That way, there'd be nobody looking out for Chance's back on the next deal. And all the deals to come.

One look at Chance's face and Maggie realized he was still mulling the problem. Reluctant to intrude on his thoughts she began to clear the table in silence.

Chance watched her as she moved around the room. Suddenly his thoughts switched from Simmons to Maggie. She worked with an economy of movement, loading the dishwasher, wiping down the oven and countertops until they sparkled.

There was a grace to her movements. An assurance. She was a woman completely in her element. So, why would someone as talented as Maggie Fuller walk away from a big city like Chicago, where her skill would earn her all sorts of rewards, to take a job on a remote ranch?

The answer that came to him was always the same. She was running. It was the only explanation.

Not his problem, he reminded himself. He had enough to deal with. He didn't need to take on her troubles. Still, he couldn't take his eyes off her.

Who the hell are you, Maggie Fuller? And what are you doing here?

"Would you like more coffee?"

At the sound of her voice he blinked, then shook his head and shoved away from the table. "Thanks. I've had enough. And my brothers were right. That was a fine meal."

"I'm glad you approved." She turned away and switched off the coffeepot. When she turned back, Chance was right beside her.

He saw the wary look that came into her eyes and kept his tone light. "When you hired on, we didn't talk about days off."

She shook her head. "I don't need any time off."

"Don't you have anywhere you'd like to go? Someone you'd like to visit?"

"No." He was staring at her so intently, she was forced to look away. Then, gathering her courage, she forced herself to meet his gaze. "But thanks anyway."

His smile was quick, hoping to put her at ease. "I know there isn't much in a town like Prosperous. But you could shop. Take in a movie."

"Maybe. At some later date, when I'm feeling tired of these four walls." His smile did strange things to her. She could feel a nervous flutter in the pit of her stomach. He was too close. Too...potently male. "But right now, I'm content to just work."

And hide out, he thought. Aloud, he merely said,

"Okay. You'll let me know if you want a day off and maybe a lift into town."

"Yes. Of course." She let out a breath, expecting him to turn away.

He'd intended to. But something perverse in his nature wouldn't allow it. Instead, he took a step closer, effectively blocking her only escape. "You smell good."

She gave a shaky laugh. "I probably smell like beef and biscuits."

"No. It isn't food I smell."

He leaned in until his face was inches from hers. It was the most purely sensuous thing she'd ever experienced, as he breathed her in. An animal instinct that left her paralyzed. She was unable to move. Even her heart forgot to beat. She stood frozen to the spot.

"Flowers. Spring flowers." As he leaned in, he found the scent stronger just there, at the base of her throat. He could almost imagine her dabbing perfume between her breasts. The thought had him sweating. "What's it called?"

"Spring Flowers." She couldn't help smiling.

"Yeah. I can smell them. Roses. Lilac. Honeysuckle." Sweet and earthy and delicate. Like Maggie, he thought.

Needing to diffuse the situation she struggled to come up with something flippant. "I didn't realize you were so knowledgeable about women's perfume."

"Neither did I." He smiled again, that quick, dangerous curve of lips, and she felt the familiar flutter of nerves. "It must be something about the company I'm keeping lately."

His mouth was so close to hers, she could feel the warmth of his breath against her lips. She swallowed, and wondered if he could hear the way her heart was pounding. "I...need you to move so I can get by."

"You don't like being hemmed in, do you, Maggie?"

"No. I feel..."

"Trapped?"

Her head came up. Her eyes narrowed. "I was going to say annoyed."

"Ah. There's that temper again. Good." His smile flashed. "I like a woman with a temper."

"Frankly, I don't care what you like. I was hired to cook for you. I didn't sign on to be your evening's entertainment."

"A pity." He lifted a hand to her arm and felt her stiffen. What was the matter with him? He'd never before had the need to spar with a woman like this. But she seemed to bring out the worst in him. Whatever the reason, he was unwilling to let it be. "I think you and I could find the evening very entertaining."

"You have a very high opinion of yourself. I suggest, if you're bored, you find a good book to read, or switch on the television."

"Is that what you do?"

"Of course."

"What a shame. You're going to have to learn to put a little fun in your life, Maggie."

"Thanks for the advice. Now if you don't mind...." She stared pointedly at his hand.

He lowered it to his side and took a step to one side, determined to put an end to this. Still...the hint of flowers and the heat of temper had him more aroused than he cared to admit.

She let out the breath she'd been holding and started past him. But as her shoulder brushed his arm, she heard his quick intake of breath. In the next moment he caught her roughly by the upper arms and brought her to a skidding halt.

He saw the look of surprise in her eyes and cursed himself. But it was already too late. Without taking time to think it through he dragged her close and, keeping his eyes on hers, kissed her.

It was the softest of kisses at first. Testing. Tasting.

She was exciting to watch. Her eyes went wide with alarm. Then the lashes fluttered. Closed. Her breath came out in a sigh, filling his mouth with the taste of her.

"I've been wanting to do that for some time now, Maggie." His fingers tightened on the soft skin of her upper arms as he drew her closer and took the kiss deeper. She tasted as cool, as fresh as a mountain spring.

Though Maggie was stunned and reeling, she had the presence of mind to keep her arms stiffly at her sides. It was a struggle. Part of her wanted to reach out and clutch at him, to run her hands over that trim, muscled body. To run her fingers through that dark spill of hair. Instead she clenched her hands into fists as his tongue tangled with hers and sent another series of jolts through her already overloaded system.

When he finally lifted his head she managed to remain standing, even though she feared her knees might buckle.

Though her throat was dry as dust she kept her tone even. "If you were hoping to show me that you're stronger, you managed to prove your point. But I'll remind you again that I agreed to cook for you. That's all the service I intend to provide."

"You won't get any argument out of me about that." He twirled a strand of her hair around his finger.

She stood perfectly still, wondering if he knew what his touch was doing to her. Heat curled like ribbons along her spine, twisting, turning, weakening her resolve.

"Of course…" he smiled, that wicked, sinful smile that had the power to melt her bones "…as long as we're both here, what's the harm in having a little fun?"

She slapped his hand away. "I may have only been in Wyoming a short time, but I've heard all about the Wilde brothers and their effect on the women around here."

He grinned. "It's been a noose around our necks since we were no more than pups."

She fought back the smile that threatened. He was so damnably appealing, he was almost irresistible. Almost. But she was absolutely determined to keep this on a strictly businesslike level. "Let's get something straight. I'm not one of those sweet, unsophisticated little girls who grew up in Prosperous, panting over one of the local legends. I'm not impressed by you or your family name or your empire. And I'm not interested in…anything you have to offer."

His smile grew. "You haven't even heard my offer yet, Maggie."

"Whatever it is, I'm not interested. Find yourself another playmate." She pushed past him and started across the room.

He stayed where he was, enjoying the way she kept her spine stiff, her head high, as she marched through the doorway.

He tucked his hands in his pockets and rocked back on his heels. She was looking better with every minute. If there was one thing he'd always enjoyed it was a challenge. And Maggie Fuller was definitely the most challenging thing to come into his life in quite a while.

He realized he'd been traveling around the world far too much lately, when what he really wanted was just to lead a quiet, uneventful life. There was no place he could think of that was more uneventful than right here in good old Prosperous, Wyoming. Eating good food. Watching his pretty new cook. And seeing just what twists and turns their lives might take.

He smiled, realizing he suddenly had a hankering to spend a whole lot more time around the ranch. Maybe, if he was lucky, he could string two or three days together, without having to leave.

Who'd have believed that he would be more interested in trying to figure out one little cook than in trying to land a few dozen multi-million-dollar contracts in far-flung countries? It just proved the power of a fascinating woman.

Chapter 4

Too agitated to settle down, Maggie prowled her room, pacing from the fireplace to the window, then back again.

The cook's quarters were no different from the rest of the ranch house. Oversize. Spacious. Comfortable. The bedroom had a big rustic bed constructed of logs, and the softest mattress she'd ever slept on. Besides the bed there was a tall wardrobe, a night table, and an overstuffed chair and ottoman. In the bathroom the shower was big enough for half a dozen people with room to spare. Off the bedroom was a sitting room with a fireplace, television and sofa and an antique rolltop desk and swivel chair. The windows looked out over the most magnificent land Maggie had ever seen. Rolling hills that seemed, in the gathering light of evening, to be black with cattle. In the distance were the snow-capped mountain peaks of the Bighorns, reaching up to touch a sky awash with millions of glittering stars.

Restless, Maggie undressed and pulled on the flannel pajamas she'd bought in the This N That Shop in Prosperous. She caught a glimpse of herself in the mirror and paused, thinking about the drawer filled with silk lingerie in her apartment in Chicago. Had it been pulled out and strewn around the bedroom? Had the mattress been slashed, the stuffing tossed about like so much snow?

She shivered at the shocking, horrifying scene she'd come upon that last night in her apartment foyer. A hall table upended. A mirror shattered. Plants and containers of dirt littering the surface of the beautiful Oriental rug.

That was all she'd been able to view before she'd been forced to run for her life. But she could imagine what the rest of the apartment must have looked like.

What would happen to all her things when next month's rent wasn't paid? Would the landlord sell it at auction to pay the bills? She thought about the mirrored buffet, the expensive dining-room table big enough to seat twenty, where she'd gathered her sister and friends together on special occasions to enjoy her gourmet meals. With a sinking feeling she pictured the custom upholstered sofa, a long curve of mauve nubby silk that faced the floor-to-ceiling windows overlooking the lights of Lakeshore Drive. Had it been ripped open and destroyed as well?

Just thinking about the destruction had the pain starting behind her eyes.

It didn't matter, she consoled herself. They were just things. And things could be replaced. Her life was more important. And life, she was learning, could be lived without an accumulation of possessions. A person could, when pushed to the wall, get by with a bed, a change of clothes and a job that occupied the mind as well as the hands.

But for how long? How long could she go on wondering about all that she'd left behind?

What about her friends? What were they thinking now? Were they believing the lies being spread about her? And what of the authorities? Were they looking for her? Had someone on the bus recognized her and notified the Chicago police?

Ray Collier had warned her that she would pay. What better way to seek revenge than by systematically destroying her? First by ruining her reputation, and then by taking away everything that had ever mattered to her. Her sister. Her friends. Her livelihood. Her sense of safety. Especially that sense of safety.

Never again would she be able to take her freedom for granted. No matter where she was, she would be forced to look over her shoulder, wondering if strangers recognized her.

Even though she'd escaped with her life, she wasn't free. Without meaning to, she'd played right into Ray Collier's hand. And now he was holding all the cards. He had rigged the evidence in his own favor, making her look like the guilty party. What's more, he was an authority figure. A man people trusted. While she was nothing more than a woman with no credibility whatsoever. A woman on the run. A woman many would believe was a criminal.

She closed her eyes, waiting for the moment of panic to pass. With her fingers gripping the edge of the desk she took in deep breaths, filling her lungs, struggling to empty her mind. She couldn't allow these thoughts to continue. If she did, she'd go mad.

She resolutely crossed the room and switched on the television. What she needed was a mindless old movie.

When she found what she was searching for, she took an afghan from the foot of the bed and wrapped herself in it, then settled into the comfortable chair, grateful that Cody had laid in a supply of firewood, and had taken the time to lay a fire that now burned cozily.

It should have been the perfect balm for her soul. Stars gleaming in a midnight sky. The comforting smell of woodsmoke on the hearth. Nothing more challenging than an old black-and-white comedy. But try as she might, she couldn't concentrate on the zany antics of the characters on the screen. Instead, she closed her eyes and found herself thinking again about that scene in the kitchen with Chance.

What was she going to do about him? He was getting to her. With that heart-stopping smile and that bad-boy image, he was hard to resist. That could prove to be dangerous. She had no business letting anyone get too close. Especially a man like Chance Wilde. If he even suspected how much trouble she was in, she'd be cut loose and sent packing without a second glance. And right now, she needed this job. Needed the safe haven of this secluded ranch.

If this had been another time, another place, a man like Chance Wilde would have seemed like a gift from heaven. But the timing was all wrong.

The trick was to keep him at arm's length. Otherwise, she was bound to get burned. But how was she going to hold at bay a man who behaved like a steamroller? She thought again about the kiss they'd shared. Being struck by lightning would have been less potent. The man kissed the way he ate. The way he lived. With all his senses fully engaged. The problem was, he'd engaged her senses as well.

That was something not many men could claim. Not that a few of them hadn't tried. But she'd always managed to put her ambitions for her career ahead of her personal life. And the truth was, most of the men she'd known had been pursuing their own careers as well.

Chance was different. A man completely at ease with himself and his life. From what she'd seen, the Wilde brothers weren't concerned with success or failure. What they relished was action. Whether it was the latest deal, or a friendly game of poker, they were completely engaged in the moment.

She opened her eyes. Stared at the ceiling. Chance Wilde would be a fabulous lover. And he would demand that his partner be as thoroughly involved as he was. There would be nothing passive in a relationship with a man like that.

She bit her lip, annoyed at the direction her thoughts were taking. It was dangerous to even fantasize about a man like Chance.

She'd always been able to keep her goals clearly in sight. And for now, her only goal should be survival. Still, it couldn't be denied. Despite the trouble she was in, she was intrigued. With one kiss, Chance Wilde had practically devoured her. Equally amazing was her response. The moment he'd touched her, she'd forgotten every rule she'd ever set for herself and had responded in the same careless way.

She found herself wondering what it would be like to just give in to the passion of the moment. To let herself be caught up in a wild, volatile explosion of feelings with a man known to be reckless.

Shocked at the direction her thoughts had taken, she

chided herself. She'd better be prepared to dig in and keep her feet squarely planted, or this man just might sweep her away.

Irritated, she switched channels until she found a raucous game show. Then she forced herself to play along with the contestants until at last she gave in to the need to sleep. But it offered no haven. Even in sleep she had to keep running to stay one step ahead of her demons, who were always in pursuit. Not just the menace that had sent her running from everything that was familiar to her. Now there was another, perhaps more perilous one, as well. A man who, with one touch, could start a fire that threatened to melt the shield she'd erected around her heart.

"Is that French toast?" Ace was the first one downstairs. This morning he was dressed in a suit and tie. All that remained of the lean, casual cowboy of the previous night were the highly polished tips of the Western boots on his feet.

He leaned over Maggie's shoulder and stared hungrily at the griddle.

"I hope you approve. I call it banana-stuffed French toast. With Scottish farmhouse eggs." Maggie turned perfectly browned sausages onto a heated tray.

Hazard paused in the doorway, his cheeks ruddy from morning chores in the barn. "If it's food, Ace approves."

"Especially," Chance added as he strolled in from the other end of the house, "when he's been out half the night carousing."

Ace shot his brother a look. "I wasn't carousing. I had a couple of beers at Clancy's, and beat Milt Ranson out of fifty bucks in a game of nine-ball."

"Poor old Milt." Hazard shook his head. "When will he learn he can't drink and gamble?"

"I hope he doesn't learn too soon." Ace picked up one of the glasses of juice Maggie had lined up on the counter and downed it in one long swallow. "I agreed to a rematch next week, and I'm already looking forward to cleaning his clock."

The three brothers shared a smile.

"The last time you said that," Hazard pointed out with a chuckle, "I believe it cost you four hundred."

"That's because I was coming down with the flu. I could hardly hold the cue stick."

"It might have had something to do with the pretty girl Milt brought along to dazzle you."

"I wasn't dazzled."

"As I recall, you spent so much time looking at her you didn't even notice that Milt was winning until he demanded another hundred."

"Okay. So maybe I got a little distracted. But I've learned my lesson. And so has Milt. Lesson number one. Never chase your money. Poor Milt was lost the minute he handed over his first twenty-dollar bill. Then it started eating at him, and he lost forty more chasing after it."

Ace started to laugh. "Speaking of eating, that's rule number two at Clancy's. Never eat the tomato paste on cardboard they call pizza. Or the burnt beef they have the nerve to call a charburger. I was up half the night paying for that mistake."

His brothers joined in the laughter.

Hazard eyed him speculatively. "You never used to have such rotten things to say about Clancy's food, as I recall."

"Well, maybe not. But that was before I tasted real

cooking. Maggie's cooking.'' Ace breathed in the perfume of cinnamon and rich, strong coffee. ''Now, that's real food.''

''Breakfast is ready, gentlemen.'' Maggie set a platter of eggs and sausage and French toast on the table and began filling coffee cups. ''You can dig in.''

While his brothers eagerly took their places at the table, Chance crossed the room and poured himself a glass of water and took his time drinking it. When she returned the coffeepot to the counter he leaned against the sink watching her.

Like Ace, he was dressed for business. The suit was custom-tailored, the tie silk.

He kept his tone low enough for her ears only. ''How'd you sleep, Maggie?''

''Fine.'' She avoided his eyes. ''And you?''

''Great. Just great.'' A lie. One he'd never admit to her. He had tossed and turned half the night thinking about the way she'd felt in his arms. The way she'd tasted. It wasn't like him to let someone get under his skin like this. It bothered him. She bothered him. Having her around was driving him crazy.

''How are your rooms?'' He inhaled her perfume, then cursed himself for more foolishness. He was behaving like an adolescent. ''Are they comfortable enough?''

''They're fine. Very comfortable.''

''Big enough for all your belongings?''

''Of course. I told you, they're fine.'' She hoped he never discovered that she'd arrived with little more than the clothes on her back.

She'd bought a few essentials in town, but they weren't enough to fill a duffel bag.

He shrugged. ''I hate to admit it, but I haven't bothered to even look in that part of the house in years. We had the suites added about fifteen years ago when we were finally able to afford to hire someone to come in and cook and clean for us. I hope they haven't gotten shabby from neglect.''

"Not at all. Don't worry about it. They're spotless. Agnes does a wonderful job of keeping them clean. The rooms suit my needs perfectly."

Ace looked over. "Hey. Are you two going to join us? Or are you leaving all this food for us?"

Chance trailed Maggie to the table.

As she took her seat, Ace helped himself to another piece of French toast and slathered it with syrup. "I saw Thelma last night. She wanted to know how things were working out, Maggie."

He winked. "I told her we'd have to chain you up and hold you prisoner if you tried to leave. And now that I've tasted this French toast, that goes double. You'd better not think about leaving us any time soon."

Maggie couldn't help laughing. "Careful, Ace. All this flattery will go right to my head." She could feel herself blushing as Chance turned to look at her. "And then I just might demand a raise."

Hazard picked up his cup and drained it. "With coffee this good, you'd be worth any price. So if you're smart, you'll ask for that raise right away. We're already hooked on your cooking." As he held out his cup for a refill he added, "I'm going into town today, Maggie. Would you like to go along and load up on some supplies?"

She shook her head. "I'd rather stay here. But if you don't mind, I'll make out a list of things I'd like."

"That's fine. Any time you find yourself in need of groceries, you can always phone Kit Korson over at

Korson's Grain and Feed, and he'll be happy to truck it out to you.''

She paused. "Korson's Grain and Feed?''

At her puzzled look, the three brothers shared a laugh.

"I guess to an outsider, that must sound strange," Ace said. "But we're so used to it, we never even question it. In our father's day, it was strictly a grain storage. But as the town grew, so did the business. More and more people were moving in, with no place to buy decent food. So Korson's became a place where a rancher could stock up on all his needs, for his herd or himself. Kit's got everything from oats to oatmeal.''

"That's really one-stop shopping," Maggie muttered as she circled the table filling their cups.

"And then there's Wanda's Bait and Party Shoppe," Hazard said, bringing another round of laughter.

She looked over at him. "Is there really such a place?''

"You bet." He winked. "I guess that tells you the kind of parties they have in Prosperous." Hazard drained his cup, then shoved away from the table and pulled on his parka. "Maggie, I'll be back to pick up your list after I've taken care of a few things in the barn. And if I get too busy, I'll send Cody around for it.''

"All right." She gave him a smile. "I'll have my list ready.''

By the time Hazard let himself out she was already checking the supplies in the freezer and cupboards.

Minutes later Ace sauntered to the door, briefcase in hand. "I'm heading over to WildeMining. Don't know if I'll be back in time for dinner. I'll have Cass phone later and let you know, Maggie.''

"Cass?" Maggie gave him a blank look.

"Cassidy Kellerman, my secretary."

"Your secretary?" Maggie suppressed a smile. It was hard for her to imagine this irreverent cowboy operating his own mining company and having a secretary. But then, she reminded herself, the fact that she was cooking on a ranch in Wyoming meant that anything was possible.

When Ace was gone, Maggie completed her list. She looked up to see Chance still seated at the table, sipping his coffee and watching her intently over the rim of his cup. When he caught her eye he carefully composed his features.

She shrugged aside the uncomfortable feeling that he'd been studying her a little too purposefully. "Would you like more coffee?"

"No, thanks. I've had enough."

"Tell me. Do you have a secretary, too?"

He'd been expecting this. "As a matter of fact, I do. Carol Ann McCormick. I don't know what I'd do without her."

Maggie had a quick impression of a tall, leggy blonde, efficiently shuffling phones and faxes—and possibly other things—for her busy boss. "Where does she work?"

"In our corporate office in Cheyenne."

"Isn't it difficult operating a business so far from your office staff?"

"Not at all. With phones, faxes and computers, we manage just fine. When the company was just starting out, Carol Ann worked here, in my office at the house. But as the company grew, we knew we needed a bigger base. I was glad Carol Ann and her husband were willing to move to Cheyenne. She used to live in Prosperous. I went to high school with her daughter, Leanne.''

Maggie was forced to alter her image slightly. A not-so-leggy blonde, possibly hoping to make a match between her daughter and her boss.

''Does Leanne work in the office too?''

He shook his head, still watching her intently. ''She used to. Leanne married Ken Bentley. He works for me. In fact, half the people in Prosperous work for us, either at WildeOil, WildeMining or the Double W. Ken and Leanne have three of the cutest little girls in all of Wyoming, and she decided to leave work to stay home with them.''

Maggie crossed the room and began to clear the table. But as she reached for his plate he put his hand over hers.

''Why don't you want to go into town with Hazard?''

She pulled back abruptly. ''I just left Prosperous a few days ago. Why should I go back?''

He tilted his head back to fix her with a look. ''Most people will do anything to avoid the isolation of this place. Our last cook came up with a reason to go into town every time someone was heading that way.''

''Is that why she no longer works here?''

''It could be. Or it could be because her cooking made Thelma's taste like something out of a gourmet cookbook.''

''Hey. What a thing to say. I thought Thelma was a friend of yours.''

''She is.'' He smiled as he pushed away from the table and stood, towering over her. She had just neatly turned the conversation away from herself. Again. He'd give her this much. She was clever. ''But Thelma can't cook worth a…'' He cleared his throat. ''Let's just say that Thelma's cooking should carry a skull and cross-bones for unsuspecting customers."

Maggie couldn't help laughing. "She made me a grilled-cheese sandwich the first time I met her. That was when her cook, Slocum, had just gone to jail, and she was carrying the workload alone."

"Yeah? How'd it taste?"

"Like something she'd scraped off the bottom of her shoe."

Chance joined in the laughter. "Yeah. That's our Thel. She's got the biggest heart in all of Wyoming. She just can't cook. It's a good thing we love her. And we really do."

Maggie was still smiling. "The feeling is mutual. She had nothing but good things to say about the Wilde brothers. When I was reluctant to take this job, because I didn't like the idea of working for three strangers, she assured me that she'd known you all her life, and that you and your brothers were honorable men. She promised me I wouldn't be sorry."

"I hope you never have a reason to be." He stepped closer and lifted a hand to her hair. "I know I'm not sorry you're here."

She had given herself a good talking to earlier this morning and was determined to avoid him at all cost. "Easy for you to say now that you've had a good breakfast."

"Yeah. There's that." She was as transparent as glass. He knew exactly what she was trying to do. Keep it light while keeping her distance. And he was just as determined to thwart her efforts. The one thing he wasn't going to allow her to do was ignore him.

He twisted one silken strand of her hair around his finger, all the while staring into her eyes, watching them widen. From fear? Distrust? Whatever the emotion, she blinked and it was gone. She lifted her chin in that gesture that always made him want to smile. It was obvious that no matter how uncomfortable she was, she wasn't about to back down. It was one more thing he couldn't help admiring about her.

"And then, Maggie, there's this."

Without warning he lowered his face and brushed his mouth over hers. The kiss was as soft as a snowflake and just as fleeting. But it packed a punch that had them both taking a step back.

He reached out a hand to her shoulder, as much to steady himself as to remain connected. "Did I just imagine that?"

"What?" She was amazed at how difficult it was to speak over the feelings that clogged her throat.

"This." He lowered his head and kissed her again, lingering over her lips until they warmed and softened beneath his.

Her fear was forgotten. As were all her well-intentioned promises to herself.

She couldn't hold back the little gasp as she felt the quick rush of heat, and the curl of desire along her spine. Without meaning to, she brought her hands to his shoulders and held on as the room took a slow dip and turn. She ignored the warning bells that were sounding in her brain as she allowed him to linger, savoring the moment.

He took his time, his hands circling her waist, the fingers splaying across her ribcage. He kept his eyes open, enjoying the play of shifting expressions across her face. She was delightful to watch. Nerves fluttering just beneath the surface. The slight flush of desire that colored her skin. The way her lashes flickered, casting shadows on her cheeks. The quick hitch of her breath. And the helpless shudder as his fingers moved upward, stopping just below her breasts.

She stepped back in alarm.

When he lifted his head, she could see by the slight narrowing of his eyes that he wasn't immune to such feelings either.

There was no denying the sparks that flew each time they touched. Sparks that, if struck often enough, were bound to ignite. It was one more reason why she had to find a way to keep her distance from this man. He was definitely an accident waiting to happen. But the truth was, each time he touched her, she forgot to be sensible. In fact, in his presence she forgot every good intention she'd ever made.

Before either of them could speak they heard the roar of engines passing directly overhead.

Chance shot her a dangerous smile. "Talk about lousy timing. It looks like my ride's here."

"Are you and Ace…" she drew in a breath and prayed her heart would settle down to its natural rhythm "…flying out together?"

He shook his head. "Ace is going over to Wilde-Mining. That's about a hundred fifty miles west of here, on the edge of our land. I'm heading to our corporate office in Cheyenne. Whether I like it or not, it's time to handle a little business."

"How far is Cheyenne from here?"

"Just a short hop on a copter." As he started past her he paused, seemed to think twice about it, then turned back. He lifted the back of his hand to her cheek and touched lightly, before brushing a butterfly kiss across her lips.

He saw the way her cheeks flooded with color.

Lowering his hand to his side, he took a step back. "Don't worry about the distance. Even if my little brother doesn't make it home tonight, you can count on me for dinner. Then maybe we can take up where we left off."

"Sorry." She was determined not to give him the satisfaction of the last word. "The only thing we're going to do together tonight is eat."

"Okay. That's a start." His lips curved in the most tempting smile. "Then we'll just see where the night takes us."

As he exited the kitchen, Maggie found herself wondering if that was a promise or a threat.

One thing she did know. Before he returned tonight, she was going to give herself a good talking-to. What kind of wimp was she that every time he so much as looked at her, she fell apart?

She was absolutely not going to allow him to touch her again. Every time he did, all sorts of strange things happened to her. Her mind turned to mush. And her bones seemed to melt. Reason enough to see that she kept her distance from Chance Wilde. No matter how difficult that might prove to be. Because this was a man who knew exactly what effect he had on her.

He was toying with her. Playing with her mind. Maybe even hoping to get even for that first encounter.

Yes, she had no doubt that Chance Wilde knew exactly what he was doing. And what he was doing was driving her around the bend.

Chapter 5

The helicopter dipped low over the land, casting a shadow on the grazing herd. Chance sat beside the pilot, adjusting mirrored sunglasses to shade his eyes. As they drew closer to the ranch, he stared at the land below without really seeing it. He was thinking about Maggie.

He'd spent far too much time thinking about her today. She seemed to hover on the edges of his mind, even during the most crucial business meetings. He had a briefcase crammed with documents that required his signature. Usually he spent the flight from Cheyenne poring over papers, making crucial decisions about future contracts. This time, he'd spent the entire flight simply staring out the window. And, though he hated to admit it, he'd abruptly cancelled his last meeting of the day in order to get back home earlier than planned.

Who was Maggie Fuller? What was she doing hiding out here? He had no doubt she was hiding. Though she tried to cover it, she was running scared. He'd never be able to forget the look on her face when she'd first caught sight of him with his rifle. She'd been absolutely terrified. That wasn't the normal fear of the unknown. In fact, she exhibited an abnormal level of anxiety.

What had brought her to this place? Had something happened to frighten her? Hurt her? Or could she be running from somebody? His eyes narrowed behind the glasses. Maybe it was a combination of both. Something and somebody. Something too terrible to talk about. Somebody too dangerous to forget.

He'd always trusted his instincts about people. And his instinct told him that whatever her problem, she was no threat to him or his brothers. If she was some sort of corporate spy, she was either the best he'd ever met, or the worst. She seemed to have no clue about the degree of their wealth or their holdings. She would have to be the most talented actress in the world to feign that look this morning when she realized that Ace had a secretary. As for his own work schedule, she didn't seem to have a clue.

He smiled in spite of himself. She had the most amazing face. So animated. So completely guileless. No, he thought as the ranch house came into view. She wasn't here to spy on them. She was here to cook. She couldn't fake that kind of talent. Or the love she had for her work. He was willing to concede that she had probably worked as a cook before she came here. But that was part of the problem he had about this whole mystery. Anyone who wanted to earn a living as a cook would make their way to a big city like New York, Los Angeles, Chicago. Talented chefs just didn't migrate to a backwater town like Prosperous, Wyoming. Unless they were foolish or desperate. And since Maggie Fuller was no fool, there was obviously one thing that drove her—desperation.

The craft landed on the concrete pad, the blades spinning as Chance jumped out.

"Thanks, Brady."

"Sure thing, Chance. Will you be needing me tomorrow?"

Chance shook his head. "I don't know yet. I'll call you."

By the time the helicopter was airborne once again, he was halfway to the house.

He tossed his jacket and briefcase on a bench just inside the front door, and loosened his tie as he strode along the hallway to the kitchen. The closer he got, the louder grew the sound of music on the oldies radio station. He recognized an old Bee Gees number about stayin' alive. Maggie was singing along at the top of her lungs.

When he stepped through the doorway, he stared around in amazement.

It looked as though a tornado had struck. Or at least some sort of disaster. The sink was littered with pots and pans. There were more in disarray all over the countertops. Maggie, in an oversize apron, was up to her elbows in dough. She seemed to be trying to beat it to death with her fists, punching against the soft mound, turning it, then punching it again, as she moved in rhythm to the music.

Chance studied her profile. Her hair curled damply around her forehead and neck. The tip of her nose and one cheek were dusted with flour. She had kicked off her shoes. Her bare toes peeked out from beneath the cuffs of wrinkled denims, her feet keeping time to the beat.

For the space of several minutes he leaned against the doorway, his arms crossed over his chest, watching her struggle with the blob of dough. Then, in a cheery tone he called, "Hi honey, I'm home."

She spun around so quickly, she nearly lost her balance. Her face registered shock, fear, then wild-eyed disbelief.

"What are you doing here? I wasn't expecting you for hours."

"I can see that. If you hadn't been playing the music so loud, you'd have heard the sound of the helicopter engines."

He uncrossed his arms and took a step closer, staring in fascination at the front of her apron. It was smeared with bloodred stains. "So. Did the other guy survive?"

She glanced down at herself and realized what he was looking at. She burst into laughter. "I hope you like Italian."

"That depends." His lips curved in a smile. "Did you kill him, or only wound him?"

"It was only a flesh wound. I took out most of my venom on the clams and the marinara sauce. I think I'll save the rest of my anger for the guy who just walked in that door before I had a chance to clean up this mess."

"Okay." He lifted a hand in mock defense. "How about if I offer to help you?"

She shook her head. "Don't be silly. You've already put in a full day at work. This is my job."

"Humor me." He began to roll his sleeves. "It's been a long time since I've washed dishes." He emptied the sink of pots and pans and turned on the tap, pouring in a liberal amount of detergent. Picking up a brush, he began to scrub, as the radio grew silent for a moment before breaking into the first notes of Garth Brooks singing "You Move Me."

"Why are you home so early?" Maggie shaped the last of the dough into a loaf pan, then draped a clean linen cloth over it.

"A little bird told me my cook was in need of assistance."

"The bird lied." She picked up a towel and started to dry. "I really would have had everything clean in time, if only you'd given me a couple more hours."

"In a couple more hours you'd have run out of pots and pans." He chuckled. "And room to put them. Do you always work in such a frenzy?"

"That depends. Today I decided to bake half a dozen loaves of bread, each one seasoned in a slightly different way."

"Why so many?"

In truth, she hadn't been able to get Cody's words out of her mind. The image of three boys losing their mother then their father had stayed with her. Maybe it was her way of erasing the image she carried of these brothers struggling to keep a ranch and a family together.

She merely said, "Seeing the way you and your brothers love to eat, I figured we'd go through at least that many in a week."

He handed her a glistening pot, enjoying the way her eyes heated up when their fingers brushed. "Sort of a big job, isn't it?"

"I'm used to taking on big jobs." She had a fleeting memory of the staff who had worked beside her at the restaurant. "But I'm also used to having someone cleaning up behind me."

"All the more reason I'm glad I showed up early. So, how big was the last kitchen you worked in?"

She thought of the expanse of stainless-steel work space, the salad chefs, the pastry chef and the crew of seven to assist. "About this size," she lied.

He'd already noted her pause and knew that she was deciding how much to tell him. It only made him want to dig deeper. "Did you work alone?"

She shrugged. "I had help when I needed it."

She was shutting him out. Offering as few details as possible. He couldn't help himself. He needed to prod a little more. "Did you need help often?"

"Only when there was a big party."

"In that little restaurant in Chicago."

"Um-hmm." She compressed her lips, knowing he was digging and wishing she could find a way to change the subject.

He glanced at her. "Would you like us to hire a helper? I'm sure my brothers would agree, if you thought it was necessary. Maybe Thelma could recommend someone."

"No." Her response was immediate and firm. The last thing she wanted was a stranger poking around, watching her. "I'm perfectly capable of handling this alone. If there were two of us working here every day, we'd be tripping over each other."

"I suppose you're right." Out of the corner of his eye he saw the way she heaved a sigh of relief. "Of course, there's always Cody."

"He doesn't look like a man who'd enjoy following me around a kitchen."

"Don't kid yourself. The old guy's dazzled by you. I could tell by the way his eyes lit up when he first saw you. And now that he's tasted your cooking, he's probably halfway in love.''

Maggie chuckled. ''Yeah. I always drive the old guys mad with my beef patties.''

''Seriously.'' Chance paused a moment in thought. ''It might be the perfect way to ease him out of the cold when the temperatures drop below zero. My brothers and I have been worrying about him. At his age, it's getting tougher to chase cows who get lost in blizzards. But he absolutely refuses to take life easy. Maybe if we told him you needed his help for a while, it would solve both our problems.''

Maggie nodded. ''All right. If I'm still here when the snows come, and if you still want to keep him indoors, I'd be more than happy to work with Cody.''

Chance gritted his teeth. *If* she was still here when the snows came? Where did she expect to go?

Her words broke through his reverie. ''Cody seems like such a sweetheart.''

''He's a true cowboy. Lives by a cowboy's code. He may be tough as nails, but he's respectful to women. Smokes only outdoors. And he taught my brothers and me more about cattle ranching than we could have learned in a lifetime.''

''How did he happen to work for you?''

''He worked for my father on and off, then just drifted away. Cowboys rarely stay in one place for very long,'' he added absently. ''But every time we needed him, he just seemed to be here. And when the work was done, he'd disappear again. Then, when he heard that we'd lost our father and were struggling to keep the place going, he just showed up on our doorstep. And he's been here ever since. Cody can do anything. Welding. Plumbing. Electrical work. He's a top mechanic.

For years he kept our fleet of trucks and machinery working. Though he had no training as a veterinary doctor, he knows almost as much as Hazard about treating sick animals.'' Chance shook his head. ''Now, after all these years, Cody's like one of the family.''

''Like Agnes.''

''Yeah.'' He laughed. ''Like Agnes. She can't cook worth a darn. Can't even properly boil an egg. Can barely get around anymore. In fact, we're hoping to hire someone to do the cleaning, so she can get off her feet. The only reason we've put it off this long is because she'll be outraged when she finds out what we've done.''

Maggie chuckled. ''I'd hate to be the one you hire. I saw how she bristled when she first met me. She's decided that the Wilde brothers are her domain. Everyone else is an intruder.''

He nodded. ''She never had any kids of her own. So she made us her life's work. She's not about to let anyone in without a fight.''

''She said your father hired her husband when nobody else would.''

Chance shrugged. ''It's a little easier now. But in my dad's day, it was pretty tough for some of the Native Americans to get work on the ranches. They always had to fight those negative stereotypes. Louis Tallfeather was a natural. He was a lot like Cody. He could do everything. He was one of my heroes when I was growing up.''

Maggie smiled. ''And to hear Agnes tell it, your dad was one of her heroes.''

Chance's tone softened. ''Yeah. My dad was an original. Not that he was any kind of a saint. He was the original juvenile delinquent. Ran away from home when he was just a kid. Spent his youth gambling and drifting from town to town. But in the things that mattered, he was the best. I don't think he ever saw the color of a man's skin, or cared about his past. He was willing to give everyone a fair shake. As long as they were straight with him, he treated them the same way.''

Chance drained the water from the sink and dried his hands on a clean towel. "It isn't always easy, but I've tried to live my life by that same code."

Maggie felt a tiny shiver along her spine at the fierceness in his tone. She had no doubt that he was a man who would do exactly what he said.

Glancing at her stained apron, hanging nearly to her ankles, he grinned. "I think we'd better order you a couple of new aprons. The one you're wearing was made to fit somebody twice your size."

"I don't mind. It serves the purpose."

"Uh-huh." His smile grew. "A few inches wider and it could be a tent. Any longer and you'd be tripping over it."

She started laughing. "I did wonder about your last cook."

"Let's just say she was big enough and tough enough that if we didn't like what she fixed, we were smart enough to keep our mouths shut. In fact, she could have answered to the name *King,* as in Kong."

Maggie was laughing harder as she turned away to stir the clam sauce and start the water for linguini. Chance leaned against the sink and watched her. And realized that he was having a great time.

"What is this?" He pointed to the rack of freshly made pasta. "You actually make your own?"

She shrugged. "Doesn't everyone?" When he didn't

answer she turned to stare at him. ''You mean you've never tried making your own noodles?''

''The closest I've come to making my own was picking up a carryout at the E.Z.Diner and heating it in the microwave oven when I got home.''

''I can see your education has been sorely lacking. All you need is a little flour and egg and...''

''Spare me the details. I can't wait to taste this.'' He leaned over her shoulder. ''Have you heard from Cass?''

Maggie nodded. ''She phoned over an hour ago to say that Ace won't be coming home tonight.'' She lifted the wooden spoon from the sauce and held it to his lips. ''Taste this. See if it meets with your approval.''

He closed his hand over hers. This time he was ready for the little jolt. He stared into her eyes as he tasted. ''Absolutely perfect.''

''I thought you'd enjoy clam sauce.''

''Oh. You wanted my opinion of the food? I was talking about the woman holding the spoon.''

He saw the color that flooded her cheeks before she pulled free and turned away. ''We aren't going to start that again, remember?''

''We aren't?''

When she shot him a look, he lifted his hands in a gesture of surrender. ''Okay. Anything you say.''

On a whim he left the kitchen whistling, returning minutes later with a bottle of red wine.

While Maggie cooked the linguini and placed a small loaf of garlic bread under the broiler, he opened the wine to let it breathe before filling two glasses. When he held a glass to her lips, she had no choice but to sip.

''Umm. That's nice. Chianti?''

''I picked it up in Rome.'' He tossed off the remark

as casually as if he'd mentioned buying it in Prosperous, Wyoming. It occurred to Maggie that he was a man who would be comfortable anywhere in the world.

He was standing a little too close and looking at her a little too carefully. She felt the prickle along her spine as he remained beside her, sipping his wine while she stirred the sauce and tested the pasta with a fork.

When the phone rang, he crossed the room to answer it. Maggie let out the breath she'd been unconsciously holding.

The man made her tense. Just being alone with him had her temperature rising. She'd be relieved when Hazard joined them. Then she'd be able to relax and just be herself. There was something soothing about the gentle middle brother. He was as calm as his two brothers were volatile.

"Okay." Chance's deep voice drifted across the room. "Tell her hi for me, bro."

He hung up the phone and picked up his glass before walking toward her.

"That was Hazard. He and Cody are in town and running late. They'll grab a bite to eat at Thelma's and pick up your supplies before they head home later tonight."

He smiled, and Maggie was reminded of the cat that had just eaten the canary. "So it looks like it'll be just you and me tonight, Maggie."

"How cozy."

He brought his face close to hers, and breathed her in. "I was thinking the same thing."

He picked up her glass, offered it to her.

When their fingers brushed, she nearly jumped back, before reminding herself to settle down. There was, after all, nothing to be alarmed about. They were two adults, about to share a simple dinner. Nothing more.

Still, the look in his eyes had her heart stuttering. She took a long, calming sip of wine and met his gaze with what she hoped was a look of cool indifference.

"The pasta is ready if you're feeling hungry."

"I'm starving. The smell is driving me wild."

She smiled and cautioned herself to relax as she began to drain the pasta in a colander. "I know. There's something about clam sauce and garlic that always makes me drool."

"I wasn't talking about the food." He stepped closer and set down his glass beside hers. "I was talking about you, Maggie. You make me weak."

She gripped the edge of the sink when she felt a trembling beginning in her legs. "You've got to stop doing that, Chance." She steadied herself. "This is crazy. I work for you. We can't…"

"Oh, we can." His voice was as cool, as calm, as if he were discussing the weather. "And we will. Of that I have no doubt."

She lifted her head and forced herself to look at him. What she saw had the blood roaring in her temples.

His eyes were narrowed on her with a hunger that spoke to a matching hunger deep inside her. When he made a move to touch her she reached out a hand to hold him at arm's length.

He paused. Then a slow, dangerous smile curved his lips. "Okay. You're not ready yet."

"Yet?" Her eyes grew as dark as storm clouds. "What arrogance. You make it sound as though it's only a matter of time."

His smile grew, which only added to her temper. "It is, Maggie. It's as inevitable as the snow that's going to be covering the ground in the next couple of weeks. But I won't rush you. You take all the time you want.''

''Thank you. How very understanding of you.'' Her tone was pure ice.

Still smiling, he took a step closer. This time she backed up until she could feel the press of the counter digging into the small of her back. With nowhere to go, she lifted her chin a fraction.

''I love the way you do that.'' He caught her chin in his hand and stared down into her eyes. ''You have the most expressive face. Did you know? Those incredible eyes flash fire. And your mouth turns down in the most intriguing pout. It almost begs a kiss.''

She saw his gaze shift until he was staring at her mouth. She felt for a moment as though all the blood had drained from her head. If he kissed her now, she didn't think she'd have the will to stop him. The mere thought of it had her blood heating and her heart racing.

Instead he surprised her by brushing his fingertips over her nose and cheek. ''Flour. I was almost tempted to try kissing it away, but I figure you'd probably let me have it with a pot of linguini.''

''I still might.''

''Is that a dare?''

''Take it any way you want.''

''Thanks for the offer. Don't mind if I do.'' Before she realized what he intended, he leaned close and brushed his mouth over hers.

The rush of heat was instantaneous. And devastating. With each brush of his lips, with each touch of his fingers along her spine, she absorbed another blow to her already overloaded system. The potent male taste of him sent little darts of pleasure streaking right through to the center of her being.

When at last he lifted his head, she was forced to stand perfectly still, fighting for breath.

"I think we should forget about eating." His lips brushed her temple. His warm breath feathered her hair. "And go right to dessert."

"Not on your life." Determined to nip this in the bud, she pushed against him and stepped away.

Handing him a basket she said, "Better get that garlic bread out of the oven before it burns."

Without bothering to look at him, she reached for a platter and heaped it with linguini, before ladling sauce over it. She removed two salads from the refrigerator and placed them on the table.

She was relieved a moment later when he topped off their glasses with wine and crossed to her.

"Very smooth, Maggie." He handed her a glass and touched the rim of his lightly to hers in a salute. "But there's no denying what's between us. One of these nights you'll decide you've made us both wait long enough."

At his words, spoken so deliberately, she had to fight the jittery feeling that curled along her spine.

"For now—" he smiled and held her chair "—let's just enjoy each other's company."

She sat and sipped her wine, waiting for the feeling to pass. "You mean, in a sane, civilized manner?"

He sat across from her and shot her a dangerous look. "Believe me, Maggie, when it comes to what I want to share with you, there's nothing civilized about it."

He saw the way she ducked her head to hide the flush that stained her cheeks. Anger? Or was it something more? Maybe she was fighting her own battle, because she wanted the same thing. His blood warmed at the thought. He couldn't be certain. Yet. But this much he knew. The more she held back, the more he wanted her.

Though he had never been a patient man, he was willing to bide his time. No matter how long it took him, he had no doubt that sooner or later he'd uncover every exciting, mysterious thing there was to know about the very private, tight-lipped Maggie Fuller. Since he was the gambling son of a gambling man, he was willing to bet everything he owned on that.

Chapter 6

"Agnes." Maggie paused in her work to watch the old woman pass through the kitchen carrying a bucket of water. "Don't you ever stop working and just sit?"

"Why would I do that?"

"To catch your breath. To just relax." Maggie picked up a china cup. "How about some tea and biscuits?"

The older woman shrugged. "Huh. I suppose I could. You going to have some?"

Maggie nodded. "Okay. I could use a break."

She filled two cups and set a plate of biscuits and a little bowl of jam on the table.

Agnes set down her bucket and took a seat, rolling her tired shoulders. She sipped. And almost smiled before she caught herself. "Don't like to take a break in the middle of the day like this. Makes it hard to get started again. What'd you put in these?"

"A little cinnamon, a little nutmeg. You like them?"

The older woman shrugged. "They're not too bad."

That, Maggie realized, was probably the closest she'd ever get to a compliment.

"What're you fixing for dinner tonight for the guys in the bunkhouse?"

"Don't have to cook. It's Friday night. Those that aren't needed here will drive into town and eat at the E.Z.Diner. Then they'll head over to Clancy's."

"What about those who have to stay?"

She shrugged. "Chili burgers."

"And for dessert?"

Agnes looked up. "Dessert? These are cowboys, citywoman."

Maggie smiled. "I'd think even cowboys would have a sweet tooth. What's your favorite dessert, Agnes?"

The older woman leaned back, holding the cup in the palm of her hand. "There was a cornbread my ma used to make. Don't know exactly how she fancied it up, but it had cherries in it, I think. And nuts on top." She shook her head. "Haven't had it in years, but I can still taste it." She finished her tea, then set down the cup and eased herself out of the chair. "Thanks for the tea and biscuits. Time I got back to work."

As she walked away, Maggie searched her mind for cornbread recipes.

"Maggie." Ace breezed in and picked up a piece of flatbread from a tray, generously slathering it with a cheese spread from the bowl beside it.

It had become routine for Maggie to have some sort of appetizer ready when the men came in from work. It eased their hunger, since they often forgot to eat for hours.

"I've got a request."

She looked up from the stove. "What would you like?"

"I'm flying in some executives from South Africa. They'll be going out to the mine site then coming back here for a business meeting. Think you could handle dinner for eight?"

Her smile was quick. At last. A real challenge. "Sure. When?"

He blinked. "Just like that?"

Her smile grew. "Isn't that why you hired me?"

"Well, yeah. But I wasn't expecting you to be so happy about it."

"Ace. I love to cook. This will give me a chance to brush up on my skills. Just tell me when and what you'd like me to fix."

"When is next Tuesday. The what is up to you. I don't care what you feed them as long as they go home happy."

"Fine." She resumed stirring. "You won't be sorry."

He picked up a second piece of flatbread, covered it with cheese, and popped it in his mouth. "Yeah. I'm counting on it."

"More veal piccata, Eric?"

"I shouldn't." Eric VanEislander patted his ample stomach then reached for the platter. "After those wonderful anchovy mushrooms and the polenta canapés, I shouldn't even be thinking about seconds. But I don't believe I've ever tasted anything so fine as this. And the filet. Tell me, Ace, is it home grown?"

"Of course. All the beef you eat here is raised on our own ranch. Thanks to Hazard." Ace glanced across the table at his brother, who was doing his best to stay awake. He'd already put in fifteen hours with the wranglers, and all he wanted was to sleep. But both Hazard and Chance had agreed to be present for this important dinner with the representatives of South Africa's largest mining consortium.

They watched as their dinner companions polished off an entire platter of steak and veal, and emptied a basket of flaky biscuits.

"More wine?" Ace topped off their glasses and grinned at his brother.

Cody, wearing a leather vest, his only concession to his new role as chef's assistant, stepped into the room and began clearing away the dishes. When he rolled the cart into the kitchen, Maggie unloaded it. Minutes later she entered the dining room with a crystal bowl containing their dessert.

"Gentlemen, this is our chef, Maggie Fuller."

While the men around the table offered their compliments, she smiled and touched a match to the contents of the bowl. There was a dramatic flare of firelight that quickly burned off. Then she spooned bananas flambé into individual bowls, which Cody passed around the table.

As quickly as she had appeared, Maggie departed. Then she and Agnes began to clean the kitchen. They were soon joined by Cody.

"Those guys are looking mighty happy," he muttered. "And Ace has that smile he's always wearing when he's just won big-time. They're about to head into his office to sign a contract. I'd say your dinner party was a success, Maggie."

"Thanks to the two of you." She opened the oven, revealing the dinner she'd been saving. "Now it's our turn to enjoy."

They were just sitting down at the kitchen table when the door opened and Eric VanEislander stepped in.

"Miss Fuller."

She smiled. "Yes? Is there something you wanted?"

"There is indeed." He looked supremely confident as he said, "Whatever you're being paid here, Miss Fuller, I'm prepared to double it if you'll agree to come and work for me."

Maggie's mouth dropped open. For the space of several seconds she couldn't think of a thing to say. This had come completely out of the blue.

Finally, composing herself, she kept her smile in place. "Thank you, Mr. VanEislander. That's a lovely compliment. But I'm perfectly happy here. I wouldn't consider leaving at any price."

He studied her a moment. Then, unaccustomed to defeat, he shook his head. "I think, when you have time to reconsider, you just might change your mind." He reached into his pocket. "Here's my business card, Miss Fuller, in case you should want to reach me."

When he had left, Maggie turned to see Cody and Agnes staring at her in silence.

"Well." She returned to the table. "I wonder if it was my veal piccata or my filet? Or maybe the bananas flambé?"

Cody merely smiled. What Maggie hadn't seen was Chance, standing just beyond the doorway, watching carefully and listening to every word of their exchange.

Cody had seen something else. The look of surprise mingled with pleasure when she'd gently rebuffed the generous offer to leave.

The days passed in a blur of work. The golden days of late autumn gave way to a sudden chill in the air, signalling what was to come. Agnes warned that winter often arrived in Wyoming without warning, blanketing this part of the country in snow that might not disappear until late in the spring.

Each day without incident seemed to lessen Maggie's tension. Though there were visitors to the ranch, the Wilde brothers knew each one by name. There had been no strangers. This far from civilization it would seem that no one arrived uninvited, or without the knowledge of half the town of Prosperous.

So many things had changed. Agnes no longer made coffee in the offices, since the three brothers disdained their rooms in favor of the kitchen each morning. More and more often, Maggie was able to persuade Agnes to allow her to send food from the kitchen out to the cowboys in the bunkhouse as well. Chili and burgers were being replaced by pasta and pot roast, salads and home-made biscuits. Maggie managed to take the sting out of it by insisting that the older woman relax in the kitchen with a cup of tea, while she personally hauled the food over to the bunkhouse in a truck. Though Agnes offered a mild protest, she seemed to relish the break in her routine. And, though Agnes continued to insist that she had no use for anything but plain food, she could be seen sampling honey biscuits, cinnamon toast and apple-spiced sticks, and sighing with pleasure. The sight of it always brought a smile to Maggie's lips.

One afternoon, as Agnes paused in her work for a cup of tea, Maggie set a plate in front of her.

"What's this?" Agnes glanced at the flaky pastry, then at Maggie.

"I call it cherry almond cornbread. I was hoping it might come close to the one you described as your favorite."

"Huh." The old woman sniffed before picking up a fork. She cut off a small piece, tasted, then sat perfectly still as she chewed and swallowed.

"Ah well." Maggie shrugged, then turned away to retrieve the pot of tea. "I guess I'll have to try again."

Agnes quickly blinked away the moisture that sprang to her eyes. "It's not bad. Maybe I'll try a little more."

When Maggie turned, the old woman had cleaned her plate.

Seeing it, Maggie placed the entire pan of cornbread in front of her. "I hope you'll take the rest of this to your room."

"What for?"

"I'm making something else for the men tonight. I thought maybe you'd want some of this later."

"I suppose I could." Agnes was careful to finish her tea before carrying the pan of cornbread to her room.

Maggie was preparing breakfast when Chance sauntered into the kitchen.

As always, she was excruciatingly aware of him the moment he stepped into the room.

He filled up a cup of coffee and sipped.

"You've been here four weeks now."

She nodded.

"I told you we'd review your employment after two weeks."

She could hardly breathe. She'd been waiting for this. And hoping maybe it had been forgotten.

"Are you happy here, Maggie?"

"Very." She could see no reason to hide her feelings. "Are you pleased with my work so far?"

"Yeah. Very pleased."

She waited, aware that he was watching her over the rim of the cup.

"My brothers and I had a meeting last night. We agreed that we'd like to continue your employment and offer you a raise if you'll stay on."

She tried to contain her excitement. The truth was, she'd stay for half the pay. "How much?"

"Fifty dollars more a week."

She nodded and hoped she didn't look too smug. "That sounds fair."

"You'll stay then?"

"I'll stay."

"Good."

She turned away to remove a pan of biscuits from the oven. When she straightened, he was standing beside her.

"There's something else."

She didn't look at him. Couldn't. His voice had taken on that low, intimate tone she'd begun to recognize.

"I'm still waiting for you to decide about us."

She swallowed. "I told you. There is no us, Chance."

"And I told you. There will be."

When the door opened on a rush of cold air, admitting Hazard and Cody, he left her and joined them at the table. But all through the meal she could feel him watching her. It left a prickly sensation along her spine.

As the days settled into a comfortable routine, Maggie was actually beginning to believe that she could make a new life for herself here in Wyoming. The slower pace of ranch life was a soothing balm to her soul. She hadn't realized how much pressure she'd been living with until it began to ease. And as the tension eased, so did the headaches she'd been experiencing.

She felt as though a steel band had been removed from around her temples.

Everything about Wyoming was new and exciting: the barns and outbuildings that she began to explore with Hazard and Cody, the vast expanse of pastureland that she could view from the windows of the ranch house. Even the blustery, bleak weather sweeping across the countryside didn't dampen her enthusiasm. After all, she'd faced some bitter winters in Chicago. How much worse, she questioned, could it be here in the West?

Though it was early October, and snow had been predicted, she blithely faced the coming winter with optimism born of innocence.

Now if only she could ease the tension when she was around Chance. Whenever she found herself alone with him, even for a few minutes, she could feel herself wavering in her determination to hold him at arm's length. There was just something about him. A feeling that beneath that smooth, successful face he showed the world lay a hint of darkness, a thread of excitement.

It was clear to her that Chance Wilde was a man who'd always followed his own path, regardless of what others thought. When he flashed that dangerous smile, she could feel all her hard-won resolve begin to crumble.

There was another side to him, as well. A playful side that broke through on occasion.

''Do I smell cookies?''

Maggie looked up from the oven to see Chance standing in the doorway. He'd changed from his business suit to comfortable jeans and a plaid shirt, with the sleeves rolled to the elbows.

"You do. Chocolate chip. I didn't hear the helicopter."

"I used the limo today. Ace and I had a meeting at WildeMining." He stayed where he was, afraid to go closer. Every time he looked at her he wanted her. That only made things worse. He'd meant what he had said. The next time was up to her. And so he kept his distance. And waited.

"How'd you know chocolate chip cookies were my favorite?"

"They're every man's." She continued removing the cookies from the baking sheet onto a plate. When she looked up she glanced beyond him. "Where's Ace?"

"Gone into town. It's time for his weekly fleecing of the suckers at Clancy's pool hall."

"Doesn't he ever lose?"

Chance grinned. "Once in a while. But he's really good. There aren't many in Prosperous who can beat him."

"Doesn't it worry you that your brother is a gambler?"

He threw back his head and roared.

Puzzled, she arched a brow. "Why was that question so funny?"

"Sorry." Unable to resist the scent of freshly baked cookies any longer, he opened the refrigerator and filled a tall glass with ice-cold milk. "If you knew our family history, you'd understand. We come from a long line of gamblers. It's in our blood."

"You mean speculators. Prospectors. Men who chased after gold or oil. That's not the same as a gambler who shoots pool or plays poker."

He shook his head and helped himself to a hot cookie, savoring the taste of it, the texture of the melting chocolate, before washing it down with a long drink of milk. "Maggie, a gambler's a gambler. Whether he's chasing after oil or minerals or another man's money, it's all the same. It takes a certain kind of man to risk everything he has on the toss of the dice or the turn of a shovel in the ground. Trust me. Ace is just doing what comes naturally to a Wilde." He looked up at the ring of the telephone. As he turned away he said, "Remind me one day to tell you about my father. Now there was a true gambler."

Minutes later he returned and grabbed a handful of cookies as he headed toward the door. "Crisis in the barn. Hazard and Cody need my help. We'll be a little late for dinner."

As he sauntered away, Maggie stared after him. It was always Chance they called when things went wrong. Whether it was a crisis in the barn or at his company, she had come to the conclusion that Chance would be up to handling it, no matter what the problem.

When another hour had ticked by, Maggie made her way to the barn with a carafe of hot coffee and a tray of sandwiches.

Chance looked up in surprise. "What's this?"

"Just enough to keep you men going until you can come in for some real food."

Chance watched as Hazard and Cody poured themselves cups of steaming coffee and devoured several sandwiches, barely chewing them in their haste.

As always in her presence, Cody tipped his hat. "Thank you kindly, Maggie. That's just what we needed. Looks like you read our minds, as usual."

"There are more here when you need them." Maggie set the tray on a bale of hay before walking away.

As soon as she was gone Chance turned to Cody. "What do you mean, as usual?"

"Oh. Didn't you know?" Cody bent to the sick calf, holding him still while Hazard drew a vial of blood. "A lot of times lately, if we get too busy to go inside, Maggie brings the food to us here in the barn."

"She's been doing that a lot lately?"

Hazard shrugged, too busy to notice the frown between his brother's brows. "Yeah. Funny. I don't know how she figures out just when Cody and I have reached the end of our energy level. Like magic she appears just in the nick of time."

Cody, watching Chance's reaction, nodded. "That little gal's like an angel of mercy. Helping us to keep body and soul together." He moved aside. "Here, Chance. Hold this while we get another sample."

He handed the vial to Chance, then tightened his grip on the calf while Hazard drew more blood.

While he waited and watched, Chance felt the beginnings of a smile playing on his lips. Maggie Fuller might be a city girl who didn't know the first thing about life on a ranch. And she might vehemently deny she was doing anything more than she was being paid to do. But he was beginning to think there was a whole lot more going on here than met the eye. Whether she wanted to admit it or not, she was beginning to connect. Beginning to really care about them.

If she wasn't careful, she might learn to love it here.

"Maggie." Cody removed his hat and held it in front of him as he entered the kitchen carrying the tray. "Hazard thanks you for the coffee and sandwiches. And so do I. We'll be in for supper in a couple of hours."

"Oh, you're welcome, Cody." She accepted the tray and set it on the kitchen counter.

When he turned away she said, "Do you have to hurry back?"

He paused. Turned. "No, ma'am. Is there something you need help with?"

"No." She took a breath, then released it. "I was just curious about something."

"Yes'm?"

"Chance's father. Was he born and raised here in Wyoming?"

Cody chuckled. "No ma'am. Wes Wilde always claimed he was raised on a hardscrabble farm in Georgia. Nobody knows for sure, because he left home when he was twelve and never looked back. If there were any family or friends who knew him, they'd be long gone by now."

"He left home at twelve? How does a boy of twelve leave home?"

"He claimed he jumped a freight train headed north."

"But why?"

"He said he had an itch that just had to be scratched. An itch to leave the farm and see the world."

"What does a boy of twelve do without a home or family? How did he eat? Where did he sleep?"

The old man scratched his head. "He claims he never gave it a thought. He figured he'd worry about survival when he hopped off the train. His first stop was someplace in Ohio. He joined a circus, and spent the summer cleaning up after the circus animals. By the following year he was running one of the sleight-of-hand games in the midway, and doing exactly what he wanted— seeing the country. The circus never stayed in any town more than a week. And he was learning to survive by his wits. He discovered he was a born gambler. He used to boast that he had the fastest hands in the business. Nobody could catch him changing cards or coins. Not even experienced con artists.''

''That was his goal? To become a con artist?''

The old cowboy shook his head. ''A gambler. By the time he was eighteen he was running his own craps game in Detroit. When he got busted, he moved to Las Vegas and worked odd jobs until he was old enough to gamble legally. But that didn't last long either. Once the word was out that he was a pro, his face became too familiar to the security people, and whenever they spotted him they'd toss him out of the game and out of the casino.''

Warming to his story, Cody pulled up a chair and straddled it.

''He took a job dealing craps at a little joint in downtown Vegas, and started saving his money. At about that same time he met another gambler, Mason Gabriel, who was working in the poker room. They pooled their money, and one night they parlayed five hundred dollars into twenty-five thousand.''

Maggie's eyes widened. ''I can't even imagine anyone willing to risk everything on the turn of a card, when they had to work so hard to earn it. But at least it paid off. Twenty-five thousand.'' She shook her head. ''Is that when he bought this ranch?''

Cody threw back his head and chuckled. ''Ma'am, twenty-five thousand dollars wouldn't buy a fraction of this place. Wes Wilde and Mason Gabriel used that twenty-five thousand to buy their way into a bigger game. A much bigger game, with much bigger fish. In a villa in Monte Carlo, they took on an oil baron, a tobacco heir and a shipping tycoon in a seventy-two-hour poker marathon. And they wound up with the deed to one hundred thousand acres of prime Wyoming land.'' He laughed, remembering the way his old friend always loved telling the story. ''The only problem was, Mason was a city boy, who wanted nothing to do with the land. All he wanted was to get back to Vegas and live the life he loved. So he insisted they sell the land.''

''Did Wes Wilde want to sell it, too?''

Cody shook his head. ''Now, mind you, Wes didn't have a dime to his name. But he suddenly realized that he wanted, more than anything in this world, to get back to the land. Not just any land. This land. It became his obsession. He begged Mason to join him in working the land. He was afraid if they couldn't work together, they'd both end up losing it. But Mason refused. All he wanted was to live the good life in Vegas. So Wes and Mason had the land appraised, and found out it was worth half a million dollars.''

''Half a million.'' Maggie couldn't seem to take it all in. ''Isn't that wonderful?''

''Yes and no. You see, the more it was worth, the more Mason would demand as his share. So, in order to buy Mason out, Wes Wilde had to mortgage the land and bury himself in debt. But he was so determined to hang on to what he'd won, he begged, borrowed and nearly worked himself to death. In the end, he did it. He was able to come up with a quarter of a million dollars, and Mason went off to Vegas, still calling Wes Wilde every kind of fool for giving up a life of ease for one of hardship. And it really was hardship in the early years. It took all of them—Wes, his wife, his three sons—working every minute of the day and night just to hold onto it.''

Maggie was shaking her head in wonder. "Is that why you helped him?"

The old man nodded. "I really admired that man and his family. Half the time they didn't know what they were doing. After all, Wes was a gambler, not a rancher. But they kept on struggling to make it all work."

"Did Wes Wilde live long enough to see that his sacrifice was worthwhile?"

Cody shrugged. "Wes used to joke that all he'd done was exchange one miserable piece of hardscrabble land for another. But the truth was, he was having the time of his life. He'd come full-circle. This was what he had wanted. All he had wanted. What was even more important to him was the fact that he was able to leave his three sons a legacy. Not just this land and their devotion to it. But more important, their devotion to one another."

His voice lowered. "I've watched them grow from boys to men. Watched them hang together through troubles that would have caused weaker men to break apart."

He related the story that most of the people in Prosperous already knew. How Chance had given up an opportunity to go on to be a college football star in order to keep a promise to his father. How he had managed college, a few credits at a time, when he could squeeze them into his schedule. And how he'd insisted that both his brothers attend university, regardless of the cost in both time and money.

As the old cowboy talked, he saw tears come to Maggie's eyes. In that instant he knew what he'd already begun to suspect. The lady might not know it herself yet, but she was hooked on Chance Wilde.

"I watched Chance give up momentary glory for the

promise of long-term goals that seemed next to impossible. But he made them happen. He and his brothers, working together. Right now, you couldn't put a price tag on this land his daddy won in a poker game.''

''You think a lot of Chance and his brothers, don't you, Cody?''

The old cowboy stood, carefully replacing the chair before crossing to the door. His voice was gruff with emotion. ''Yes'm. I guess they're the sons I never had. And I'm as proud of them as though they were my own.''

Maggie watched as he stepped out the door before placing his hat on his head and striding toward the barn.

It occurred to her that the Wilde brothers were a whole lot more than she had first thought. Thelma wasn't the only one who had only good things to say about them. Not one, but two old people were absolutely devoted to them. Both Agnes and Cody had watched them grow from boyhood to manhood. Knew all their flaws. And still loved them without question.

And Chance Wilde, despite his reputation for being a tough guy, could meet a lot of people's definition of hero.

Chapter 7

"Another fine meal, Maggie." Hazard leaned back, sipping his coffee and looking completely satisfied.

Maggie carved a slice of apple pie and offered it to him. She was surprised when he shook his head in refusal.

"I thought this was your favorite."

"It is. But I can't eat another bite. I guess I overindulged to make up for the day I put in with the herd."

"Trouble?" She topped off Chance's cup, then paused beside Hazard.

"You could say that." He sighed and took another sip of coffee before pushing the cup away. "Got some sick cattle. Got to find out why. Now it's back to reality. I'll leave Cody in the barn while I head on up to the north ridge and check up on Peterson. He phoned earlier to say he's laid up with a rotten cold. He assured me everything's fine, but I'll feel better after I've seen for myself."

Chance put a hand on his brother's arm. "Hold on. You've got enough to do. You stay and finish your work with Cody. I'll check on Peterson."

"You don't mind?"

Chance shook his head. "It's a nice, clear night for a ride. I'll take the truck and be back in a couple of hours." He glanced over at Maggie, who was loading the dishwasher. "Want to come along? There's a terrific view of the ranch house from up there."

She paused to consider. Except for a few brief tours of the surrounding area, she'd rarely set foot out of this house. And though she'd begun to consider it her safety net, she couldn't see the harm in leaving for an hour or two.

She'd rather be going with Cody or Hazard. Those two overly courteous cowboys didn't affect her the way Chance did. But it was only a quick ride and then back to the ranch. What could possibly be wrong with that?

"I guess I could go along. What'll I need?"

"A warm parka." Chance pointed to a room off the kitchen. "There ought to be several in there. See if one of them fits."

She finished loading the dishes then dried her hands and left the room. Minutes later she returned wearing a cowhide jacket. "How's this?"

Chance picked up the keys to the truck and studied her with a grin. "It looks a whole lot better on you than it does on Ace. Come on."

Wearing a similar cowhide jacket and a wide-brimmed hat and carrying a rifle over his shoulder, he led the way outside.

Her eyes widened at the sight of the rifle. "Do you really need that?"

He shrugged. ''I hope not. But it's best to be prepared.''

He put a hand under her elbow as they crossed a wide expanse of lawn. Just that simple touch had her blood heating.

They stepped into a garage that housed half a dozen vehicles, most of them Jeeps and four-wheel-drive trucks, as well as several all-terrain vehicles.

''We'll take this one.'' Chance unlocked the door of a truck and helped Maggie inside, then walked around to the driver's side and let himself in.

He stowed the rifle behind the seat, then turned the ignition and backed out. Within minutes they had left the ranch house behind and were headed into the hills.

''Oh. Just look at that sunset.'' Maggie drew in a breath of pure appreciation as she stared at the sky, streaked with ribbons of red, pink and gold. ''Why does everything here seem so much bigger and brighter, and clearer?''

'''Cause you're in God's country, ma'am. We just do everything better in Wyoming.''

She had to laugh at his perfect imitation of Cody's drawl. ''I guess I can't argue with that. I've never seen anything quite so spectacular. Oh, and look at that.'' She pointed to the billowing clouds hovering just above the peaks of the Bighorn Mountains in the distance. Each cloud was tipped with gold. ''They don't even look real. They look like a painting. You know the kind. A heavenly scene with angels coming down from the clouds.''

It occurred to Chance that she could be in a painting as well. There was a certain goodness, a sweetness about her, that he found most attractive. And a vulner-

ability that had him wanting to protect her from un-
named danger.

He nodded toward the distant mountains. "It's funny.
I've been all over the world. I've seen the most amazing
sights. The Pyramids in Egypt. The ruins in Greece. I've
ridden gondolas in Venice and camels in the Saudi des-
ert. But nothing compares with this place. It's still the
only one that takes my breath away."

Touched by the fire in his tone, she turned to stare at
his profile as he maneuvered the truck across a rocky
expanse of hillside. "It must be wonderful to love a
place that much."

He shot her a sideways glance. "Don't you have anything that means this much to you?"

She looked away, avoiding his eyes. "I thought I did.
But my feelings don't even come close to what you've
just described."

"Tell me about your home in Chicago. Got any family there?"

"I did. A sister."

"She moved?"

"She died."

"I'm sorry." He glanced over, noting the pain in her
eyes. He had the most overpowering urge to take her in
his arms and comfort her. Not that she'd accept it. She
was so damnably independent. Another thing he
couldn't help admiring about her.

He forced his attention to the rocky path ahead of
them. "Did she die recently?"

"It's been three months now." Three months. Hardly
time to grieve. There'd been no time. She felt the beginnings of a lump forming in her throat.

"That's really tough. No other family?"

She shook her head. "Our parents have been dead

for years. Eve was the oldest by four years, and was really more of a mother to me than my own mother. I…'' she turned to stare out the side window, so that he couldn't see how deep the pain was ''…I miss her a lot.''

He held his silence, remembering his own losses. Though the years had healed the wounds, the scars were still there. And sometimes, at the oddest times, he'd feel a twinge. He'd learned not to probe those scars too deeply.

To change the subject he pointed to a ranch house in the distance. ''That's Peterson's place.''

''I thought all this land belongs to you and your brothers.''

''It does. But it's too big to maintain alone. So we hire ranchers who are willing to help. If they're single, they stay at a bunkhouse with the rest of the wranglers. We have eight, scattered across the ranch wherever the herds are concentrated. Then we have a few married ranchers as well. We build them a house, and pay them to live on the land in exchange for the care of a herd.''

''Do they have children?''

''A couple of them do.''

''Where do they go to school?''

''Most of them go to school in Prosperous. Especially if they're in high school. A couple of them are homeschooled, just because it's easier than spending hours on the road to school and back.''

''Don't the women and children mind the isolation?''

He shrugged. ''It comes with the territory. If you're going to earn your living out here in cattle country, you'd better be prepared to like being alone. There are always trade-offs in life. For the cowboy, the opportunity to live the life he's always wanted means he might have to spend a lot of hours alone with his thoughts. And his cattle.'' He grinned. ''Of course, they all have computers now. They chat on the internet, not only with each other, but with people halfway around the world.''

Maggie realized there might have been a time when such isolation would have seemed unendurable to her. Now, it sounded like a safe haven from the most troubling of worlds.

The truck pulled up in front of the darkened ranch house. Chance turned off the ignition. ''I'll be right back after I check on Peterson.''

For an instant a razor of fear sliced through her veins, and it was on the tip of her tongue to insist on going with him. Then she drew in a deep calming breath. She would not allow her imagination to run wild. There were no crazed gunmen lurking in the darkness.

Chance climbed down from the truck and made his way to the back door. Minutes later he disappeared inside. Maggie watched as light flooded the windows. A few minutes later the lights were extinguished and Chance returned.

''Peterson's feeling lousy, but nothing that a good night's sleep won't cure. Nothing serious. Just a cold. He claims to have everything he needs.'' He climbed into the truck and turned the key.

''Does he live alone here?''

Chance shook his head. ''His wife and kids are in Casper, visiting her family. They'll be back by the weekend. I told him I'd check on the herd and report back to Hazard.''

They left the ranch house behind and started off across the darkened hills. After nearly an hour of navigating rocky hills, they came to a stop. Below them, the land was black with cattle.

For several long minutes Chance studied the scene in silence. Finally he turned to Maggie. "This is something I never get tired of seeing. Isn't it beautiful?"

She nodded, touched by the serenity of the animals and the land.

"How many cattle are here?" Maggie's voice was hushed in the darkness.

"This herd is one of the smaller ones. Maybe a thousand head."

"A thousand head. And you call it small." She swiveled her head, straining to see through the darkness, and marveling at the sheer numbers. "It must make you proud, to know that you and your brothers accomplished all this."

"I guess so. When I take the time to reflect on it. Most of the time I don't even stop to think what we've done. There always seems to be one more fence to mend. One more ranch house to build. One more business to spin off and one more contract to sign. But at the end of the day, I have to admit, I'm just happy to be here, on my father's land, doing what he always dreamed of."

"What about your dreams?"

He turned to her. She was struck by the moonlight glinting in his smoky eyes. He looked dark and dangerous and mysterious.

"I've already accomplished most of them." As he spoke, his fingers played with a strand of her hair curling at her neck.

She sat very still, fighting a rush of strange sensations.

"As for the rest." He shrugged. Allowed his movements to still. "Though I never thought I could say this about myself, I've learned that I'm a patient man." He turned and pointed. "Look—way down there. See those lights?"

Maggie nodded, relieved to have his attention diverted for the moment.

"That's the Double W."

"And we're still on your land?"

"Yeah. As far as the eye can see." His tone softened. "I guess that was my first dream. Just to hold on to it. Then the dream got bigger and I decided I wanted more. I wanted to buy more land. Develop the land. Find its hidden riches and use them. And now..." he grew silent a moment "...now I guess I just want to make certain that my brothers and I can always live here, on the land we love." His voice fairly trembled with emotion. "Doing the work we love."

He leaned back, taking pleasure in the view before him. "Since I was a kid, I always thought this would be the place to build my home. High up on this hill, where I could be close enough to see the ranch house and far enough to have my own space, apart from my brothers."

"Why don't you do it?"

He shrugged. "It's just never been the right time. And I'm not in any hurry to live alone. I guess I always thought I'd wait until I found the right person to share it with. But I can see it in my mind. The long, low house. Lots of windows. And a fireplace in every room. And maybe a couple of kids who loved this place as much as their old man."

He glanced over at her, surprised by the depth of passion he'd revealed. "I guess we'd better get back."

He turned the key in the ignition. When nothing happened, he looked puzzled as he tried it a second time. There was only silence.

He stepped out of the truck and lifted the hood, poking around the engine for several minutes. Then he called, "Try it now, Maggie."

She did as he asked. There was no sound, except for his muttered curses.

He worked for several more minutes, then asked her to try the ignition again. When the engine remained dead, he snatched his cell phone from the truck and punched in some numbers. After a quick exchange of words, he pocketed the phone and picked up his rifle before opening her door and offering his hand.

"What now?" She slid from the truck, surprised by the blast of frigid air.

"There's a range shack about a mile from here. It'll be a lot warmer than the truck."

Drawing her parka around her, she struggled to keep up with his long, impatient strides. "Anything would be warmer than this. What's a range shack?"

"We have them scattered around the countryside for our wranglers. They're equipped with bunks and food and plenty of wood for the fireplace."

"Great." She was already beginning to shiver from the bitter cold. The thought of a cozy fire and some hot food lifted her spirits considerably. "Will somebody come and pick us up there?"

"Yeah. Watch your step here."

He pointed a flashlight at a rock, and she stepped around it before heaving a sigh of relief and accepting his hand. "That's good. I was a little worried."

"Nothing to worry about. Hazard said he can spare Cody to come by and pick us up first thing in the morning."

She stopped dead in her tracks, tugging on his hand. "In the morning?"

He paused. Nodded.

"But what about tonight?"

"No such luck. If Peterson felt better, he'd come by for us. But with Peterson out sick, there's nobody else who can do it. We're just too far away from the main ranch, or from any of the bunkhouses. Come on." When she ignored his hand, he turned.

"What about Peterson's house?"

"It'd take us the better part of two hours on foot. You'd never make it." He turned and started ahead.

She stayed where she was, staring at him until she could barely make out his form in the darkness.

His voice came from up ahead. "What's the matter? Aren't you coming?"

She stalked toward him, fighting a wave of fury. "Do I have any choice?"

"Hey." He put a hand on her arm and felt her stiffen. "I know you're not happy about this, but from the tone of your voice, I'd guess that you think I'm somehow enjoying it."

"Aren't you?" She hated the note of sarcasm in her voice. But she was too angry to control it. "Of all the trucks you could have picked, you chose the one that won't take us back to the ranch."

"You think this was deliberate?"

"I think you'll have a great time relaying this little joke to your brothers. You can have a couple of laughs over the night you and the ranch cook spent in the range shack."

"Believe me..." he dropped his hand to his side and curled his fingers into a fist, annoyed that even now, in the heat of anger, she had the power to make him feel this way—like a jolt of electricity was shooting through his veins, "...it's been a lot of years since I needed to fake engine trouble in order to have a girl spend the night with me. Now let's get going. Before we both freeze to death.''

He turned away and started up the hill without bothering to see if she was following. For the space of a heartbeat she thought about making her way back to the truck and spending the night there just to spite him. But she rejected the idea at once. Not only was she too much of a coward to spend the night alone in a cold truck, she wasn't a fool. If it got cold enough, she could actually freeze to death. She wasn't about to pass up the comfort of a safe haven just to prove a point.

Though it galled her, she started forward, knowing she had no choice but to follow Chance, no matter where he led her.

The range shack was a small log building that had been set in a stand of trees to offer shelter from the wind. Because the night had turned bitterly cold, Maggie was grateful to step inside. She was even more pleased to see that the cabin had a generator for electricity. Along one wall were sturdy bunk beds made of logs. More logs were stacked on the hearth beside a stone fireplace. Above the fireplace was a shelf of stone that formed a mantel.

Chance crossed the room and yanked one of the blankets from the foot of the bunk, wrapping it around her shoulders.

"Sit here," he ordered, pressing her into a sturdy wooden kitchen chair. Then he placed his rifle beside the closed door and shrugged out of his parka, before setting to work making a fire.

While he worked, Maggie studied the width of his shoulders and the muscles of his back and upper arms straining beneath the plaid shirt. What would it be like to be encircled in the warmth of those arms? To be free to run her hands over that muscled back, those corded shoulders? The thought of it caused her heart to skip a beat.

Annoyed at the direction of her thoughts, she forced herself to look away, noting the small bathroom beyond an open door and the apartment-sized stove and sink on the far side of the room. Above were open cupboards, stocked with staples. Sugar, flour, coffee, canned meats.

As warmth began to fill the room, she felt herself relax. This might be an inconvenience, but it was far from primitive. She thought about her first reaction, back there on the trail. She must have sounded like a whining, self-absorbed little girl. Suddenly she was ashamed of herself.

Clutching the blanket around her she crossed the room and rummaged through the cupboards until she located a coffeepot. "I could make some coffee."

Chance got to his feet, wiping his hand on his jeans. "That'd be great."

She busied herself at the small stove. Soon the aroma of coffee brewing added another layer of comfort to the room. When the coffee was ready she filled two cups and handed one to Chance.

As he accepted it she cleared her throat. "I'm sorry for what I said back there."

"Hey, I don't blame you. I guess it did look suspicious. Besides, you had no way of knowing what you were getting into." He sipped. With an easy smile he turned away, rummaging through the cupboards until he found what he was looking for. Uncorking a bottle of whiskey, he poured a liberal amount into both their cups. "Drink this. It'll take away the chill."

He drank, and Maggie did the same. She could feel the warmth begin to snake through her veins.

"Well." She had thought the tension would be relieved, but now that she was warm and safe, there was another kind of tension to deal with.

He was standing entirely too close. She was beginning to feel the room closing in on her. Especially when each time she looked at Chance she felt that quick little flutter around her heart.

Looking for something, anything, to distract her from her thoughts, she pointed to the kerosene lanterns on a shelf. "What are those for?"

It didn't work. Chance was still looking at her as he said, "They're a backup. In case there's no power."

"Does that happen often?"

He nodded. "The weather up here is unpredictable. We get plenty of ice and snowstorms. We try to be prepared for any emergency."

"Do all the ranchers around here have places like this on their land?" She knew she was babbling, but she needed to keep the conversation focused on something bland and safe.

"Most of them." He drained his cup, set it aside. "It isn't just the winters that can cause problems. We've been known to have ice storms in April and May and snow squalls in August."

Maggie shivered and drew closer to the fireplace. "I had no idea. I can't even imagine snow in August."

"It doesn't happen often. But we've learned to be prepared for anything nature wants to throw at us. Speaking of which…" he slipped into his parka, "…I'm going to bring in another supply of logs. I wouldn't want that fire to go out in the middle of the night."

As he stepped outside, Maggie stared at the closed door, relieved that, for the moment, she could catch her breath. The truth was, being alone with Chance Wilde absolutely terrified her.

She'd never known a man quite like him before. There was something...uncivilized about him.

If it was true that people were shaped by their environment, then Chance Wilde had come by his tough-guy attitude and fierce determination naturally. It would take a special kind of man, a man with superhuman strength and extraordinary courage, to succeed in a place as demanding as this. And now that Cody had filled her in on some of the family history, she realized that Chance Wilde was as much a gambler as his father had been. He was just following the example of Wes Wilde—a man who had left everything that was comfortable and familiar to make his own way in the world. She had no doubt that Chance Wilde would survive no matter where he found himself.

He was the exact opposite of her. She'd always liked everything safe. Safe and comfortable. Until recently. She was reminded again how far she'd come from all that was familiar. And yet, though she ought to feel completely out of her element, the truth was, each day in this Wyoming wilderness brought her one step closer to a sense of calm within herself.

By the time Chance returned with an armload of logs, she had pulled herself together. If she could survive all that had happened to her before this, she could certainly survive one night alone with Chance.

He deposited the logs and stood by the fire a moment, rubbing his hands together. Then he filled his cup with more coffee and splashed it with whiskey before lifting it to his lips.

"I'm sorry about the long, cold walk here, Maggie. But I think you'll agree that this is a much better place to spend the night than my truck."

"Definitely." She stared out the small window of the shack. "Is that snow on the windowpane?"

"Just a few flakes. It's nothing to worry about. I don't think we're going to get any measurable amounts of snow for a few weeks yet."

"Good. I don't mind a night here. But I don't think I'd like to find myself snowed in."

"Oh, I don't know." His voice warmed with a hint of laughter. "I can think of worse things."

Something about his tone caused her to turn. He was staring at her in that dark, dangerous way that had her heart doing somersaults.

Needing to do something, she walked to the fireplace. With her back to him she said, "I asked Cody to tell me about your father. It was an amazing story. If everything Cody told me is true, your father was an unbelievably confident man."

"Yeah. It runs in the family."

She turned to face him and saw that he hadn't moved. There had been no change in the inflection in his voice. And yet Maggie had the distinct impression that he was no longer talking about his father or his family history.

This was personal. Just the two of them. And the knowledge frightened her, even while it excited her.

Chance saw the flush that colored her cheeks and knew that, although she was trying to ignore him, she was having a hard time of it. Maybe it was the whiskey and the exertion of the long walk in the cold night air. Or maybe it was finally being alone with the woman who had caused him so many sleepless nights. Whatever the reason, he decided to simply enjoy himself. And let this night write its own ending.

"Funny." He took a step closer, watching her eyes. "You've only been in this shack an hour or less, and already I can smell your perfume in here."

"I think that's coffee you smell."

"No." He stepped closer, breathing her in. "It's you. I'd know you anywhere. Even in the dark."

She was reminded of a wild animal catching the scent of another. She swallowed as he touched a hand to her hair.

"What is it about your hair, Maggie? It's so soft." He plunged both hands into the tangles and drew her head back.

Without warning he skimmed his mouth over her temple, then lower to her cheek, then lower still, until his mouth was on hers.

She'd meant to avoid this. But now that his lips were on hers, now that his tongue was whispering ever-so-lightly over hers, she couldn't even recall what it was she was supposed to avoid.

"Every morning I see you in some prim little blouse." His hands skimmed down her sides, then up again, his thumbs brushing the sides of her breasts. "And I find myself wondering how you look when you go to bed at night."

"Chance, I..."

"Shh." He pressed his lips to hers. "Don't spoil my illusions. I like imagining you in some sheer, slinky little harem number."

She chuckled. "Sorry to spoil things for you. I look even worse at night than I do when I'm baking bread."

"Umm." He ran hot, quick kisses over her face. "Bread. Now there's a real turn-on. When I see you dusted with flour, I want to kiss it away.'' He pressed soft kisses to her cheek, the tip of her nose. ''And when I see you stirring something on the stove, I just want to come up behind you and…'' he lowered his mouth to her neck. ''Until you came along, I never thought about sex in the kitchen. In fact, I never dreamed a woman could make me feel this way just by cooking. But you do, Maggie.''

She wanted to laugh. But instead the sound came out in a shaky little sigh. ''I had no idea. So far you've only tasted simple fare. I wonder how you'll control yourself when I cook something exotic.''

''Who says I need to control myself?''

''I do.'' She struggled to remember the plan. To hold him at arm's length. But it wasn't easy when his mouth was doing such pleasurable things to her skin. ''I came here to cook, remember? I'm so glad I found the Double W.'' She arched her neck, loving the dizzying feelings that were stirring inside. She was hot and cold and her legs felt a little too weak. But she was safe here. And the knowledge loosened her tongue. ''I'm so tired of running, Chance. I just want to be here. Safe in your arms.''

''Safe?'' His head came up. His eyes narrowed. All his movements halted. ''Is that what you want? To be safe?''

She started to backtrack. ''Did I say that? I meant to say…''

He lifted his hands away, and took a step back, breaking contact. To keep from touching her again he stuck his hands in his pockets and turned away. ''If you think you're safe with me, you must really be desperate.''

''I'm not desperate. I'm…'' She hung her head, but

not before he saw the fear in her eyes. Fear, mixed with regret.

"Yeah. I know. Backed into a corner, with nowhere to go." His voice was harsher than he intended. But anger and frustration were warring inside, and he was in no mood to be gentle. What had started out as seduction had suddenly become deadly serious. And right now, one of them had to act responsibly. He'd pushed her too far, too fast. And taken her in the wrong direction. She was looking for safety, while he was looking for hot sex.

"Go to bed, Maggie. And take the top bunk. That way, you can be sure I won't attack you."

Seeing the temper in his eyes she kicked off her boots before skittering up the ladder as fast as she could.

He stared at her backside as she climbed up and snuggled under the blankets, and fought another rush of heat.

With just the light from the fire, he kicked off his boots and pulled off his shirt before climbing between the covers of the lower bunk.

He heard a soft rustling above, and knew that Maggie was trying to get comfortable.

He crossed his arms under his head and resolutely closed his eyes. But he knew sleep would never come now. All he could think about was the woman who lay just an arm's length above him. How she tasted. How her body felt pressed against his. How his body responded each time he touched her.

He got up and walked to the window, peering into the darkness. He may as well not even try to sleep. Instead of what he'd been hoping for, it was going to prove to be nothing more than a long, miserable night.

Chapter 8

Maggie was back in Chicago. Stepping off the elevator, heading toward her apartment. She was upset by something she'd been told. What was it? Something about Eve. Something too horrible to recall. She'd blocked it from her mind.

She stopped to fit the key in the door when she realized it wasn't locked. As she touched the knob, the door swung inward.

Puzzled, she peered inside. What she saw had her heart stopping. The foyer table had been overturned. The front hall mirror shattered. There was broken glass everywhere. Potted plants upended, their broken stems and trails of leaves and dirt streaking the Oriental rug.

And then she caught sight of the man's shadow as his head came up and he spotted her, standing in the doorway. In his hand was a gun. He slowly raised his arm, pointed the pistol, aimed, fired.

With a cry she sat bolt upright, her heart racing, her breath burning her lungs.

As she came fully awake, she realized it had been the dream again. That terrible, blood-chilling dream that haunted her, giving her no rest.

It took her a moment to remember where she was. Wyoming. The range shack. A thousand miles away from any danger.

She glanced around. The room was in darkness. The fire had burned to embers. Shivering, she gathered up her blanket and climbed down the ladder. As she crossed to the fireplace, she caught sight of a man's shadow by the window. Her heart leaping to her throat, she froze.

"Chance." His name came out in a whoosh of air.

"Sorry. I didn't mean to frighten you."

He stayed where he was, reluctant to go to her. He'd heard her thrashing about. Had realized that she was in the throes of a nightmare. But there was nothing he could do to help her. Not unless he climbed that ladder and offered to hold her. And that would have taken him over the line. And so he'd merely waited, hoping she'd come out of it and drift back to sleep.

He held up a glass of amber liquid. "Maybe this will help."

"Thanks." She accepted the glass and drank, grateful for the warmth and the bitter bite of the whiskey.

She watched as he crossed to the fireplace and tossed another log on the hot coals. He straightened, turned. He was barefoot and naked to the waist, wearing only his jeans, unsnapped at the waist.

He stayed where he was as flames began to lick along the bark and ignite. It was far better if he kept his distance.

"I'm sorry I woke you. I guess I cried out."

He shook his head. "I was awake. I couldn't sleep."

"I wish I could say that. If I had my way I'd never fall asleep."

He did go to her then, but only to take the empty glass from her hands. "Does this happen often?"

She nodded, struggling to shake off the tremors that still rocked her. "Often enough to cause a lot of sleepless nights."

"Is there nothing you can do about it?"

She shrugged, already feeling embarrassed by what he'd seen and heard. She turned away. "I think I'll make some coffee."

"I'll make it. You sit here by the fire."

Before she could protest he walked away. She drew the blanket around her shoulders and settled herself on a chair in front of the fire. Soon the little cabin was filled with the rich fragrance of coffee.

Chance filled two cups and offered one to her.

She gave him an embarrassed smile. "I'm not used to being waited on. I'm usually the one doing the serving."

"Maybe you ought to be waited on more often."

She gave a shaky little laugh. "Now why would you say a thing like that?"

"You strike me as a woman who deserves to be pampered."

To keep from touching her he walked to the fireplace and rested his hand along the stone mantle. "I know you're in some kind of trouble, Maggie."

She gave a sound that could have been a laugh or a sob. "It wouldn't take much to figure that out. I'm not very good at hiding it."

"Want to tell me about it?"

She shook her head. "I can't."

"Can't?" His tone was harsh. "Or won't?"

"Both, I suppose." She stood and crossed to the stove, intent upon re-filling her cup. She kept the blanket wrapped around her like a mantle of dignity.

She was startled when he caught her arm and turned her to face him. On his face was a look of fury. "How can I help you if you won't confide in me?"

"You can't help me, Chance. Nobody can."

"Let me try."

"No." She tried to pull away but she was no match for his strength.

His fingers closed over her upper arms, and he dragged her against him with such fury she cried out.

At once his touch gentled. "God, Maggie. I don't want to hurt you. I can tell you've already been hurt enough. All I want to do is help you. With whatever trouble you're in."

"I don't want to talk about it. I just wish…"

When she fell silent he held her a little away. "What do you wish?"

"That it would all disappear." She shook her head. "Oh, Chance. Just hold me for a minute."

Without a word he gathered her against him, his hands soothing, massaging, as they wandered up and down her back. The blanket fell to pool at their feet. Neither of them noticed.

Oh, she felt so good, so right, here in his arms. But he didn't know how much longer he could do this without taking them both down that path she was so determined to avoid.

He wanted her. Desperately. And he was afraid that giving in to his desire would only make things worse. For both of them. It had to be her choice, not his. And there were too many things going on in her life right now. Whatever they were, they were causing her too much pain.

She lifted her head. Her voice was little more than a whisper. "That feels so good. If you wouldn't mind..."

"What?"

She took in a quick breath. "Just kissing me. Once."

His eyes narrowed. She was asking too much of him—offering herself, but limiting him to a single kiss. Still, only a saint would refuse. And he was far from saintly.

"Hell, I don't mind." He lowered his head and brushed his lips over hers.

At the touch of their mouths he absorbed the shock. A kick from an angry bull would have been less potent.

He lifted his head and stared down at her, unwilling to believe what he'd just felt. But he could see by the glazed look in her eyes that she'd felt it too.

He started to step back. "Sorry. I can't do this. Even for you, Maggie. It's getting too serious for me."

She brought her arms around his neck, holding him still. "Didn't you tell me the next step was up to me?"

He hesitated, then looked down into her eyes. And could see the invitation there.

His smile flared. That hot, dangerous smile that did such strange things to her insides. "Yeah. So, what did you have in mind?"

"This." She lifted herself on tiptoe and brushed her mouth over his.

Instead of the reaction she'd expected, he merely kept his eyes on hers. His hands were still held stiffly at his sides.

When she stepped back he said, "Okay. I get it. You

want to forget your problems by losing yourself in some mindless sex.''

She started to pull away. ''I didn't...''

He caught her roughly by the arm. ''No. You didn't say so. But it's what you meant.''

When she didn't offer to defend herself, his tone roughened. ''Be warned, Maggie. What I have in mind isn't mindless. And it sure as hell won't be civilized.''

She swallowed, fighting the icy fingers of fear that were curling along her spine. She lifted her chin, determined to swallow back the fear. ''All the better. I just want...''

She barely got the words out when his mouth covered hers in a kiss so hot, so hungry, it wiped every thought from her mind.

For one tiny moment she almost resisted. It was a purely reflexive movement. One second her hands were at his bare chest, about to push him away.

Her gasp of alarm had his heart pumping, his loins tightening. He nearly devoured her with kisses.

Suddenly her fingers opened and splayed across his chest. She could feel the frantic beating of his heart, as out-of-control as her own.

He lifted his head. ''What were you trying to say?''

She took a breath to steady herself. ''All I want is you, Chance. Right here. Right now.''

''You're sure?'' His eyes were hot and fierce. His breath was hot against her cheek.

''I'm sure.''

And then there was no need to speak. She was lost in pure pleasure as their tongues mated, their mouths fed. With his mouth still on hers his hands tightened on her shoulders and he drove her back against the rough wood of the cabin wall and feasted on her lips until they were both gasping for breath.

When he lifted his head, she almost groaned with despair, wanting to feel his lips back on hers. Instead he ran nibbling kisses down her throat. She clutched at his waist and arched her neck to give him easier access. With each brush of his lips, her breathing became more ragged and labored.

His fingers were impatient as they fumbled with the buttons of her blouse. He tore one, then another, in his haste. But when he slid the fabric from her shoulders, he found delicate lace, and his movements slowed. He shoved aside the lace to find her flesh—and lowered his head to feast.

She heard a voice and didn't recognize it as her own—a gutteral sound that was more animal than human as she experienced a series of sensations unlike anything she'd ever known.

He unsnapped her jeans and slid them down her legs, then found more lace. He nearly tore it in his haste.

He heard her sigh as she moved against his hand while her mouth nibbled his ear. His blood throbbed in his temples, and he thought about taking her on a fast, dizzying ride that would bring them both the relief they sought.

But he had waited too long for this. Dreamed about what he would do. Now that they had come to this, he would have more than quick release. He would have it all.

He took a step back, so that he could see her face. Her eyes were dark with desire. Her skin flushed with heat.

"I've wanted you for so long."

"I know." Her lips curved in a smile. "You've made no secret of how you feel."

"You think you know what I'm feeling. But you don't have a clue yet, Maggie." The flickering flames of the fire cast his face in light and shadow. He looked as dark, as dangerous as any outlaw of the old West.

His gaze was fixed on her as he lowered his mouth to hers. Against her lips he whispered, "I won't be satisfied until I have everything. All of you. Your heart." He saw her eyes widen. "Your body." He cupped her breasts in his hands while his thumbs stroked her already erect nipples. "Even your soul, Maggie. I want it all."

When he bent his head to nibble and suckle, she felt her knees give way. Before she could fall he scooped her up and laid her gently on the blanket at their feet, then bent once more, his greedy mouth taking her higher than she'd ever been.

His eyes darkened with desire as he reached down. He found her, hot and moist. His mouth covered hers, stifling the little gasp that escaped her lips. At his first touch she shuddered and felt herself exploding in a burst of feeling. But he gave her no time to recover as, with teeth and tongue and fingertips, he took her on another wild, dizzying ride.

Maggie had never felt like this in her life. Her senses battered. Her body fluid and boneless. Her mind disconnected.

Each time she thought it would end, that she could absorb no more, he took her higher. Then higher still.

She needed to touch him the way he was touching her. She tore at his jeans, nearly swearing in her frustration, until he kicked them free. Her hands, her mouth, were as greedy as his, touching him everywhere.

He shuddered at the feel of her fingertips on his naked flesh. He'd waited so long. So long. And now that they were here together, he would savor each touch, each kiss.

For the first time he understood the meaning of madness. Needs clawed and scraped, struggling for release. One step, and he would slip over the edge.

And still he held back, drawing out the pleasure until they were both clinging to a desperately thin line.

She clutched at him and sobbed his name.

"Say it, Maggie. Say the words." He wanted, needed to hear them.

"I want you, Chance." She strained against him. "I want you so much."

"And I want you, Maggie."

They came together, flesh to flesh.

All she could see was Chance. Those dangerous, smoky eyes on hers as he watched her with a fierce determination that had her heart stuttering. All she could taste or smell was him. A musky, male scent more potent than the faint odor of whiskey that clung to his breath.

He was in her. Filling her as they both climbed higher and higher.

With his muscles straining, he leaned down and covered her mouth in a kiss that spoke of possession as much as passion. "You're mine, Maggie Fuller. Only mine."

She cried out his name. Or thought she did, as she held on for the ride of her life.

Maggie drifted on a warm cloud of contentment. Strong arms held her. Her lips were pressed to moist flesh. She breathed in the purely male scent that could only be Chance.

"Chance." Her eyes opened. She pushed a little away to see him watching her. "I...I guess I fell asleep."

"Only for a few minutes."

They were still lying, arms and legs tangled in the blanket on the floor of the cabin. He had wrapped a corner of it around them both, though it barely covered them.

"Are you cold?"

"No." Unsure of how she should react in this situation, she turned her head away.

He caught her chin, forcing her to look at him. "Sorry. I was a bit rough. Are you okay?"

"I'm fine."

He could feel her withdrawing by degrees. "Look. I'm not sorry this happened. But if you are…"

"I'm not. It's just…" She sat up, shoving hair from her eyes. "It could be awkward, Chance. I work for you."

"Is that what's bothering you?"

She looked toward the fire. "That's part of it. We live in the same house. We have to see each other every day. And if you should suddenly decide you don't want…"

"But I do want." He caught her hand and pressed it to his lips. "I want very much. Maggie, I never intended this to be a one-night stand." He studied her eyes. Felt his heart stop. Dear God. Was she already regretting her impulsive decision. "Did you?"

"Of course not." She shook her head, sending the dark curls dancing.

"All right." His heart began to beat again. "That part's settled. And the other part?"

She took a deep breath. This was what she'd been so studiously avoiding. The other half of intimacy. "You expect me to tell you about my problem."

He linked his fingers with hers. Looked directly into her eyes. "I guess, if you trust me enough for what we just shared, you ought to trust me with the rest."

She shook her head. "I don't want you to get involved, Chance."

For a moment he couldn't seem to believe what he was hearing. Then, determined to make this as easy as possible for her, he drew her back down into his arms and pressed his mouth to her throat. "Too late. I'm already involved."

"But I…"

"Shh." His fingers moved along her back, igniting little fires up and down her spine. "If you don't want to talk, we won't. But at least I'm satisfied that I can make you feel."

"Oh, yes. You can certainly do that." She shivered. "Do you know what you're doing to me?"

He shot her a wicked smile. "I hope it's the same thing you've been doing to me all these long weeks." He covered her mouth with his and was amazed to realize he was already fully aroused.

How was it possible to want her again so soon? But there was no denying that he did. He took the kiss deeper, loving the way she fit so perfectly in the circle of his arms. As though she'd been made just for him.

He ran soft, moist kisses along the smooth column of her throat.

At a sudden knock on the door he swore before they both drew apart. Maggie's eyes went wide with fear.

Without a word, Chance found his jeans and pulled them on. Then he snatched up his rifle just as a series of blows sounded on the door.

"Who is it?" he yelled.

"It's me. Ace."

He whipped open the door to see his younger brother standing in the bitter cold, huddled inside a parka.

"About time," Ace called as he stepped inside, slamming the door behind him. "I nearly froze."

"What're you doing here?" Chance's voice was a snarl.

"What am I...?" At the sight of Maggie hastily wrapping herself in a blanket, Ace stopped, stared, then managed to find his voice. "When I got back from Clancy's, Hazard told me I had to drive out here with a battery charger. Where'd you leave your truck?"

"A mile or so from here. Why don't you go see to it?" Chance started easing him toward the door.

"Hey. I won't be able to find it in the dark. I'm going to need you to show me the way, big brother."

"Not tonight." Chance gritted his teeth.

"Okay." Ace walked to the fire, held out his hands to the heat. "We'll do it first thing in the morning. That's better anyhow. I've already put in a long night. Which bunk do I get?"

"You aren't getting any. You're leaving. Right now." Chance caught him by the arm and started dragging him toward the door. "Three's a crowd, remember?"

"What? Are you crazy? I've just been on the road for hours, and you're telling me..." Ace caught sight of the hot, fierce look in his brother's eyes. Then he glanced over again at Maggie, who had managed to maneuver herself toward the lower bunk, still completely wrapped in a blanket. Except that her shoulders were bare. And her clothes were lying in a heap across the room. "Did I, uh, interrupt something?"

"Yeah. You did." Chance lifted the rifle menacingly. "And if you're not out of here in one minute, I may forget you're my brother."

"Yeah. Sure." Ace backed toward the door, with a sudden, silly grin on his face. "Nothing I like better than a two-hour drive at four in the morning."

"Then you ought to have a really good time on the drive home." Chance opened the door and shoved him out into the night.

As he was hustled out, Ace could be heard shouting, "It's a good thing I beat Milt out of two hundred bucks, and I'm in a really great mood, or I'd have to kick your…"

The door slammed and Chance drove home the bolt.

Then he turned to Maggie, ready to apologize for the embarrassment. "I'm sorry about that. Sometimes Ace is just like a big, dumb puppy."

She couldn't help herself. She started to laugh. "He was so sweet."

"Sweet?" He tossed aside his rifle and knelt down in front of her. "You think that pain in the… You think he's sweet?"

She nodded. "He's adorable. And you were so mad at him."

"I had every right to be mad. Ace's timing is always like that."

"He was so proud of himself for coming to our rescue. And you treated him like a…"

"A pest. Little brothers are always pests." He opened the blanket, and crawled in beside her. "Now. Where were we?"

She wrapped her arms around his waist and drew him close. "We were just about to..." She dragged her mouth across his throat. "This." Then, running nibbling kisses down his chest, she whispered, "And this."

He gave a moan of pleasure.

Suddenly, everything was wiped from his mind. His brother, the cold beyond their cabin and whatever trouble plagued Maggie, were all forgotten, as she took him once more into that warm, dark tunnel of love.

Chapter 9

"**Y**ou okay, Maggie?" On her return the following day, Cody poured a cup of hot coffee and held it out to her as she entered the kitchen.

She was touched by his concern. "I'm fine, Cody. Really," she added when she saw him looking at her so carefully. "I was a little scared at first. But once I realized how comfortable the cabin was, I knew there was nothing to worry about."

"Yeah. Especially with Chance looking out for you. No harm's going to touch you while he's taking care of things." He saw the flush that colored her cheeks. So, Ace hadn't exaggerated the situation. "Well." Seeing her discomfort he decided to change the subject. "Hazard and I are heading into town later. Anything you'd like us to bring you?"

"I'll check my supplies and make a list." She was grateful to have something to do. Cody was watching her a little too closely. Not that she blamed him. He'd known Chance since he was a boy. And probably felt about him the way a father would. That gave him the right to be concerned about every aspect of his life. Even his love life.

She figured that by now, half the Double W knew that she'd spent the night with Chance at the range shack.

"You take your time with that list, Maggie. I'll come back for it in a while. When we're ready to leave." Cody took up his hat and sauntered out to the barn. Leaving Maggie alone in the kitchen to mull over her own feelings.

Just what was she feeling? She lifted her hand to her cheeks. They were a little too hot. Like her blood. A little too hot whenever she was around Chance Wilde. That was the problem. She wasn't sure just what she was feeling. Or what he was feeling. Was it love or lust?

To be fair to Chance, she had to admit that he'd always been perfectly honest about what he wanted. He'd been pursuing her from the day she arrived here. And he'd never bothered to lead her on with love words. So much for his feelings.

As for her, if she loved him, why couldn't she trust him with the truth? The realization that she still hadn't confided in him brought a rush of shame. How could she share what they'd shared, and still not be honest?

She turned away and busied herself at the stove. Cooking always had a calming effect on her. When she puttered around a kitchen, she was better able to put things in perspective.

Now, just what was she feeling for Chance? She admired him. The way he'd taken charge of his life when he'd lost his father. The way he'd kept his family together. The way he'd chased his dreams. She even admired the fact that, though he'd made it clear he wanted her, he'd waited for her to make the choice. And there was no doubt about that. Last night had been her choice. But when he had accused her of trying to hide her fears in mindless sex, he'd hit a nerve. True, it wasn't with just anybody. She'd been fighting her attraction to him for weeks. But would last night have happened if she hadn't had that nightmare again? Was it fear—terror— that had propelled her into his arms?

The thought nagged at the edges of her mind.

It was true that she felt safe in Chance's arms. And it was equally true that he was a fantastic lover. But she didn't want to be unfair to him. She hated the thought that she might be using him.

She turned away from the stove and crossed her arms over her chest, deep in thought. Then she suddenly smiled as the answer came, quickly and simply.

Maybe she didn't know quite how he felt about things yet. But this much she knew. Whether or not he loved her, she was head over heels in love with him. And she couldn't wait to be alone with him again.

Hazard stood in the doorway of Chance's bathroom, watching him shave. "Everything all right?"

"Yeah." Chance turned on the faucet, rinsed his razor. "Peterson just has a cold."

"I know. I wasn't worried about Peterson."

Chance lifted the razor to his lathered face for another swipe, then glanced at his brother's reflection in the mirror.

Hazard met his steady gaze. "Ace told me what he saw."

"So? You got something on your mind? Spill it."

Hazard didn't bother mincing words. "It's you and Maggie."

"What about us?"

Hazard shrugged. "It's not like you to mess around with hired help."

Chance dropped the razor into the sink with a clatter. In the silence that followed he turned. "Maybe I don't think of Maggie as hired help."

Hazard kept his tone even. "How *do* you think of her?"

Chance's first thought was to grab his brother by the front of his shirt and throw him out of his room. It's what he would have done yesterday. And all the days before. It was the way they'd always resolved problems. Somehow, in the course of a single night, something had changed. He didn't feel like fighting. There was only one thing he felt like doing. All day. All night. Until he was too tired, and too sated, to move.

"Maggie's special."

Hazard blinked. He hadn't been expecting this. In fact, he'd come in here spoiling for a fight. Now he'd have to change tactics.

"Special in what way? As in…marriage?"

The thought of commitment slammed into Chance's gut, and he had to take a deep breath. He'd been too many years riding herd on responsibilities. The family. The land. The businesses. Sometimes he thought he'd never had a childhood. There had always just been hard work. Commitment? He'd had his fill of it. Still, when it came to Maggie, he couldn't reject it completely.

"I don't know. But I know this. I have feelings for Maggie. Feelings I've never had before. I need…I need time to sort them out."

"Okay." Hazard digested that and nodded. "I just

want you to know that I think she's special, too. And I don't want to see her hurt.''

''You don't want to see her... Why you condescending...'' Chance lunged forward and did what he'd wanted to do earlier. He grabbed a handful of Hazard's shirt and dragged him close, until their faces were inches apart. ''I don't need my smartass little brother telling me how to act.''

Hazard's hard, calloused fingers closed around Chance's shoulders and squeezed as he shoved him backward. His eyes were as hot and fierce as the smokey ones looking back into his.

''In case you haven't noticed, I haven't been your *little* brother in too many years to count. So if you're spoiling for a fight, I'll be happy to oblige.''

Still holding on, fingers digging so deeply they could snap bones, the two brothers circled each other like a pair of angry bucks.

Hazard's voice was low with anger. ''But that won't change anything. I still intend to look out for Maggie. In case you've forgotten, she came here looking like a wounded bird. Anybody with half a brain can see she's been hurt and is running scared. And I won't have her wounded any deeper. Not even by you, Chance. So, unless you intend to treat her very carefully, be prepared to answer to me.''

With their breath coming hard and fast, the two men stared at each other for the space of several more seconds. Then, as if by mutual consent, they released their holds on one another and stepped back.

As Hazard turned away and started out of the room Chance's voice stopped him. ''Hazard.''

He refused to turn around. The anger was still a hard, tight knot in his gut. He paused. Lifted his head.

"You're right. She is special." Chance's voice was little more than a whisper. "And I...I think I'm in love with her."

Hazard's scowl turned into a smile. He pivoted slowly. "There now. That wasn't so bad, was it?"

"What?"

At Chance's look of fury he calmly said, "I've been seeing it coming on for weeks now. The only ones who couldn't see it were you and Maggie. I just figured you were too dense to recognize what was happening."

"Why you..." In one swift motion Chance's fingers closed around the can of shaving cream.

Seeing what he intended, Hazard managed to pull the door shut seconds before the can slammed against the wood and crashed to the floor.

"That was a great meal, Maggie." Cody sat back and drained his third cup of coffee.

The others nodded their agreement.

"You sure do know a million different ways to cook beef. What do you call that?"

"Herb-and-spice-roasted beef tenderloin in a red wine and shallot sauce. It's really not that hard to make."

"Not for you, maybe." Cody accepted another refill of coffee. "You ever give any thought to writing a cookbook?"

At his question Maggie paused before returning the carafe to the kitchen counter. A smile touched her lips. "I did think of it once. My sister really wanted me to try my hand at it. She was so proud of me when I graduated from culinary school and got my first job."

Chance looked up in surprise. It was the first time

that she had actually volunteered anything about herself
or her life before coming here.

"Cody's right," he said quickly, before she could
close off the thought. "You ought to consider it. You'd
be a natural."

She shrugged, pleased with the compliment. "Cooking's one thing. Writing a cookbook is another. But
maybe some day."

"I have a great title." Ace downed another slice of
homebaked bread. *"Maggie's Fabulous Ranch Recipes."*

Hazard stabbed another piece of tenderloin. "I've got
a better one. *All About Beef.*"

Cody drawled, "Naw. You should call it plain old
Cooking with Maggie Fuller."

Chance put in his two cents. "I agree with Ace.
Something about ranch cooking. And you could try out
all your recipes on the cowboys in the bunkhouse and
use their remarks. I think it would be sensational."

Maggie laughed as she shook her head. "Amazing. I
haven't even written the first page, and you guys already have titles and quotes in mind. Now, who's ready
for chocolate cake?"

"I might have just a sliver." Cody patted his stomach.

"Me, too." Hazard polished off his second helping
of tenderloin.

"I'll have what they don't eat," Ace said with a
laugh.

"Chance?" She glanced over and saw that Chance
was watching her without saying a single word.

She felt the familiar tingle along her spine and wondered if he would manage to find some time alone with

her. Since their return from the cabin, they'd both been too busy to find even one minute together.

"No, thanks. I've had enough." He stayed where he was, watching as she moved around the table, serving dessert and coffee.

He'd been sitting here thinking that ever since her arrival, everything had changed. There was a warmth here at the Double W that had been missing for so long. It wasn't just the wonderful fragrances of cooking and baking permeating the air. Or the fact that he and his brothers were eating food they wouldn't have even considered tasting just weeks ago. It was Maggie. Her smile. Her smell. Her sense of humor. The house felt like a home again.

He and his brothers had stopped hiding out in their offices, drinking the disgusting mud Agnes used to pass off as coffee and taking endless business meetings whenever they could, just to escape. As for Agnes, there was a spring to her step that hadn't been there for years. She could be found these days sipping tea and smiling as she worked. Even old Cody lit up like a Christmas tree every time Maggie walked into the room.

Chance drew in a breath. Just seeing her made him realize how much he'd missed her all day. And now, this minute, he wanted her. Desperately.

"...go with us, Chance?"

He blinked, and realized Ace had been talking to him. "What?"

Ace swallowed back his smile. If his brother could see the look on his face right now, he'd realize he wasn't fooling anybody. He practically went into a trance every time he looked at Maggie Fuller. And she was just as transparent.

"I said the rest of us are going into town tonight. Do you want to go with us?"

Chance shook his head. "I'm tired. I think I'll just hang out here."

"Sure. Suit yourself." Ace winked at Cody.

Then he turned to Maggie, who had begun to clear the table. "Great dinner, Maggie. You sure you don't want to go with us to Prosperous? You could visit with Thelma."

"Thanks, Ace. I think I'll just stay here and tidy up."

"Well." He pushed away from the table and managed to bite back the smile that tugged at his lips. "I hope you two aren't too bored out here all alone."

"I've got a lot of paperwork to catch up on." Chance even managed to yawn. "I think I'll get to it."

"Yeah. Right." Ace signalled to the others. "Come on, Hazard. Cody. Clancy's waiting."

The three men retrieved their parkas and called their goodbyes as they exited the ranch house.

As soon as they were gone Chance stood and walked to Maggie. Wrapping his arms around her, he drew her back against him and pressed his lips to the little hollow between her neck and shoulder.

"I thought they'd never leave."

She leaned into him, loving the feel of his arms around her.

"I've thought of nothing but..."

Just then Ace slammed back into the kitchen. "Sorry. Forgot my keys." He plucked the keyring from a hook beside the door and shot them a knowing grin. "Um. The coast is clear now, bro. We won't be back for hours."

Chance glowered. "Good. Is that a promise?"

"Yeah. Sure." Ace was still chuckling as he sauntered away.

Chance gave a hiss of impatience. "If he comes
through that door again I'm going to have to kill him."

As he swept Maggie into his arms and started toward
her suite of rooms she protested, "Chance. What about
the dishes?"

"We'll do them later." He covered her mouth with
his to stifle any further protest, enjoying the quick rush
of heat and the eager way she responded.

Once in her bedroom he kicked the door shut behind
him and set her on her feet. "I wonder how you'll look
wearing nothing but an apron?"

She gave him the kind of heart-stopping smile that
always seemed to melt his bones. "I could show you."

"I'll hold you to that. Later." His hand moved to the
buttons of her blouse. "Right now I'd like to see you
wearing nothing at all."

He undressed her slowly, though he was tempted to
tear off her clothes. And then, just as slowly, he carried
her to the bed and laid her down, before settling himself
beside her.

"Do you know how beautiful you are?"

She sighed and touched a hand to his heart. "Tell
me." She needed the words. Needed to hear him say
them aloud.

"I love your skin. The softness of it." He kissed the
curve of her cheek. Traced his tongue over the outline
of her lips. "The sweetness of your mouth. I can't seem
to get enough." He took the kiss deeper, before lifting
his head to study her. "I love your hair. The way it
curls around your face just so." He caught a strand of
her hair and watched it sift through his fingers.

He leaned close and brushed a kiss over her eyelids.

"I love the color of your eyes. Like honey. And I love the way they warm when I touch you like this." He traced a finger around the curve of her breast and watched as her eyes darkened.

"And the taste of you." He bent to touch his lips to her breast and heard her soft sigh. Felt the sudden tightening of his loins.

"I love everything about you, Maggie. Everything."

And then there was no need to speak as he showed her all that he was feeling.

Chance stood by the window of Maggie's room and watched the dawn light just beginning to color the horizon. The entire night had been like a special gift. A gift he would always treasure.

They had made love as slowly, as lazily, as though they had all the time in the world. Afterward they had remained in Maggie's big bed, whispering, laughing, as comfortable as old lovers.

They had even found time to return to the kitchen and clean up the mess left from dinner. They had been as playful as children, laughing for no reason at all, savoring all the guilty pleasures as they sipped wine and nibbled the last of the cake. And true to her word, Maggie had allowed him to see how she looked wearing nothing but an apron.

That, of course, had led him to carry her off for another round of lovemaking. And then they had slept in each other's arms.

It had been the sweetest pleasure of his life to watch her as sleep overtook her. To watch her eyes shutter and close. To feel the soft, sweet rhythm of her heartbeat, keeping time to his own. And when at last sleep had claimed him, he had drifted off, still holding her in the circle of his arms.

He would be sleeping still if it hadn't been for Maggie's nightmare. Afterward he had held her and rocked her and soothed her until she'd fallen back to sleep.

But sleep was impossible for Chance. Though Maggie's nightmare bothered him, what bothered him even more was the fact that she still didn't trust him enough to confide in him.

He closed his hand into a fist at his side. He loved her. Loved her enough to be thinking about a commitment. A lifetime with her. But until she was willing to trust him with her secret, it was proof to him that she didn't return that love.

The knowledge ate at him.

He thought about the firm he'd hired to look into the discrepancies in the Miller contract. Thorpe and Associates were thorough, efficient and discreet. They ought to be, considering the fee they charged. But he trusted that they would get to the bottom of whatever trouble was brewing at WildeOil.

He made the decision instantly. He would contact them in the morning, and hand them another assignment. If Maggie couldn't bring herself to tell him what was going on in her life, he'd find out for himself.

The thought of another man, a husband, an ex-husband, flashed through his mind. Just as quickly he dismissed it.

Whatever Maggie's trouble was, it wasn't marital. He'd gotten by on his instincts too long to have them fail him now. If there was one thing he knew, it was that Maggie Fuller didn't give her love lightly. If there were another man, she would have never permitted herself to come to his bed.

It was one more reason why he loved her. And why he was determined to protect her the only way he knew how—by knowing everything he could about her past. And then, once he knew, he would deal with it. No matter what the cost.

His eyes narrowed. No matter what the cost. But what if the cost proved to be too great? Knowing how independent Maggie was, he could be treading on dangerous ground. She could very well consider his involvement too intrusive. There was the real risk that she would not only refuse his offer of help, but also run away again, once she found out that he'd violated her right to privacy.

Chance turned away. He came from a long line of gamblers. He knew how to weigh the odds before jumping into the game. He wasn't going to back out of this now. He was already in over his head. Now he'd just have to play the cards that were dealt him. And trust they were enough for a winning hand.

Chapter 10

"Well." Maggie turned from the stove as Chance walked into the kitchen. "Don't you look dashing."

"Thanks." He grimaced. "It's funny. I love everything about my job. The risks. The freedom to go where I want, when I want. The chance to see the world, deal with knowledgeable businessmen. But I absolutely hate wearing suits. I've always hated them. They're the one thing I'd change if I could."

"I don't know why, when you look so good in them." She cast an admiring glance at the custom-tailored fabric that draped his muscled body to its best advantage. "Of course, I like you just as well in jeans and an old plaid shirt." Her smile was quick and naughty. "Or in nothing at all."

"You're turning into one very wicked woman, Maggie Fuller." He set down his suitcase and crossed the room to wrap his arms around her waist.

"And whose fault is that?" She leaned against him,

loving the feel of his mouth on her temple. "You've brought out the worst in me."

"Or the best." His mouth whispered over her cheek, her jaw. "I wish I didn't have to leave for Dallas."

"You said you'd only be gone a day or two."

"Yeah. But that could turn into three or four days, if anything else goes wrong with these contracts."

"Are you expecting trouble?"

He shook his head. "Simmons and I went over everything yesterday in Cheyenne. He knows I'll have his head if there are any more delays."

Just then Cody and Hazard walked in from the barn. Chance moved aside and busied himself pouring juice from a pitcher.

The two men wrapped their hands around mugs of hot coffee and sipped gratefully, pretending they hadn't noticed the way Maggie and Chance had been all but crawling inside each other's skins just seconds earlier.

"Getting colder out there." Cody breathed in the fragrance of cinnamon rolls fresh from the oven. "Darned if that isn't just about the best smell in the world, Maggie. Are those for eating or just for looking at?"

She laughed. "You know better than to ask that, Cody. Everything I bake is for eating. In fact, I just sent a platter of these out to the wranglers in the bunkhouse. And this time, Agnes didn't even mention tossing the leftovers to the critters."

At their laughter Maggie pointed to the platter of cinnamon rolls. "Help yourself, Cody."

"Don't mind if I do." He bit into one and closed his eyes. "I think maybe I've died and gone to heaven."

Maggie filled a plate with omelettes. "Do you think you could hold off dying long enough to eat breakfast first?"

He grinned, then shot a meaningful glance at the oldest of the Wilde brothers. "With food like this, a man'd be a fool to ever leave."

They looked up at the drone of airplane engines.

Chance picked up his bags and gave a sigh of resignation. "Well, this fool has no choice. My plane's here." He shot a grin at Cody. "And somebody has to drive me out to the landing strip."

The old man heaved himself out of the chair. "Looks like I'm elected." He turned to Maggie. "Think you could save me some of that food?"

"I'll not only save it, I'll keep it hot in the oven. I promised Agnes I'd keep hers hot, too." She touched a hand to Chance's arm, wishing they had a moment of privacy, so she could send him off with more than a mere touch. "Safe trip."

"Thanks. I hope I'll be missed at least a little."

"You'll be missed a whole lot."

She watched as he led the way out the door, Cody trailing behind. When she caught sight of Hazard staring at her with a grin, she turned away and busied herself at the stove.

It occurred to Maggie that her romance with Chance was just about the worst-kept secret at the Double W.

"Maggie Fuller."

At Thelma's scratchy voice, several customers in the E.Z.Diner turned to stare at the woman in the doorway.

"I was beginning to think you were never going to leave the Double W and come back for a visit."

"Hi, Thelma." Maggie hurried forward to hug the woman who had first hired her when she'd stepped off a bus from Chicago. "You look..." She couldn't help staring at Thelma's bright orange hair and green lipstick and matching nail polish. "...very colorful today."

"Thanks, honey." Thelma's throaty laugh was a cross between a growl and a wheeze. "Park it, and I'll pour you a cup."

Maggie sat at the counter and watched as Thelma planted a cup of coffee in front of her.

"So. How'd you finally get a day in town?"

"Hazard was coming in for supplies, and I thought I'd come along."

"About time. Well?" The older woman leaned a hip against the counter. "How's it working out with the Wilde boys?"

"It's fine. Just fine."

"Fine?" Thelma's already arched brows shot up like exclamation points. "Is that all you can say about it?"

"Okay. It's a wonderful place to work. Thelma, I had no idea how big it was. I guess I was expecting an ordinary ranch house. But it's huge. There's so much space to just wander around and get lost. And the working conditions are the best. I'm free to cook whatever I want."

"How about Agnes? How are you getting along with the old grouch?"

"Shh. Thelma." Maggie glanced around, hoping nobody had overheard. "She's not an old grouch. She and I are getting along just fine."

"Well, that's some kind of record. You mean to tell me the two of you aren't at each other's throats?"

Maggie grinned. "She wasn't very fond of me at first."

"Fond of?" Thelma snorted. "Come on, Maggie. This is me, Thel. No need to use fancy words."

"Okay. She didn't like me at all, at first. But I think

that's changing. Now that she's stopped seeing me as a competitor, she's actually starting to come around. I think, in time, we might even become friends.''

"Will wonders never cease? That old woman hasn't liked anyone in the entire state of Wyoming, except the Wilde brothers, since her husband died."

"Maybe she's just lonesome."

Thelma shook her head. "Okay. Tell me about working for the Wildes."

"They seem really happy with my cooking. At least, so far there have been no complaints."

"Didn't I tell you?" Thelma's voice lowered. "And didn't I tell you they were great guys?"

"Yes. You did." Maggie stirred cream into her coffee. "I'm really grateful, Thelma. For everything."

"Uh-huh." The older woman brushed a speck of imaginary lint from the lacy handkerchief pinned to her pocket. It was plain that she was uncomfortable with any expression of gratitude. "I didn't do anything. You're the one with the talent. I just steered you their way when I knew I was going to have to make room for Slocum to come back to work."

"I understand."

Maggie glanced at the man busy working at the grill. Thelma followed her glance.

"I know," the older woman said under her breath. "He's not much to look at. And not very dependable. But he's good to me. And he keeps my bed warm on cold winter nights."

Maggie couldn't help chuckling at her honesty.

"How about your bed?" Thelma studied her more closely. "You're not looking nearly as scared as when I first met you. In fact, you're looking downright satisfied."

Maggie was relieved when two customers chose that moment to walk in, causing a distraction.

Thelma pulled the pencil from behind her ear and made her way to their table. Minutes later she returned, shouting the orders to her cook. A short time later, after serving them, she sidled up beside Maggie.

"Don't think I haven't forgotten where we left off." She leaned close. "So. Which brother snagged your interest?"

"Thelma!" Maggie tried to look indignant, but the older woman wasn't fooled.

"Save that for somebody else, honey. Now tell me why you're looking so good. Is it Ace?" She gave an exaggerated sigh. "He's my little sweetheart. If I was twenty years younger." She paused. "If I was thirty years younger." She winked. "Okay. If I was forty years younger, I'd make a play for that one."

Maggie couldn't help laughing. "Thelma, you're outrageous."

"Okay. Forget Ace. Is it Hazard? That big, muscular rancher makes all the girls' hearts flutter. But he's a shy one. That'd probably appeal to you."

"Oh, Thelma." Maggie shook her head. "I'm not interested in any of the Wilde brothers."

"Uh-huh." Thelma studied her a moment, then said, "It's not Ace, and it's not Hazard. I guess that only leaves Chance."

Maggie schooled her features and held her silence.

Thelma slapped her on the shoulder and gave a loud hoot. "Well, if you aren't the coy one. And why *not* go for the oldest brother? He's so sexy, I nearly swoon every time I look at him. But honey, you've got a tough bull by the horns with that one. I hope you're up to it. He's resisted every advance ever made on his hide.

Why, every woman in Wyoming over the age of reason has tried and failed with Chance Wilde.''

Maggie shook her head. "I don't know what you're talking about. I've got to run, Thelma.''

"Yep. I know just what you're saying, honey. That's your story, and you're sticking to it. But old Thel knows better.''

Maggie could feel her cheeks growing hot. She stood, leaving half a cup of coffee. "Sorry I have to run. But I promised to meet Hazard and Cody over at the This N That Shop.''

"Sure thing, honey. You run along.'' Thelma winked. "And next time you stop by, you'd better be ready to fill me in. Or you might just find me parked on your doorstep out at the Double W looking for all the juicy details.''

Maggie made a fast exit, grateful that she actually did have to make a couple of purchases at the This N That Shop, so that she wouldn't feel like such a liar. The truth was, she just wasn't ready to talk about her feelings where Chance was concerned. She was in way over her head. But there was too much going on in her life. Too much that could send her off and running without a moment's notice. Until she could sort through the baggage she'd brought with her, she couldn't possibly sort out what to do about her feelings for Chance.

Mulling over her dilemma, she wandered through town, stopping at Wanda's Bait and Party Shoppe, then moving on to the This N That Shop, where she made several hasty purchases.

As she walked through the town, it occurred to her that it was the first time since she'd fled Chicago that she had felt safe walking alone. But, she reminded herself, this was Prosperous, Wyoming. Who could ever find her here?

"Mr. Wilde." The voice on the other end of the phone spoke in quick, staccato phrases, with a hint of Long Island roots.

Chance sat a little straighter in the leather recliner of his jet. The trip to Dallas had gone smoothly, and the business had been concluded in two days. Now, as the plane crossed into Wyoming, he held the phone to his ear. "What did you find out, Thorpe?"

"It didn't take much digging. Most of it was common knowledge in Chicago. But I knew you'd want a thorough report, so I dug a little deeper."

As the voice droned on, Chance's eyes narrowed. "Fax me that report. Now."

"Yes, sir. Right away. And as soon as I turn up more, I'll get it to you. Besides the newspaper accounts, I think I'll be able to get hold of the police report. I've got an old friend in the Chicago D.A.'s office."

"Good. And Thorpe—keep digging. As deep as you have to. I want it all."

After he hung up, Chance drummed his fingers on the arm of the chair, waiting for the fax to come through. As soon as it did, he read every word, before looking up with a hiss of disgust. So much for his hope of a simple solution to Maggie's problems. According to this, she was up to her eyebrows in trouble.

"Oh, how I've missed you." Maggie could barely get the words out as they tugged at each other's clothes and rolled around on the bed.

His hands and mouth were everywhere, burning a trail of fire across her naked flesh.

"Not as much as I missed you." He couldn't believe the feelings that poured from him. Feelings he hadn't even known he was capable of until he'd walked through the door and caught sight of her standing there at the table, just tidying up after dinner.

One silent look at his brothers and they'd given him a wide berth, finding chores that suddenly required their immediate attention.

"I didn't believe it was possible to be this homesick in just two days." He lingered over her mouth, loving the clean, fresh taste of her.

"Has it been only two days?" She wrapped her arms around his waist and pressed her lips to the hollow of his throat, loving the way he sighed with pure pleasure. "It felt like weeks."

"I know. The first night in the hotel was the longest of my life. Last night wasn't nearly as bad, because I knew the contracts would be signed this afternoon, and barring any delays, I'd be on my way home to you." He paused. Lifted his head. "I like the sound of that. Home to you."

Maggie thought her heart might explode with happiness as he lowered his mouth to hers. And then, with soft sighs and whispered words of love, they melted into one another. The need for words was long past.

"I'm relieved to have those contracts signed, sealed and delivered." Chance handed Maggie a tulip glass filled with champagne, before settling himself in bed beside her.

"Were there any problems?" She looked pleasantly sated, with her hair mussed and her skin flushed from lovemaking. She had pulled on his starched white shirt to cover her nakedness.

He found himself thinking that a woman could look far better in white shirts than any man. The thought had him smiling as he shook his head. "No problems. This time it went without a hitch."

"I'm glad." She handed him a crusty roll piled with thin slices of prime rib left over from dinner.

He took a bite, then washed it down with champagne, before handing the glass back to her.

"I wasn't expecting any problems. The firm I hired boasts a ninety-five-percent success rate on all their cases."

"Cases?" Maggie looked up. "What sort of cases?"

"Fraud. Theft. Corporate spying."

"You think Avery Simmons is involved in corporate spying?"

"I think someone is. That contract didn't just change itself. Before they're through, Thorpe and Associates will know as much about my employees as they know about themselves. And someone in my employ is going to get more than he bargained for in his paycheck."

"A pink slip?"

"More than that. A summons. I intend to sue the guilty party for fraud."

"Serves him right." She sipped champagne and leaned back against the pillows. "I hate stealing."

He heard the venom in her tone and paused for a beat, hoping to give her as much time as she needed. "Thieves rarely just steal our money or possessions. They steal much more: our confidence. Whether it's confidence in ourselves or in someone else. In my case, I've begun to mistrust all those employees who deal with the contracts. And that's so unfair to them. They deserve better. They deserve my trust. But lately, I can't trust any of them."

When she remained silent he turned to her. "How about you, Maggie? Any problems while I was gone?"

She shook her head. "No problems. I had a visit with Thelma in town. Kit Korson had all the supplies I needed. Life's good."

"Yeah." He was staring at her in a way that always made her uncomfortable. As though studying her under a microscope. "It could be a whole lot better."

She felt a tiny flutter around her heart. "How?"

"If you'd trust me."

Her smile slipped a notch. "I told you, Chance. I do trust you."

"But not enough to share any real secrets."

She flounced off the bed, unwilling to sit quietly under his scrutiny. "Maybe I just don't have any secrets to share."

He watched as she stalked to the window and stared into the darkness. He could read her agitation—in the way her hands clenched into fists at her sides, in the way she held herself so rigidly as she stared pointedly out the window, refusing to look at him.

"Don't you?"

"No."

His voice was ominously calm. "All right. I didn't want to have to say this. But it's time for some honesty."

He stared at her stiff spine, her jutting jaw, and wished he knew how to soften the blow.

On a sigh, he said tiredly, "Maybe Maggie Fuller doesn't have any secrets. But Margaret Mary Trainor has a closet-full."

Chapter 11

Maggie's head came up sharply.

"You spied on me!" With a look of fury she turned so quickly the champagne sloshed over the rim of the glass and stained the front of the white shirt. She took no notice. All she could see was Chance's eyes, narrowed on her.

"That's right. But only because I want to help you."

She was already shaking her head. "You can't help me, Chance. Nobody can."

"How do you know that, unless you give me a chance." He shot her that silly, heart-stopping grin, hoping to diffuse the volatile situation. "After all, it is my name. Now, about yours…"

His ploy worked. Defeated, she took a deep breath. "I've always been Maggie. I was christened Margaret Mary Trainor."

"And the Fuller?"

She looked down at the glass in her hand. "Fuller

was my mother's maiden name. It was the first thing that came to mind when Thelma offered to hire me and asked my name.''

''And you couldn't use your own name.''

''No.'' She looked up. ''I'm not very good at lying.''

''So I've noticed.''

''How much do you know?''

He crossed the room and removed the fax from his suit-coat pocket then read aloud, ''Margaret Mary Trainor, cook and co-owner of Feast, a four-star restaurant in Chicago, has been missing now for more than a month. After her disappearance it was learned that the restaurant's bank account had been emptied and the books were missing. The authorities believe that she absconded with funds to thwart her business partner and brother-in-law, Ray Collier, who had arranged for the sale of their restaurant. The *Chicago News* reports that Detective Ray Collier, a much-decorated police officer with the Chicago force, had been married to Eve Trainor, late sister of the missing woman. Collier has stated that, despite the charges of embezzlement against Ms. Trainor, he will reserve judgment until she can be found and brought to trial. The restaurant will continue to operate under his management until such time.''

He looked up. ''Did the report miss anything?''

She shook her head. ''Not much.''

He paused. ''So?''

Maggie shrugged. ''It's true that the funds are missing. By my account there was a hundred thousand in the bank to pay salaries and taxes. As for the books, I'm sure by now they've been destroyed, so there's no way to determine just how much money has been stolen or misappropriated. But I give you my word, Chance. I didn't have anything to do with it.''

"Okay." Chance smoothed out the pages of the fax and handed them to Maggie.

She accepted them without looking at them. She was too busy staring at him.

She perched on the edge of the desk. "What do you mean *okay?*"

"Okay. You didn't do it. Was it your partner, Ray Collier?"

She swallowed, then nodded. "Yes. But I...didn't expect someone like you to accept me at my word."

"Someone like me?"

"You know what people say about you. You're tough and shrewd and demanding in business. I've heard you admit as much."

"What's that got to do with believing you?"

"I don't know." She shook her head as if to clear it. "I just thought..." she gave a long, deep sigh. "I have no proof."

"That doesn't matter, Maggie. I know you." He took her hand and studied it, so small against his. "Now why don't you tell me what really happened?"

She took a deep breath. "I'll try. I've never had the chance to say the words aloud until now." She waited a moment, sorting her thoughts. "Ray Collier was married to my sister, Eve. At the time I was working as head chef at the Drake and dreaming about owning my own restaurant. It was Eve who got me to agree to be Ray's partner in business. I think she thought it would bring us all closer together."

"So you agreed to go into business with him?"

She nodded. "Eve and I each put up one hundred thousand dollars."

"That's a lot of money."

"I know. It was part of the estate left us by our parents. Along with the money, I pledged my time and talent in the kitchen, while Ray pledged to handle the business end of the partnership. He would hire and fire and deal with the ledgers before they went to the accountants. It seemed a fair division of time, money and talent.'' She paused a moment and looked away. ''Shortly after we got the business up and running, Eve died suddenly. An aneurysm, the doctor said. I was so stunned, I guess I walked around in a fog for weeks. I couldn't have told you what was going on around me. All I did was show up for work, cook for hours and then fall into bed. And then I got hit with another blow. My kitchen manager had an argument with Ray and was fired. Before she left, she told me I'd be wise to open my eyes and take a good, hard look at what was going on with the business. When I did, I found dozens of unpaid bills for food and liquor orders. Some of the suppliers wouldn't even deliver any longer, unless we were willing to pay cash. What was worse, I found my signature forged on documents. They weren't even a good forgery. There was no attempt to make the signature look like my writing. So I decided, then and there, to start taking a closer look at the business end of the operation.'' Her tone lowered. ''I found that none of the figures Ray was giving to the accountant matched mine.''

''Doctored books.'' Chance was watching her closely.

''Yes.'' She nodded. ''Doctored books. An elaborate set of phony receipts. I confronted Ray, expecting him to admit what he'd done and to apologize.'' She shook her head. ''The funny thing is, I still wasn't concerned about the money. I made a good living. So did he. I figured I'd give him time to reimburse me, because I still considered him family. After all, he and my sister, Eve, had been married for more than five years. I guess that's why I didn't see any of this coming.''

Chance waited patiently, though his mind had already leaped ahead. It was an old story. One his father had warned him about repeatedly. The quickest way to lose everything was to take in a greedy partner.

She glanced up, then away. ''Instead of an apology, Ray told me he had found a buyer for the restaurant. He had put it up for sale without even consulting me. When we'd started the operation, we had been equal partners, even though his money came from Eve. Now he was telling me he was selling what wasn't his to sell. And when I mentioned the unpaid debts and the inflated income on the books, things turned ugly. He warned me that unless I kept quiet, I'd suffer the same fate as my sister.''

Chance saw the change in her. The sudden agitation. She turned toward the window, then began to pace. ''I couldn't believe what I was hearing. His words were so chilling, I couldn't accept them at first. But they kept playing over and over in my mind.'' She pressed her hands to her ears, as though hoping to shut out the words, the thoughts. ''Had he had a hand in Eve's death? It had never occurred to me to think such a horrible thing. But now I was beginning to doubt everything. Still, I wasn't really convinced. I figured those things just happened in novels. They don't happen in real life. Not to me.''

She hugged her arms about herself, suddenly cold. ''How could I have been so blind?''

''What happened to change your mind, Maggie?''

''That same night, with Ray's threat still ringing in my mind, I arrived home to find my apartment door unlocked. I pushed it open just far enough to see inside.'' She shook her head, trying to blot out the image. ''At first I thought it was just a random act of violence. There was broken glass, upended furniture. But then, I caught sight of an armed man waiting for me. He was trying to make it look as though the apartment had been ransacked and robbed, but he was really there to kill me. When he caught sight of me in the doorway, he raised the gun and aimed it directly at me. I ran, with nothing but the clothes on my back, and whatever money was in my wallet.''

''Why didn't you run to the police?''

She shook her head. ''You read that fax. Ray is on the police force. I couldn't go to the police about one of their own.''

''Do you really believe they wouldn't protect you from him?''

''I couldn't take that chance. I was suddenly terrified of him. I thought I knew him. But I didn't know him at all. If he had killed Eve, and if he had hired a gunman to kill me, he would stop at nothing to silence me. I needed to run, until I was far enough away that he couldn't find me. I was so afraid. Afraid to take a cab. Afraid my movements could be traced. So I ran through back streets in the dark. All the way to the bus station. I was afraid to use my credit cards for the same reason. So I bought a one-way ticket on the first bus leaving Chicago. That's how I ended up in Wyoming. I thought…'' she shivered. ''I don't know what I thought. I was scared. No,'' she corrected. ''I was terrified, and looking for a place to hide until I could sort things out. The only trouble is, I still can't see any solution to the problem. Even though everyone believes that I'm a thief, that's better than returning to Chicago and having to face the man who could destroy me.''

He walked toward her, attempting to soothe. ''Your instincts were right, Maggie. You did everything you could to buy some time. As for the location, it couldn't be better. You came to the right place.''

She shook her head and backed away. ''No. Don't you see? I wasn't thinking about anyone but myself. But now that I…'' she took a deep breath ''…now that I care about you and your brothers, I can't stay here.''

''Why not?''

''What if I'm found here? I could be bringing my troubles to your doorstep.''

''Your troubles are already here, Maggie. I'm already involved. What affects you affects me as well.''

Shaking her head, she backed up until she bumped into the wall.

Chance caught her by the shoulders and stared down into her troubled eyes. ''You don't really think my brothers and I are going to let you deal with this alone?''

''But don't you see?'' Her voice rose on a note of hysteria. ''All Ray has to do is notify the authorities here that I'm wanted by the police in Chicago, and they'll arrest me. And your name will be smeared.''

''Do you think that would bother me?''

''All right. If you're not worried about your reputation, think about this. Ray has a license to carry a gun. He can come here and arrest me himself. And I'll have to go with him.''

Chance's eyes grew hot and fierce. ''Let him come.''

''Chance, if you tried to stop him, he'd have the right to shoot you. To shoot us both. He can kill us, because he's already killed once.'' Her eyes widened. Her voice took on a note of panic. "He killed Eve. He killed my sister. Oh God, Chance, how could this be possible?"

He could read in her eyes the shock and horror that had suddenly dawned. Until this moment she'd kept it all locked inside. Now, having spoken the words aloud, it hit her with all the force of a physical blow.

"Go ahead, Maggie. Let it all out." He drew her into the circle of his arms and could feel her stiffen, determined to hold it all inside.

"I can't. Don't you see? If I start, I'll never stop." She shook her head, her spine rigid, her body trembling. "I can't. I just can't."

She wouldn't think about the fear. About the never-to-be-filled hole left in her life by her sister's death. About the fact that her good name had been muddied by a man bent on destruction. If she did, she might become paralyzed with terror and grief.

"All right." Chance watched as she took in a deep, shuddering breath and struggled to find some calm. Her strength in the face of such trouble amazed him.

"The first line of defense is to know your adversary. I'll have Thorpe get us everything he can on Ray Collier. Then we'll plan our next step."

"Our next step?"

"How to get Collier before he gets us." He smiled, and she was reminded of the first time she'd seen him. Hadn't she known then that he'd be a dangerous opponent?

"Oh, Chance." She closed her eyes a moment, feeling a welling of relief. "Of all the things you've said, the thing I like best is *us*. I've felt alone in this for so long."

"See? And all along, you were trying to shut me out."

She gave a shaky laugh. "Sorry."

"Yeah. Me too." He lifted her chin so that she was forced to look into his eyes. What she saw had her heart stuttering.

"You're not alone any more, Maggie. You can count on my brothers and me. We won't let you down."

He scooped her up and carried her to the bed.

Before she could speak, he kissed her. Then he gently laid her on the bed and stretched out beside her.

"From now on, we're a team. You're going to have to learn to trust us completely. Deal?"

She stared up into his eyes. "You're sure about this? You're sure you want to get involved in something this vicious, this dangerous?"

"As sure as I've ever been about anything." He held out his hand.

"Okay." She took a long, deep breath. "You've got yourself a deal." She placed her hand in his and watched as he took it to his lips.

"Now, partner, let's seal this bargain." He drew her into the circle of his arms and kissed her. And then, with exquisite patience, he slipped the shirt from her shoulders and showed her, in the most profound way, just how much he cherished her.

"I have to let my brothers know what's going on."

"I wish you wouldn't." Maggie turned from the stove, where she'd already started breakfast. "Why can't we keep this between the two of us?"

"Because." He walked up behind her and began massaging the knot of tension in her shoulders. "They have a right to know."

"What if they believe the lies that are being spread about me?"

His movements halted. He slowly turned her to face him. "Do you really expect them to think less of you when they hear the truth?"

"I don't know." She shook her head. "I'll bet plenty of my old friends are reading about me in the press back in Chicago, and thinking the worst."

"You can't help what people choose to think, Maggie. But I'm willing to wager any amount of money that my brothers will become your staunchest defenders." He tipped up her chin. "Besides, we need to alert everyone here at the Double W to be on the lookout for strangers."

"But there are hundreds of thousands of acres of wilderness. If Ray should find out I'm here, it wouldn't be too hard for him to send someone after me."

Chance had already come to the same conclusion. To put her at ease he merely smiled. "It's one thing for Collier to send a gunman to your apartment in Chicago. With all the people in that city climbing stairs and riding elevators, it's a pretty easy matter to go unnoticed in a crowd. But it won't be the same here. First of all, Collier has to find you. Then he has to hire someone who can blend in with the locals. In case you haven't noticed, everybody in Prosperous knows everybody else. Within days of hiring you at the E.Z.Diner, half the people in town and the surrounding ranches had been in to sample the newcomer's cooking. Remember? We may be a small community, but we have a grapevine that handles gossip with the best of them."

"But that's just it. Everybody knew I was new to the area. And the word could have spread beyond Prosperous."

"That's true. But nobody from Chicago has come through town asking about you."

Maggie nodded. "I guess you're right." She sighed, trying to talk herself out of the tension. "In all this time, nobody's tried to contact me." She turned away and began to pour fresh orange juice into several glasses.

Chance picked one up and drank. "You don't mind then if I fill my brothers in over breakfast?"

She shook her head. "I guess it's impossible to keep this to ourselves any longer. Go ahead and do what you have to."

He'd already intended to do just that. But as he'd learned early on in business, it always helped if he could exact permission before going ahead and doing what his instincts told him was best.

Hazard and Ace listened in silence as Chance filled them in on what had happened to Maggie. When he was finished, Hazard glanced at the woman seated across the table.

"That's a heavy load to have to carry alone, Maggie. I'm glad you decided to share it."

She sighed. "I guess I'm glad, too. Though, until this moment I wasn't sure just how I'd feel."

Ace set down his cup of coffee. "How long do you intend to hide out here?"

"I don't know. I didn't really have a plan when I got off that bus. I guess I just wanted some time to sort things out. But with each passing day, it just got easier and easier to stay put and not face up to what's going on back in Chicago. And then things got…" she avoided Chance's eyes, "…even more complicated."

"Yeah." Ace and Hazard exchanged a knowing look. They were well aware of the complications. Chance and Maggie wore their feelings on their sleeves.

"Sooner or later you're going to have to notify the

authorities.'' Hazard turned to Chance. ''Do you agree?''

Chance nodded. ''But I'd like to wait until we have all the facts. I've put Thorpe on the case. He claims to have a friend in the Chicago D.A.'s office. It would help if we could find out just what they have so far. And I'd like time to dig into Collier's past. Why did a good cop turn bad? Is his motive money? Revenge? Lust? There's always something going on in a criminal's mind. And this didn't happen overnight. He was taking his time, laying a trail of evidence that would lead directly to Maggie.''

''So.'' Hazard drained his cup and shoved back his chair. ''For now, we wait and watch. And report any strangers in town or here on the Double W.''

''Right.'' Chance watched as Maggie walked to the counter to retrieve the coffeepot. ''And we try to arrange our schedules so that one of us is always around.''

Hearing him, Maggie shook her head. ''No. I won't have you babysitting me. This is just what I was afraid of. You can't start rearranging your schedules to accommodate me. There are enough people around the ranch all day that no stranger could ever sneak up on me.''

Chance was about to argue until he saw the determined look on her face.

He held up his hands in a gesture of surrender. ''Okay, Maggie. You're right, of course. We'll all go about our business and wait for Thorpe to come up with his report.''

''That's more like it.'' Maggie breathed a sigh of relief. The last thing she wanted was to disrupt everyone's life and have them constantly watching her to determine the depth of her fear.

A short time later, as the three brothers walked away,

Chance waited until they were out of sight of Maggie before halting. "If you'll give me your schedules for the next couple of weeks, I'll try to plan mine accordingly."

Ace and Hazard wore identical grins.

"I'd advise you not to let Maggie know what you're doing," Ace muttered. "She just might drop a little arsenic in your soup."

"Yeah." Chance's voice was warm with laughter. "She does have a thing about being independent, doesn't she?"

"That's right. And you heard what she said about hoping we'd continued with our usual plans."

"I heard. I just don't happen to agree."

"I'm with you," Hazard said.

Ace nodded. "Me, too."

"All right. Then it's agreed that one of us will try to be here at the ranch with Maggie at all times?"

"Agreed." The three brothers gave solemn nods of their heads.

As Chance sauntered away, Ace turned to Hazard. "You think he knows he's in love yet?"

Hazard merely grinned. "I don't know about that. But I do know that he's lost his heart to someone who's his equal. I'd hate to have to make book on which of them is the stronger." He shook his head at the thought of Maggie running from an armed man. "At least now we know why she freaked at their first introduction, when Chance walked into the kitchen carrying his rifle."

"I'd forgotten about that." Ace threw back his head and roared. "You know something? Our big brother is lucky he's still got a heart to lose. If Maggie had been a little stronger, or her aim a little better…''

Hazard shivered at the thought.

The two of them walked away, still shaking their heads.

Chapter 12

"Chance." Maggie looked up. "I was just making a list of things I needed from Korson's Grain and Feed."

He leaned down and glanced over her shoulder while he idly rubbed at the knot of tension in her neck and shoulders. These long days of freedom should have given her a reason to hope for the best but if anything, she seemed to be getting more tense by the day. She hadn't left the ranch house in over a week. And each time the door slammed, he saw the fear in her eyes.

What's more, he'd seen an increase in the frequency of the nightmares.

"Cumin? Coriander seeds? What are you trying to do to poor Kit? Make him feel like a backwoods hick?"

She flushed. "I didn't know if he carried them. But since you mentioned a trip you once took to Morocco, I was thinking of making Moroccan spiced beef."

"You were?" The previous night he had told her about the trip to Morocco, taken when he was young and eager to build WildeOil into an international competitor. It had started out to be the journey of a lifetime, but it had soon evolved into a disaster, with everything going wrong that possibly could. He had not only lost the contract, but was forced to sleep in the lobby of a fleabag hotel, and on the return home, his luggage had been lost.

He had told her the story in order to get her mind off her own troubles. But later, shortly after laughing at his troubles, she'd been awakened by her own, pursuing her like a demon in her dreams.

He studied her, then couldn't help smiling. "I have a better idea. Why don't we eat out tonight?"

"Out? You mean at the E.Z.Diner?"

He shook his head.

"But that's the only place to eat in Prosperous."

"Then we'll just have to go somewhere else."

"No. I couldn't…" She looked up. "Where?"

He caught her hand. "Let me surprise you. Pack a bag."

She drew back, embarrassed. "I don't have a bag."

"What about all the things a woman needs for survival? Clothes? Makeup? All those great-smelling soaps and lotions and perfumes?"

She shook her head. "All I have is what was in my purse when I ran, and what I could buy at the This N That Shop in Prosperous."

He paused to give her a long, speculative look before plucking a cell phone from his pocket and punching in a series of numbers.

When he heard a voice at the other end he winked at her. "Hazard? You and Ace are on your own tonight. I'm taking our cook away." He grinned. "That's right. See you tomorrow."

Then he dialed another number. "Alex? I'm on my way. And I'm bringing along a friend. Chill a bottle of Dom."

He shoved the phone into his pocket and linked his fingers with hers. "Come on, Maggie. You're way overdue for a little pampering."

"Maggie, this is Alex Rand, my pilot." Chance kept his arm around Maggie's shoulders as he said, "Alex, Maggie Fuller."

"Hi, Maggie." Tanned and fit with prematurely silver hair, the pilot offered his hand. "Welcome aboard."

"Thank you." Her mind was still whirling from the limousine ride out to the airstrip.

Now the sight of the gleaming jet with its engines idling, and the eager crew standing at the foot of the stairs, had her feeling more than a little breathless.

Chance turned to a boyish-looking redhead with blue eyes glinting with humor. "This is Jimmy Cormeyer, our backup pilot."

"Hello, Maggie." He offered a firm handshake.

"And this is Frank Truscott, our navigator."

Dazed, all Maggie could do was smile and nod at the stocky man as Chance led her up the steps and inside the plane.

"You didn't tell me we were flying."

He paused. "I hope you aren't afraid to fly?"

She shook her head.

"Good. That's a relief."

"But how did they have the plane ready on such short notice?"

"Because I was about to fly out on a quick business trip. But this is even better. I'd much rather combine business with pleasure. Now, quit asking so many questions and make yourself comfortable.''

The interior wasn't at all what she'd been expecting. There were no rows of seats. No baggage compartments overhead. The main cabin was laid out like a comfortable sitting room with half a dozen leather recliners arranged in a semi-circle.

"What's back there?" She nodded toward the closed door.

"Bedroom and bathroom. Come on. I'll show you."

He led the way to a luxurious bedroom, complete with a king-size bed. The bathroom had gold fixtures, and was even equipped with a shower.

"This is yours?" She couldn't seem to take it all in.

He nodded. "WildeOil and WildeMining share the cost. Our first plane was just a puddle-jumper that Ace and Hazard and I used to fly from one county to the next."

"You're all pilots?"

At her look of amazement he laughed. "If I'd have known that would get such a reaction from you, I'd have told you weeks ago. But don't be too impressed. Practically everybody in Wyoming has a pilot's license. Without it, we'd never get anywhere. When Ace and I started finding ourselves out of the country as often as we were home, we realized it was time to lay out the expense of a jet, and the crew to maintain it."

He led her back to the main compartment and indicated a chair. "Buckle up, Maggie. We'll be out of here in a few minutes."

"You're not going to tell me where we're going?"

He shook his head. "And spoil the surprise? But I will tell you it's an easy flight. So just sit back and enjoy the next couple of hours."

Maggie fastened her seatbelt. As Chance had promised, within minutes they were airborne.

A short time later Jimmy Cormeyer ducked in and conferred with Chance, then opened a refrigerator and produced a bottle of Dom Perignon. With a pop of the cork he filled two flutes and placed them on a silver tray, then set the opened bottle in a crystal ice bucket before disappearing into the front cabin.

Chance handed Maggie a glass, then lifted his own. "To surprises," he said.

Maggie sipped, then sighed as it slid like liquid silver down her throat. "I wouldn't mind if we just flew around for a few hours and landed again at the Double W. That would be enough of a surprise for me. I'm already feeling as pampered as a princess."

Chance gave her a mysterious smile. "As a cook you can understand. This is just the appetizer. The real feast is yet to come."

And what a feast!

Maggie recognized the Golden Gate Bridge as they flew over it, then circled the airport below.

"Chance." Her eyes were wide. "That's San Francisco."

"That's right."

"Oh. It's one of my favorite cities."

"I'm glad. It's one of mine, too." He reached over and caught her hand as the plane landed smoothly, then rolled to a stop at the private terminal. Minutes later they were seated in a limousine, and whisked into the city.

As they rolled along Geary Street, Chance called to the driver, "We'll stop here first."

"Very good, sir."

The vehicle pulled to a stop at the curb. Chance stepped out and offered his hand to Maggie. Shielding the sun from her eyes she looked up at the building and turned to him in surprise.

"You're taking me to a spa?"

"I'm dropping you here. Since I have a little business to take care of, I want you to be somewhere relaxing."

He led her inside and spoke with the woman behind the desk. Then he turned and brushed his lips over Maggie's. "I'll be back in a couple of hours. I'm leaving you in Gerda's capable hands. Enjoy yourself."

When he was gone, the tall woman led Maggie to a dressing room and handed her a thick terry robe.

As Maggie undressed, Gerda offered her a menu of the services available. "Would you like to make your own choices, Miss Fuller? Or would you like to hear what Mr. Wilde suggested?"

Her curiosity got the better of her. "I guess I'm open to his suggestions first."

"Mr. Wilde suggested that you might like a massage first, Miss Fuller. Then a facial, a manicure and pedicure. Then an appointment with Yves to have your hair trimmed and your makeup will be with François."

Maggie couldn't help laughing. "Oh, I think I'm going to like every single one of Mr. Wilde's suggestions."

Gerda joined in the laughter. "I thought you might. Shall I go ahead and schedule them?"

"By all means."

As Maggie allowed herself to be led to the first room, she could already feel herself relaxing. She disrobed and settled herself on the massage table. The lights were dimmed and the strains of Debussy began to play softly in the background.

The woman's hands were strong and firm as they moved over Maggie's neck and shoulders, up and down her spine. And as she lay in a half-sleeping, half-wakeful state, all the little knots of tension began to evaporate like the mist over the bay.

For the next few hours, while she was required to do nothing more demanding than choose the color of polish for her nails, Maggie emptied her mind, and allow herself to drift on a current of contentment.

"What's this?" With her hair softly curled, her nails a gleaming bronze, and her skin feeling as soft as a newborn's, Maggie stepped back into the dressing room.

Instead of the denims and shirt she'd left there, she found the room filled with mysterious boxes and bags.

"Mr. Wilde said they were all yours. And he hoped everything fit." Gerda held up a honey-colored silk dress and matching cashmere coat. "He suggested you might want to wear this tonight."

"You're not joking?" Maggie's eyes warmed at the sight.

"Indeed not. And I must say, Mr. Wilde has excellent taste." Gerda's tone held a note of approval. "I recognize these as part of the newest collection from Armani."

When Maggie slipped the dress over her head, she was delighted with the way the exquisite fabric glided over her body. An hour later she was wearing the dress and coat, along with little bronze strappy sandals. At her throat was a gold and amber choker, with matching earrings. There was even perfume. Something light and airy with just a hint of wildflowers.

When she walked to the foyer, Chance was waiting. In his hands was a clutch of white violets.

"Oh, Chance." Maggie was so touched, she bent her head to the flowers to hide the tears that sprang to her eyes. "I can't tell you how wonderful I feel."

"Not half as wonderful as you look." He draped an arm around her shoulders and led her outside to the waiting limousine.

As she settled herself inside she turned to him. "Don't you think all this…" she indicated the clothes, the shoes, the jewelry, "…is a bit much to wear while I'm cooking for you and your brothers?"

"Not at all. I'm sure I speak for Ace and Hazard when I say you'll certainly be the most glamorous cook we've ever employed."

She joined in the laughter. "Where will I possibly wear all this?"

"You're in San Francisco, Maggie. They have some of the finest restaurants in the world here. It would be a crime to leave without trying a few."

"A few?"

He gave her a mysterious smile. "Just sit back and enjoy. That's an order, Miss Fuller."

After several blocks their limousine glided to a stop. Chance caught her hand and they began threading their way among the tourists who crowded the shops and walkways at Fisherman's Wharf.

"Have you been here before?" he asked.

Maggie nodded. "Several times. The last time, I came with my sister. We stayed at a little hotel just a few blocks from here. And every day we'd prowl all the shops and restaurants here at the wharf."

The memory of her time spent with Eve was so vivid,

she had to stop talking to swallow the lump that threatened to choke her.

Seeing it, Chance squeezed her hand and walked in silence beside her, giving her time to compose herself.

The breeze carried the tang of the ocean. It mingled with the wonderful scents of seafood from sidewalk vendors, and the unexpectedly cloying perfume of scented candles from gift shops.

Chance turned to her, loving the way her eyes seemed to reflect the colorful lights along the wharf. The breeze ruffled her hair, and had her skin glowing.

"Here we are." He led her inside a restaurant with a wall of windows that overlooked the bay.

As soon as the owner caught sight of them, he hurried over.

"Chance Wilde. It's been a while."

"Yeah, Tony. Too long. Tony Massari, this is Maggie Fuller."

"Hi, Maggie." He was a big, burly man with tousled gray hair and laugh lines deeply etched around pale blue eyes. His shirt and tie were slightly rumpled. He would have looked just as natural handling cargo on the docks as he did the menus in his big, work-worn hands.

He gave her an admiring glance. "Welcome to Massari's, Maggie."

"Thank you. It smells wonderful in here."

"Garlic." He brought his fingers to his lips. Kissed them and closed his eyes. "There is nothing like the perfume of garlic."

"I agree. I can never have enough."

He shot a grin at Chance. "Now this is a girl after my own heart."

"In more ways than you know, Tony." Chance

caught her hand. "She's the finest cook I've ever known."

Tony gave her a lingering look. "We'll have to share recipes some day."

"I'd like that."

With a smile he beckoned them. "Come on. I have a special table for the two of you."

He led them through the restaurant to a secluded booth with the most amazing view of the bay.

"Thanks, Tony." Chance looked around. "How about the menus?"

Tony shook his head and smiled. "You won't need them. In honor of the occasion, I'll give you something special. I'll see to it myself."

"What occasion?"

He merely smiled. "I'll be back with some appetizers. What would you like to drink?"

"Something dry and red." Chance lifted Maggie's hand to his lips. "Merlot."

"Coming up."

Tony walked away, hustling towards the kichen.

"Feel like walking?" Chance caught Maggie's hand and led her along the sidewalk, while the limousine glided along the street, keeping pace with them.

"I think we'd better. It'll take a couple of miles to walk off all that wonderful food."

"Yeah. Tony loves to cook." Chance wrapped an arm around her shoulders. "Ready for dinner now?"

"You must be joking!"

He shook his head. "I warned you. That was just the beginning of the evening. Now it's time for some real food."

He stopped in front of a small, elegant restaurant,

then led her inside. As soon as the maître d' caught
sight of them, he hurried over.

"Mr. Wilde. Your table is waiting."

"Thanks, Michael."

They made their way to a small, raised banquette. As
soon as they were seated, four servers circled the table
to see to their every need.

"Champagne, Mr. Wilde?"

"Yes." Chance watched as two flutes were filled.
Then he touched his glass to Maggie's. "To surprises."

She smiled. Without hesitation she added, "May they
always be as pleasant as these. And may we escape this
fabulous city with our hearts intact."

"Not possible. But we can try." He sipped, then said,
"What are you in the mood for?"

"Anything but steak," she said with a laugh. "How
about lobster?"

He nodded. "Lobster it is."

While the waiters bustled about, preparing a feast,
Chance and Maggie spoke in hushed tones and sipped
champagne. And felt the cares of the world slip away.

It was past midnight when Maggie and Chance
stepped into the cabin of the plane and fastened their
seat belts.

Maggie leaned back and sighed. "This whole thing
seems like a dream. A wonderful fairy tale. I still can't
believe it. The spa. These clothes. All that wonderful
food."

"I can't believe how much you ate. In all the time
you've worked at the Double W, I've never seen you
eat so heartily."

Maggie laughed. "That's different. It's my job. And
though I love cooking, I'm not much for eating my own

food. But this.'' She sighed. ''This was pure heaven. Those moules marinieres at Massari's! And the garlic shrimp!''

''Yeah. Tony knows garlic.''

''I wangled the recipe from his cook. I'm going to fix them next week.''

He unfastened his seat belt and stood by the window, watching the lights of the city fall away. ''How about that lobster at Stefani's?''

She looked over at him. ''I'll never be able to think about San Francisco again without thinking about that restaurant. I don't know when I've had such a meal. Champagne and lobster. And the view of the city. It was incredible.''

''Not half as amazing as the view from the top of the St. Francis.''

She sighed again. ''Crème brûlée and brandy. And the best coffee in the world. I feel so incredibly light-hearted.''

Suddenly she unfastened her seat belt and crossed to him. Catching his hands in hers she said, ''Chance, this has been the most amazing day. I still can't believe we did this.''

''It was great, wasn't it?'' He stared down at their hands, then brought her hand to his mouth, pressing a kiss to her palm. When he lifted his head to stare at her, she saw the hunger in his eyes. A hunger that matched her own.

''I feel the way I felt that night at the range shack, Maggie. Wanting you so badly, I'm afraid to touch you. Afraid I'll be too rough.''

She lifted his hand to her cheek, then moved it slowly to her mouth. ''I'm not fragile, Chance. I won't break. And I want you, too. Desperately.''

Without a word he lifted her in his arms and carried her to the bedroom. Even before he kicked the door shut his mouth was on hers. The fire between them blazed out of control. And then his hands were on her. Touching her everywhere. They barely made it to the bed as their greedy hands and mouths found each other.

And as the plane sped through the midnight sky toward Wyoming, they lost themselves once more in the dark, silken web of passion.

Chapter 13

Maggie was humming as she planned the week's menus. She paused, chewing on the end of the pencil.

Ace was off to Colorado and had promised to bring her some portobello mushrooms. She smiled, knowing just how she intended to use them. If Kit Korson had fresh spinach, all the better. Hazard had promised to check at Korson's Grain and Feed when he drove to Prosperous later today.

She laughed to herself, remembering how, when she'd first been offered the job at the Double W, she had scorned the thought of cooking for the three Wilde brothers. She'd expected their appetites to run to chili and overcooked burgers. What a surprise they'd had in store for her. Not only were they far more sophisticated than she'd anticipated, but their worldwide travels had given them eclectic tastes more suited to the head of some international conglomerate.

Come to think of it, she corrected herself, that's ex-

actly what the Double W was. With all the businesses
these men were involved in, it had become as big as
any multinational corporation. Still, what amazed her
most was that these three men continued to operate as
a simple family unit.

Family. It was something she'd always missed. Having lost her parents so young, she'd considered herself
lucky to have a sister. She and Eve had been as close
as two sisters could possibly be.

And now Eve was gone.

The sudden, unexpected ache around her heart caught
her by surprise. It had been hard enough to accept when
she'd thought that Eve's death had been from an un-
detected aneurysm. But the knowledge that she'd been
murdered made the pain so much worse. Murdered by
a man who had claimed to love her. A man sworn to
uphold the law.

Maggie walked to the window and studied the peaceful countryside. Out here, so far from the bustling
crowds of Chicago, it was hard to imagine that violence
existed. Even now, if she hadn't seen the deliberate destruction in her apartment, and hadn't witnessed first-
hand the gunman waiting for her, she still would find it
hard to believe any of it. Her sister's murder. Her
brother-in-law's involvement in it. The systematic theft
from the restaurant.

And yet Chance had been willing to believe it, simply
because she had said it was so. She shook her head in
amazement. Would she have been as willing to believe
in him, given the circumstances?

Her answer was swift and certain. She would believe
in Chance. No matter what.

As she stared out the window, big fat flakes of snow
drifted down. And though they melted on the pane, they

were already beginning to stick to the ground. She found herself shivering in anticipation of a Wyoming winter. Would she be around long enough to experience it? Or would she face up to her obligation to put aside her own fear in order to see that Eve's killer was brought to justice? Though she dreaded all thought of facing Ray Collier, she knew it was only a matter of time before she would have to stare down her demons.

She shook her head to chase away such disturbing thoughts. Not yet. She wouldn't allow herself to think about her uncertain future. Instead, she would think about something pleasant. She smiled. She'd think about the amazing story she'd been told about the circumstances that had brought Wes Wilde to this place so many years ago.

What kind of vision had he possessed that he had understood, before anyone else, just how important this land was? And what sort of man had he been, to have given life to three such fascinating sons?

From what Cody had told her, he was the stuff of legends. A man larger than life, with the ability to see what others overlooked. From what she'd seen so far, his three sons were just like him. Especially the one who owned her heart.

Deep in thought, Maggie almost didn't notice the sudden movement by the barn. A man, hat low on his head, was peering around as though searching for something. She felt a sudden trickle of fear along her spine. Then, as she watched, the man was joined by Cody, who was holding out a long, thin piece of metal.

She let out a sigh of relief. Hadn't she overheard Cody telling Hazard this morning that Peterson would be coming by the ranch today to see if he could weld a pump handle?

She chided herself for her nervousness. She was going to have to stop letting her imagination rule her common sense.

So that was Peterson. She watched as he made his way to a nearby truck. He had the long-legged gait of a cowboy. And wore the unmistakable garb of all the ranchers in these parts. Jeans, cowhide jacket and wide-brimmed hat.

She glanced at the clock and decided she'd better get started fixing dinner. The menus for the rest of the week could wait. Right now she'd deal with her own hungry cowboys.

The helicopter skimmed low over the trees. Chance watched its shadow dance unerringly below them. It was snowing harder now. Not enough to hamper flight, but enough to spin a soft white cocoon over the land. It was strange to see sunlight above and snow below.

To the north were darker clouds, bringing in the heavier snow. By morning, they'd be digging out.

When the cell phone rang, he lifted it to his ear.

"Mr. Wilde?" The staccato voice could be heard above the roar of the engines.

"Yeah, Thorpe. What've you got for me?"

"I think I can safely say that Simmons was not the one who gave you grief over the changes on the Miller contract."

Chance felt some of the tension seep from between his shoulders. He'd been hoping for this. He had not wanted to believe that he'd misplaced his trust.

Thorpe's voice broke through his thoughts. "Do you remember an employee named Burton Caldwell?"

"Yeah. He worked in our accounting department about six years ago. He was caught stealing."

''There's no record of his dismissal.''

''I didn't want to destroy the man's reputation. He had a wife and four kids. So I offered him a deal. He could stay and make restitution a little at a time until the debt was cleared.''

''Then what happened?''

''The next thing I knew, he was gone. I found out later that he ran off with another woman, leaving his family with a pile of bills. So I just wrote off the debt and never bothered to pursue it. Prosperous is a small town. Having their father branded a thief would stain his kids for a lifetime.''

Thorpe paused. ''Well, at least your intentions were honorable. But you may have done yourself more harm than good. Do you know an employee named Iris Arnold?''

Chance frowned. ''The name sounds familiar. Is she a new employee in Cheyenne?''

''She is. One of Simmons's assistants, hired for her computer skills. When I checked her background, I discovered that her maiden name was Caldwell.''

''Burton's daughter?''

''That's right. Unfortunately, her mother, hoping to shield her children from the truth, led them to believe that the reason their father ran off was because he'd been about to lose his job. That little lie has caused Iris to carry a grudge, and someone used that anger to get to you. Upon further investigation, I discovered a rather large deposit in her account just a week before she hired on at WildeOil. It would seem that one of your competitors had her in their employ as well. In the short time she worked for you, she was also accepting payment from them. A pretty hefty payment, by the way.''

Chance's eyes narrowed. Under his breath he muttered, "The sins of the father..." Aloud he said, "So. Somebody wanted to see our company take a fall?"

"That's what it looks like."

"You'll fax me the supporting evidence? I want names. Dates. Cancelled checks. And anything you can dig up in this woman's background to prove our case."

"Yes, sir. It's on its way. I'll fax you what I have so far."

"Good. This will earn you a bonus, Mr. Thorpe."

"That's much appreciated. Now about the Margaret Mary Trainor case."

Chance tensed, listening in silence as he strained to hear every word over the sound of the helicopter's engines.

As Thorpe's voice droned on, he gave a sigh of relief. At last. This was what he'd been hoping for. "Thanks, Thorpe. Fax that report as well. I appreciate your thoroughness. There'll be an additional bonus in this for you. A very substantial one. Now, contact the Chicago authorities. Let them know that Ms. Trainor is alive and well, and will be making a statement to them as soon as possible."

He clicked off the phone and sat back with an air of satisfaction. The mirrored sunglasses hid his eyes, narrowed in thought.

On a whim he picked up the phone and punched in some numbers. When he heard his youngest brother's voice on the other end he shouted, "Ace? Where are you?"

"Aspen. Just finishing up lunch."

"When will you be heading back?"

He strained to hear the answer. Between the copter engines, and the voices in the Aspen restaurant, the words were being distorted.

''When?''

''Tonight, I hope. I got the contract I was hoping for. And I've had enough of this place. I just want to get back home to a certain pretty lady's good cooking. Now, what are you calling about? I know you didn't want to ask me about the weather on the slopes.''

''I just heard from Thorpe. He has what we need to nail Ray Collier.''

He had to hold the phone away from his ear when Ace let out a yelp of pleasure. It brought a smile to his lips. ''Yeah. My sentiments exactly. I think I'll phone Hazard with the news.'' He paused. Listened to the question. ''No. I'll wait until I get home to tell her. I want to see her face.''

He disconnected, then dialed another series of numbers. When he heard Cody's drawl, he shouted, ''Hey, Cody. Give me Hazard.''

''Sorry, Chance. He's not here. He drove into Prosperous. He'll be back in a couple of hours.''

''Who's with Maggie?''

''She's alone, but she's fine. I was just in the house half an hour ago, right after Peterson left. The last I saw of her, she was starting dinner.''

''Okay. Stick close until I get there. Tell her I'll be home by six. And tell her I'm bringing something she's going to love.''

''I'll give her the message.'' Cody's voice was abruptly cut off as Chance disconnected.

He couldn't wait to see her face when he told her they had enough to nail the bastard who'd killed her sister.

He leaned back, idly drumming his fingers on the cell phone. He was sorely tempted to call her now, just to hear her voice. But she'd know there was something up.

He'd spoil the surprise. Instead, he shoved the phone into his pocket and turned to stare out the window. He could wait a while longer.

Life was good, he thought with a smile. And it was about to get much better.

Maggie was feeling inspired. She chopped shallots and sautéed them until tender, then stirred in some dry red wine and a little dark red port, all the while humming along with the Temptations on the radio.

She set the steaks on a broiler rack and placed it on the counter, then returned her attention to the sauce. She added some beef broth and dried rosemary and brought the whole thing to a boil. All that was left to do was to stir vigorously for ten or twelve minutes, until it reached the right consistency. Then she'd be ready to broil the steaks the minute Chance and Hazard got home.

If she were adding this to a restaurant menu, she'd call it a man's meal. Hearty. Robust. The thought had her grinning. It certainly suited the Wilde brothers. Those were words she'd use to describe all three cowboys.

She heard the door open and continued to stir.

With her back to it she called, "Hey, Cody. You're early. But that's okay. There's some cheese dip on the counter behind me. And a basket of sesame sticks I baked earlier. Sorry I can't stop right now. I don't want to burn this sauce. Just help yourself."

"Well, golly gee whiz, thanks, little sis."

At the sound of that familiar sarcastic tone, Maggie dropped the spoon with a clatter and turned to find herself staring at the man who had been haunting her dreams ever since she'd fled Chicago. Only this wasn't a dream. It was her worst nightmare.

Ray Collier was tall, well over six feet, and layered with muscles from years of compulsive weight training. It had always been a source of pride to Ray that he was considered one of the most physically fit officers on the force. It was a well-known fact among his fellow officers that he had a taste for violence—the tougher the better. He was always at his best when he was compelled to use brute force against a lawbreaker who was foolish enough to challenge him.

Despite his violent nature, he had a deceptively boyish face and a lopsided grin that endeared him to women. It's what had initially won Eve over.

Eve. The pain came, sharp and swift and deep.

Maggie's heart forgot to beat as she stared at Ray's hand. In it was a small, deadly gun.

"Ray. How did you...?"

"How did I find you? Hey, you haven't made it easy. I had half the Chicago police force looking for you." He grinned. "But you made a fatal error, little sis. You had some wiseguy checking out the D.A.'s files. What he didn't know was that most of those legal eagles are on my side. I'm the law, remember?"

He threw back his head and laughed. "You look about as happy to see me as that old geezer out in the barn."

"Cody." She felt her heart stop. "Did you...hurt him?"

"Naw. I kissed him." He couldn't help laughing at his own joke. "The old fool grabbed up a pitchfork and came at me. I was tempted to shoot him, but I was afraid the sound would send you running for cover. And we wouldn't want that, would we, little sis? You've been running long enough. So I just hit him over the head hard enough that he'll never wake up."

"He's…" she licked her lips, "…dead?"

"Unless he's got a head made out of concrete."

She started to sink to her knees. "No. Oh, no. Not Cody. He didn't deserve this."

Collier waved the hand holding the gun. "Shut up. Stop your whining. You'll be next if you don't do exactly as you're told."

She looked about wildly and began to back away. She knew instinctively that it didn't matter if she stayed or ran. Either way, Ray Collier wasn't about to let her live. He'd come here for one reason. To keep her from telling what she knew. And there was only one way to be certain of that.

In desperation she turned and ran.

"Why you little…"

Ignoring Ray's savage oath, she struggled to reach the door. Before she could grasp the knob, she was caught by a bruising blow to the back of the head. She dropped to her knees as a shower of stars seemed to dance through her line of vision.

He stood over her. "You just keep on making things worse, don't you?"

Before she could clear her head, she was yanked roughly to her feet. At the same moment she felt the tip of the pistol jammed against her ribs.

"You and I are going for a ride, little sis."

She blinked, trying desperately to clear away the dizziness. "Where are you taking me?"

He wrapped a beefy arm around her throat and hauled her backward. "That's enough questions. Just shut your mouth and do as you're told."

She reached up to claw at the offending arm, but her strength was no match for his. He merely tightened his grasp, cutting off her breath. She struggled against a wave of blackness as he dragged her out the door and down the back steps to where a truck stood idling.

He opened the driver's door and shoved her roughly inside, then climbed in beside her. Then he reached into his back pocket and removed a pair of handcuffs.

"Just in case you're thinking about getting away," he muttered as he fastened one to her left wrist, and the other to his right.

He slammed the door shut and, juggling the pistol, put the truck into gear. The wheels spewed gravel as they left the ranch house far behind.

Chance felt the familiar rush of affection as the helicopter passed over the roof of the Double W. No matter how often he left or how far his travels took him, he loved coming home. And now that Maggie had become a part of his life, the homecoming was even sweeter.

As soon as Brady Warren had landed the craft, Chance was out the door and sprinting across the field toward the ranch house.

He couldn't wait to see Maggie's face when he gave her the news.

By the time he hit the front door he had removed his suit jacket and was loosening his tie. He strode quickly through the front room and paused in the doorway of the kitchen. The high, sweet notes of Otis Redding sitting on the dock of the bay had him smiling as he peered around expectantly. Anticipation hummed through him.

"Maggie?"

He paused. The acrid odor of something burning assaulted his nostrils. He crossed to the stove and turned off the burner, shoving the scorched pan to one side.

He felt a prickly feeling along his scalp. It wasn't

like Maggie to allow any distraction to get in the way of her cooking. She wasn't the type to just forget something on the stove and walk away. Unless...

His voice took on a note of urgency. "Maggie?"

His pulse started pounding in his temples as he raced across the kitchen to her suite of rooms. The bed had been carefully made. Nothing was out of place.

His heart was racing as, minutes later, he flew out the back door and headed toward the barn.

Inside he found Cody, dazed and moaning, struggling to lift his head from a pool of blood.

With a string of oaths, Chance gathered the old man into his arms and helped him to a sitting position. "Did you see who did this?"

"Big guy. Driving a truck. Packs a hell of a punch. Feels like he slugged me with a couple tons of stone." Cody shook his head, struggling to clear it. "He had a pistol. All I had was a pitchfork, Chance. Don't know why he didn't shoot me."

"I do." The realization came to him instantly. "He didn't want to warn Maggie he was coming."

"Is it...?"

"It's Collier."

Seeing Chance's face, Cody knew instantly. "Does he have Maggie?"

Chance nodded as he lifted the old cowboy in his arms and headed toward the house.

Inside he laid him gently on the sofa and phoned for a medevac team from the hospital in Cheyenne. When he turned, Agnes was just walking in after delivering supper to the cowboys at the bunkhouse.

Seeing Cody she clapped a hand over her mouth to stifle the cry that escaped her lips. Her eyes were wide with concern as she whispered, "What in heaven's name has happened here?"

Chance dropped an arm around her shoulders. "I don't have time, but Cody will tell you everything."

He knelt beside the old man. "I have to go after Collier. Are you going to be all right here with Agnes until the medical team gets here?"

"Yeah." Cody caught his arm as he started to scramble to his feet. "You've got to stop him. You know what he plans to do to her."

Chance's tone was grim. "I know."

"You've got to get her back, son."

"I will." Chance spun away. "You can count on it."

Chapter 14

Maggie watched with a mixture of horror and fascination as their truck careened across a field and plunged into the woods. "Where are we going?"

"Someplace where we can be alone. We've got some unfinished business to take care of, little sis."

She gritted her teeth at that hated nickname. He'd begun calling her that when he'd first married Eve. The more she'd railed against it, the more Ray seemed to enjoy using it. It had been one more indication of his cutting brand of humor.

Thinking back, she couldn't recall a single time when he'd called her by name. Nor could she remember a single pleasant conversation between them. In the five years he'd been her brother-in-law, the only thing they had had in common was Eve. Dear, sweet Eve, who had loved them both. And had begged them to find a way to get along. It had been Eve who had talked them into going into business together, hoping the venture would bring them closer.

"Tell me why, Ray? Why are you doing this?"

"You're a loose end. And you know how I hate them."

"So you're going to eliminate me? Just like that?"

"Yep. Now you're getting it." He snapped his fingers. "Just like that. I like things neat and tidy." He grinned at her. "I'll bet you thought you'd messed things up for me." The truck shot out of the woods and Ray was forced to pull his attention back to driving as they roared up a steep incline.

Maggie stared around in dismay. They were going deeper and deeper into wilderness. He hadn't given her time to grab a jacket. In the chill of the truck, the thin shirt and denims gave her little protection. She was already shivering. Her teeth were chattering, whether from cold or fear, she wasn't certain.

He gave a snort of laughter. "Actually, you did me a big favor, little sis. 'Cause now that you've become a fugitive, a respected officer of the law like me has every right to shoot you if you resist arrest."

Her heart nearly stopped. "And you're going to see that I resist, aren't you?"

"You got that right." The truck came up over a hill, and made a wide arc, avoiding the Peterson house.

In the distance, Maggie could see the range shack where she and Chance had spent the night. She closed her eyes against the pain. Chance. She would never see him again. Or the Double W. A violent tremor shot through her before she swallowed back her fear and lifted her head. If it killed her, she wouldn't give Ray Collier the satisfaction of seeing just how terrified she was.

"You won't get away with it, Ray. There's bound to be an investigation over why you were the one to find me and then kill me. You're not just another Chicago cop. You were my brother-in-law. My business partner. When they piece all that together, you'll be sending up all kinds of red flags in the department."

"Don't you worry about me handling the department. Right now I'm a hero. Maybe you haven't kept up with the news from the big city. I saved an old woman from a burning building last week. My face was on the front page of the *Chicago News*. I'm going to get another citation." He shot her a sideways glance. "Who knows? Maybe they'll give me another reward after this is over." He laughed at his own joke. "For my dedicated, single-minded pursuit of justice. Why, I might even make top cop for bringing in the infamous Margaret Mary Trainor."

Chance drove like a madman, barely taking the time to slip his arms through the sleeves of his cowhide jacket as he did so. He'd hated to waste even a minute, but it had been necessary to go upstairs for his rifle and the keys to his truck.

At the first ring of his cell phone, he snatched it from his pocket and held it to his ear. "Yeah?"

"Chance?" Hazard's voice was tense and strained.

"Where've you been?" Chance snapped. "I've been trying to reach you."

"I just came from the E.Z.Diner. I left my phone in the truck. Thelma said a stranger stopped by with a photo of Maggie. Before she had a chance to ask him any questions, Slocum spoke up and told the guy where Maggie's working. Thelma's mad as a wet hen. She's always known Maggie was running from something.

Now she's worried that he might be an abusive husband.''

"I wish that's all it was."

At Chance's muttered oath Hazard shouted, "Do you think it's Ray Collier?"

"Yeah." Chance swore again. "It's him."

"Is Maggie all right?"

"Collier got to her before I got home. I'm on their trail now."

It was Hazard's turn to swear under his breath. "Tell me where you are, and I'll join you."

"First you'd better get to the ranch and see to Cody. He took a nasty blow to the head. I've phoned for a medevac team from Cheyenne. But with this snow, they're going to be lucky to get through. I hated leaving him alone with Agnes. I'm worried about him. About both of them."

"All right. I'll go to the ranch first. Do what I can. Then you can let me know where you are, and I'll get there as soon as possible."

"One more thing." Chance crested a hill and stared around in frustration. There wasn't a sign of a truck anywhere on the horizon. "Phone the sheriff and Brady Warren. Tell him to get the helicopter in the air right away."

"That's going to be risky, Chance. You said yourself the snow's a problem."

"We have no choice. We're running out of time. There's not a minute to lose."

"What's your plan, Ray? Where are you taking me?"

He kept his eyes on the trail. "What's this about a plan? What makes you think I have any plan?"

"You're not just driving aimlessly. I saw the way

you avoided that ranch house. You know exactly where you're headed, don't you?''

Now he did glance at her. The look in his eyes was one of seething hatred. ''You know, little sis, that's what I always resented most about you. You always had to know everything.'' His voice took on a sarcastic whine. ''Why did I carry my gun even when I was off duty? Why did I want to take on the extra duties of tallying the restaurant ledgers and daily sheets, instead of letting the accounting firm handle it? You and your questions made me sick. Why couldn't you have been more like your sister? Eve was so trusting, she never questioned a thing I did.''

Maggie felt her eyes fill and blinked hard. ''Don't you mention her name. Don't you dare mention my sister's name, after what you did.''

He tugged hard on the handcuffs, catching her off-guard and dragging her across the seat of the truck until her face was inches from his. ''What I did to your sister is nothing compared to what I'm planning for you. You'd better be grateful that I'm such a good marksman. I'll have no trouble dropping you with one shot. But watch out, Miss Know-It-All. If you try pulling a fast one, maybe I'll just be a little off the mark. I'll let the first bullet rip through your thigh. Or shoulder. I'll do just enough to inflict pain, but not enough to kill you right away.'' He gave a high-pitched laugh that scraped over her already raw nerves. ''Have you ever seen somebody rolling around on the ground in agony and begging to die? That'll be you if I miss with the first shot. I'll take my sweet time and just watch you suffer for a while before I put you out of your misery.''

When she tried to push away he tugged her back, then shot a glance at their joined wrists. ''You've got no chance against me, little sis. You're not going anywhere until I unlock these.''

The truck crested another ridge, and he peered ahead until he spotted what he was looking for. Then with a smile, he gunned the engine and the truck skidded sideways down the snowy hill toward a narrow dirt trail in the distance.

Chance viewed the snow as a blessing and a curse. A blessing because he had picked up a faint trail he knew had to be the truck Collier was driving. A curse because the heavy snow was quickly obliterating what was left of the tire tracks. Chance knew that before long the snow and the approaching darkness would work against him.

When his phone rang he snatched at it.

''Yeah?''

''Chance, it's Brady. I'm up over the south ridge. I probably don't have more than a half hour of daylight left. And the snow's getting heavier. Have you found anything?''

''Yeah. Come on over to the north ridge. I've already alerted Peterson. He's taking his truck as far as the foothills. I'm just passing the range shack, but there's no sign they stopped here.''

Chance disengaged the phone, and peered through the curtain of snow. From the path Collier had taken, it was plain that he was determined to avoid returning to the town of Prosperous. But where could he go up here?

He might be planning to kill Maggie and dump her body where it wasn't likely to be found until next spring. But that wouldn't solve his problems. She would still be considered missing.

If what Thorpe told him was true, Collier needed

money now. He was eager to sell the restaurant. And that meant he needed Maggie returned to Chicago. Or— Chance felt his heart lurch as the more plausible thought intruded—he needed Maggie dead, so that he would be declared the sole owner of the restaurant.

Chance closed his eyes a moment and pressed his forehead to the steering wheel. He'd flown over this countryside a hundred times or more. In his mind's eye he pictured the land from above, charting the familiar hills and valleys, the river beds, the foothills. And then he remembered. His eyes snapped open. Of course. If Collier had studied a map of the area, he would know that there was a little-known trail that had once been used for mining. It led to a new, two-lane road that crossed the northern half of the Double W and led to the interstate.

It traversed some of the most primitive land in the area. They had no chance of running into anyone. And anytime Collier chose, he could kill Maggie, without fear of witnesses.

Chance gunned the engine, veering from the trail he'd been following. They were too far ahead of him. His only hope now was to take a shortcut and surprise them.

He prayed he could outrun the snow as well. One slip of the wheel and he could find himself buried in a snow-covered ditch, where he'd be of no use whatsoever to the woman he loved.

The woman he loved.

For the space of a heartbeat, he struggled with a rush of dizzying fear. It occurred to him that he had rarely in his life experienced such an emotion. The first time had been at the death of his father. But that had been a childish, selfish fear for himself and his brothers. A fear that they wouldn't be up to the challenge issued by Wes Wilde.

This was different. A cold, gut-wrenching fear that all his wealth and all his power and all the discipline he'd demanded of himself over the years wouldn't be enough to save the woman who was now at the mercy of a madman.

Ray Collier drove slowly along the old rutted trail. Through the curtain of snow he watched for the turn-off. From the map he knew that this part of the terrain was rough and rarely travelled. He'd planned this carefully. He didn't want some cowboy riding up to spoil his carefully laid plans.

Not that he'd mind adding to the body count. Killing didn't bother him. He'd always thought it amusing when his fellow officers got all bent out of shape over an accidental shooting. They'd spend time with a shrink, baring their souls, going over every little detail of their childhood, in the hope of getting past the trauma of killing some hooker or crackhead who'd happened to get in their line of fire.

To Ray, dying was part of living. And he intended to squeeze as much out of this life as he could. If that meant eliminating a few roadblocks, it didn't matter to him. A criminal. An innocent victim. They were all the same. So, if some cowboy happened along, that was his tough luck. As for Ray, he'd do what he had to and find a way to get rid of the bodies.

He had a tarp in the back of the truck for Maggie. He grinned. She'd be going back to Chicago in style. He'd phone in his report and let the force pay for his ticket home and the ride in the luggage compartment for her casket.

If anybody got in the way of his plans for her, they'd find themselves becoming food for the wolves.

He suddenly veered to the left and the truck skidded off the trail and into a section of dense woods.

"Showtime, little sis." He decided to leave the engine idling. It was getting colder, and this business shouldn't take long.

He yanked on the cuffs, dragging her out of the truck alongside him.

Chance drove up to the point where the old trail intersected the new highway. There wasn't a single track marring the snow. For as far as he could see, the landscape was pristine.

He fought back a wave of despair. Had he miscalculated? If so, Collier could be miles from here. And this mistake would cost Maggie her life.

The phone rang. He snatched it up.

"Yeah?"

"Chance." Brady's voice broke through static. "The snow's getting too thick. Can't see anything but blinding white from up here. But I thought I spotted something moving in the woods just off the old trail."

"I'm just north of there." Chance paused a moment. "Can you land anywhere around here?"

There was a moment of silence before Brady said, "I can try."

"Good. Try to put it down on the highway."

"If I can find it," Brady muttered.

"You'll be able to spot it by the electrical wires that run parallel to it. You should see a line of telephone poles in the snow."

"All right. I'll keep an eye out for them."

"If you can land there, it'll block any escape if Collier tries to make a run for it."

"I'll give it my best." Brady's voice seemed to fade in and out. "Visibility up here is almost zero."

Though he'd never done so before, Chance whispered a prayer as he parked his truck at the edge of the woods and started walking. This was, he realized with a feeling of dread, the perfect place for a killer to commit murder and expect to get away with it.

Maggie's sneaker-clad feet sank into the snow up to her ankles. She didn't even notice the cold. She was beyond feeling. Her mind, her body, had gone numb. She merely moved along beside Ray as he led her deeper into the stand of trees.

Ray paused and tested the weight of a tree limb. Satisfied, he reached for the key to the handcuffs and unfastened the one around his wrist. Maggie made a sudden jerk of her arm, hoping to break free, but he was too strong for her. With a vicious tug, he snapped the handcuff around the branch of the tree.

"That ought to hold you." He had to shout over the howling of the wind.

Maggie swallowed and turned to face him.

"Nope. That won't do." He grabbed her by the shoulders and forcibly turned her around. "There. That's better. Just stand that way."

She spun back. "What's the matter, Ray? Afraid to see my face when you shoot me?"

He threw back his head and laughed. "You've got to be joking. Do you really think it'll bother me to kill you? Hell, little sis, what's one more death now? You really want to know what I think about killing? I drove the needle into Eve's arm right after she'd given me the best loving of our marriage.''

Maggie's stomach clenched, and she had to fight a wave of nausea. How could her sister have trusted this monster? How was it that no one could see through that charming façade to the real Ray Collier?

''I just want you to turn around because you're resisting arrest, remember?'' Ray stared down at her with an amused grin. ''Can't have any powder burns on the body. And if you're a good girl, I'll do it with a single shot. The guys on the force know I'm an expert marksman. They'd expect me to take you with one bullet.''

Maggie's mind was suddenly alive with anger. Her eyes misted with tears. Not tears of sorrow, but tears of seething, burning fury.

As she blinked them away, she thought she saw a blur of motion in the trees behind Ray. She blinked again, and felt her heartbeat quicken. Was that Chance? Or was her mind, so befuddled by cold and despair, simply conjuring up his tempting image to taunt her? Whether it was fact or hallucination, she was determined to keep Ray distracted.

''Why did you kill Eve, Ray?''

He paused in his movements. ''Why? Because she made a fatal mistake, little sis. She got in my way.''

Maggie's eyes narrowed. ''In your way of what?''

''Of my happiness.''

''Your happiness? She didn't make you happy? Then why didn't you just divorce her? Why did you have to kill her?''

''Because,'' came the voice from somewhere behind Ray. ''He needed the insurance money.''

Ray whirled. Seeing a man with a rifle aimed directly at him he took a quick step behind Maggie and wrapped

his arm around her neck, holding her in front of him
like a shield.

"Put down the rifle, cowboy." He pressed the barrel
of the pistol to Maggie's temple. "Or the lady buys it."

When Chance hesitated, Maggie shouted, "Don't do
it, Chance. He's going to kill me anyway."

"No, he isn't." Chance tossed aside the rifle and took
a step closer. "Not if I can help it."

"Hold it right there, cowboy." Ray released his hold
on Maggie and stepped away.

Chance caught sight of the handcuffs. His heart sank.
He'd hoped to distract Collier long enough to allow
Maggie to escape. Now, whatever plan he'd had had
just evaporated. He'd have to think of something else.

He turned to Maggie, forcing himself to ignore the
man with the gun. "Collier took out a half-million-
dollar life insurance policy on Eve. He thought that
would be enough to finance his recently acquired lavish
lifestyle. But he's already blown through that and is
currently running on empty. You see, he's been string-
ing along a very wealthy socialite for the past couple
of years. Once they're married, he'll have a new supply
of cash, until he blows through her bankroll, too. But
until then, he needs the money from the sale of the
restaurant. And in order to sell it, he needs to get rid of
you, Maggie."

She blinked back her tears and nodded. "Just a loose
end. Ray hates loose ends."

"You do?" Chance lifted his head. "If that's the
case, you're going to really hate this."

Collier took aim with his pistol. "I don't consider a
cowboy who just wandered in a loose end. Just a nui-
sance that I'll soon be rid of."

Chance laughed. "I didn't mean me. I meant that."

He pointed skyward. Above the howling of the wind could be heard a faint sound that seemed to grow louder with each second. Soon the air vibrated with the sound of a helicopter hovering above the treetops.

Seconds later, the sound changed, growing in intensity as Brady Warren brought it in for a landing several hundred yards beyond the forest.

"That isn't going to stop me. By the time the pilot makes his way in here, I'll be through with my business. And this badge will make it all legal."

Collier turned and aimed the gun at Maggie. "Turn around, little sis. Your number's up."

Though her legs were trembling so badly she could no longer feel them, Maggie stood her ground. "Sorry, Ray. If you want to shoot me in the back, you'll have to knock me unconscious first."

"Why you little…" In a rage he started toward her, his arm raised to strike.

Chance seized that moment to leap across the space that separated them, taking Collier down with him. The force of their fall caused the pistol to slip from Ray's fingers. It landed in the snow. The two men rolled around on the ground, exchanging blows and struggling to retrieve the gun.

"Come on, cowboy." Collier's voice was high-pitched with rage. "Nothing I like better than a good brawl. We'll see how handsome you look when I'm through with you." His fist exploded against Chance's jaw.

Chance shook his head to dispel the shower of stars that clouded his vision. Before he had time to recover Collier brought both fists into his midsection, doubling him over. Then for good measure, Collier kicked him savagely in the chest, sending him backward into the snow.

Chance struggled to his knees and heard the click of the safety as Collier snatched up the pistol and pressed it against his temple.

"Say bye-bye, cowboy." Collier was laughing as his finger caressed the trigger.

Chance felt the adrenaline pumping as he stared into Collier's eyes and saw the glint of madness. In one quick motion he brought his head up under Collier's jaw, and heard the sound of bone grinding against bone. A gunshot from Collier's gun echoed and re-echoed across the frozen silence.

Unsure whether the bullet had gone wild or had hit Chance, Maggie let out a scream. Her heart nearly stopped as she watched the two men facing each other for what seemed an eternity.

Then, as if in slow motion, Collier dropped the gun and clutched his hands to his broken jaw.

"Sorry you missed, Collier. You won't get a second chance. This is for Maggie." Chance's fist connected with Collier's nose, sending a fountain of blood pouring down his shirtfront, as he slumped to his knees.

"And this one's for me." Chance hit him again, sending him sprawling face-down in the snow.

He reached into Collier's pocket and retrieved the key to the handcuffs, then crossed to Maggie and released her.

Her legs seemed unable to support her. Her hand gripped the trunk of the tree as she sank to her knees.

"Hold on, sweetheart. One minute more. I'll just put these on Collier for good measure."

As Chance turned away, he found himself staring down the barrel of his own rifle. He tasted the cold, metallic bite of fear in the back of his throat. Not fear for himself, but fear for Maggie. He'd failed her. After all this, he'd made a fatal mistake. He hadn't counted on Collier's determination.

Collier, swaying slightly as blood streamed down his face, gave an evil laugh as he took careful aim and pressed his finger to the trigger.

Before he could squeeze off a shot, there was a tremendous roar of gunfire, that seemed to echo and re-echo through the frozen stillness. He stiffened, then looked beyond Chance to where Maggie stood leaning weakly against the trunk of the tree. In her hand was his pistol.

With a look of surprise mingled with pain he dropped to the ground.

"That one was for Eve," Maggie said as tears ran in little rivers down her cheeks.

The gun slipped from her fingers and she slid bonelessly to the ground.

Chapter 15

"Oh, Chance." Maggie couldn't stop shivering. "What have I done?"

Chance wrapped his cowhide jacket around her and lifted her into his arms. "Shh. It's over now, Maggie. It's all over."

"But I've killed a man."

"Don't think about it." He pressed his lips to her temple and closed his eyes. He'd come so close to losing her. So close. Relief rocketed through him.

"But you don't understand." Her teeth were chattering so badly, she could barely get the words out. "I'm no better than he was. I hated Ray for what he did to Eve. For what he almost did to us. And I wanted him dead. Oh, Chance. I killed him."

"Shh. Oh, baby. It's all right." He wondered if his heart would ever return to its normal rhythm. He felt as if he'd been running up a mountain for hours. And now, even when he'd reached the peak, he was afraid to stop.

Afraid if he did, he'd find that it was all a dream. That she wasn't really here, safe in his arms, and he'd have to start climbing all over again until he found her. "All I know is, you're safe. And I'm alive because of your courage. You were so brave."

She shook her head. "I wasn't brave. Just desperate."

"That's good enough for me. Either way, you saved my life."

"And you saved mine." She buried her lips in his throat and shivered again. "He was going to kill me. Not because of something I'd done, but just for the sake of money. If he'd given me a chance, I'd have gladly turned the restaurant over to him. Especially if it would have given my sister back to me. But it can't." She began weeping again. "Oh, Chance. Nothing will ever bring Eve back. Why did he have to kill Eve? Why couldn't he have let her live?"

"I don't know, Maggie." Out of the corner of his eye he saw Brady Warren come barreling out of the woods and suddenly halt when he reached the clearing.

Brady stared around with a look of complete disbelief. "I heard gunshots."

"Yeah." Chance turned, keeping Maggie firmly against his chest. He wasn't about to let go of her.

Brady glanced at the bloody figure in the snow. "Is that guy…?"

Chance nodded. "He's dead. Think you can get the chopper up in this weather?"

Brady looked dazed. "I can try. How about your truck?"

"We'll deal with it later. Right now, I'd like to get Maggie back to the ranch as soon as possible."

Brady needed no coaxing to get away from the

bloody scene. As he spun away, Chance trudged through the snow behind him, keeping a firm grip on the woman in his arms.

If he had his way, he'd never let go of her again.

Maggie could have wept when the ranch house came into view. It occurred to her that the Double W had, in these short weeks, begun to feel like home to her.

As soon as the chopper had landed, Chance climbed down and carried Maggie across the space that separated the landing pad from the ranch house.

When they stepped through the door, they were greeted by a scene that was sheer bedlam.

Ace had dropped everything to return from Colorado. He was shouting into a telephone. The pilot and crew of the medevac team sat crowded around the big open fireplace, along with two uniformed state police officers and two men in suits, as well as a reporter and a photographer from the *Wyoming Report*.

Agnes Tallfeather was moving among them, handing out mugs of coffee as thick as mud. Most were set aside after a single taste.

All conversation came to an abrupt halt at the sight of Chance and Maggie.

Ace and Hazard came rushing toward them, then stopped short.

"Blood?" Hazard's eyes narrowed on Maggie. "Has she been shot?"

"No." Chance lowered her to the sofa. "I need some blankets."

Hazard snatched an afghan from the foot of the sofa and began tucking it around her. "Where's Collier? Don't tell me he got away."

Chance shook his head. "We left him out by the old trail."

"You did what?" Ace's jaw dropped.

"Don't worry. He's not going anywhere." Chance knelt beside the sofa and began rubbing Maggie's hands together between his.

Grateful for the warmth, she closed her eyes. At once, nightmare images began playing through her mind.

One of the uniformed officers stepped forward. "Mr. Wilde, I'm Detective Frank Hinson. The medevac team alerted us that there had been an injury as a result of a crime committed here at your ranch."

"That's right." In a few terse words Chance told him what had happened, aware that the reporter was jotting down every word. "If it weren't for Maggie, I wouldn't be here now. She saved my life."

Cody leaned over the back of the sofa to pat Maggie's shoulder. "That's my girl, Maggie Fuller. I knew the first time I met you that you were a tough little survivor."

Her eyes snapped open. "Cody. You're alive." Her voice caught in her throat. "Ray told me he'd killed you." One big tear squeezed from the corner of her eye.

Seeing it, the old man pressed a big hand to her shoulder. "Hey, now. Don't you worry. He gave it a good try. Lucky for me I've got a very hard head."

Chance fixed him with a look. "What're you doing here? Why aren't you resting on a stretcher somewhere? Aren't the medevac doctors taking you to the hospital?"

"They tried. I wouldn't let them touch me." The old cowboy grinned. "Who needs them when I've got Hazard? I figure if he can doctor all those cows, he can do the same for me."

Hazard met his brother's look and rolled his eyes.

"You know how stubborn he is. Not only would he not let the medics touch him, but he wasn't about to let them take him back to Cheyenne without knowing whether you and Maggie were safe. I'm lucky he even let me patch him up. If I hadn't physically restrained him, he was going to saddle up and head out after you with a string of horses."

"Hell, that's how we did it in your father's day. We didn't worry about getting stuck in snowbanks, or having some big, fancy whirlybird brought down by a blizzard. As long as we had our horse, our rifle and a jug of brew, we could survive anything." The old man's eyes twinkled. "I miss those days."

Ace's tone was warm with laughter. "I just bet you do." In an aside he muttered, "The truth is, I was just about ready to join you."

The detective crossed the room and peered down at Maggie. "I'll need a statement, Ms. Trainor. That is your name, isn't it? Margaret Mary Trainor?"

"Yes, it is." She opened her eyes and took in a deep breath. It would seem that she was about to bounce from one problem to another, without any time to clear her mind.

"I'm told that you're being sought by Chicago authorities. These gentlemen," he turned, indicating the two men in suits, "would like to ask you a few questions."

Chance glowered at the intruders. "Can't this wait? Do you have any idea what she's been through?"

"Sorry, Mr. Wilde. We'll be as brief as possible. But we have to do our job."

With a sigh of resignation, Chance sat beside Maggie and held her hand as she answered dozens of questions about the ownership and operation of the restaurant. She

studied documents, examined records, identified her signature and pointed out the forgeries. Through it all, she
clung to Chance's hand, grateful for his quiet strength.

At last, satisfied that they'd heard enough, the inves-
tigators offered their handshakes. "Thank you, Ms.
Trainor. You understand that you'll have to return with
us to Chicago and give an official statement?"

She nodded.

"There's something else." The investigator shot a
quick worried look at Chance's tight, angry features before saying, "We'll need to exhume your sister's body
in order to confirm that she did indeed die not of natural
causes but at the hands of Ray Collier."

Maggie took a deep, painful breath. "I understand."

She was grateful when, a short time later, they turned
their attention to Brady Warren, asking him to take
them to the location of Ray Collier's body.

While the others were occupied, she made her way
to the kitchen. She would make herself a cup of tea and
pray it would dispel the cold that seemed to have settled
deep into her bones.

Chance ducked inside, out of the bitter cold. Once
the snow had let up the medevac team had headed back
to Cheyenne aboard their helicopter, Brady had taken
the police officers to retrieve Collier's body and ex-
amine the site and the journalist and photographer from
the *Wyoming Report* had been delighted to be allowed
to accompany them to take official photographs. Chance
had no doubt the entire story would make the front page
of tomorrow's edition. He gave a sigh of resignation.
Though he knew Maggie would resent the notoriety,
there were more important things she had to deal with.
Besides, given enough time, the press would uncover a

newer, juicier scandal and this would all fade from the interest of a fickle public. Then, the only one who would remember and grieve would be Maggie.

He stepped into the great room and glanced around. It was empty. He wasn't surprised. He figured by now she was probably collapsed in her bed.

When Agnes waddled in he turned. "Is Maggie asleep?"

The old woman shook her head, sending her braids swinging. "You better take a look at her. I don't like the way she looks."

"What do you mean?"

"She's just not acting right. See for yourself."

Chance made his way down the hall. When he opened the kitchen door, he stared around in surprise.

The rich fragrance of cinnamon rolls baking in the oven filled the room. Mugs of hot chocolate stood in a neat row on the counter, their steam rising to add to the perfume.

Maggie, still wearing the damp, bloody clothes, was scrubbing the blackened pot that had held the sauce for the steaks. Not just scrubbing it, but attacking it with a vengeance.

"Maggie."

She made no response.

"Maggie. Agnes said you were in here. What are you doing?"

She seemed not to hear him.

He stepped closer. "Maggie. What the hell are you doing?"

She didn't even pause in her work, but kept scrubbing, even though her knuckles were raw and bloody.

"Maggie." He crossed to her and wrapped his arms

around her, forcibly stilling her movements. "Oh, baby. What's wrong?"

"Wrong? Nothing's wrong." She shook off his hands and returned to her work. "I just have to clean up this mess."

"Let it go, Maggie."

"There's nothing to let go. I simply can't stand looking at this mess. Don't worry. I'll have it cleaned up in no time."

"And the food?"

She glanced idly at the cinnamon rolls and hot chocolate, as if seeing them for the first time. Her eyes seemed a little too bright. And her voice, when she spoke, was far too controlled. "Comfort food. Those men have been out in the cold. They'll need something to warm them."

"And what about you?"

"I'm fine." She turned away and continued her task. "I'm just fine."

"Yes, you are." He wrapped his arms around her again, and this time he pressed his lips to her temple. "You're the finest woman I've ever known, Maggie. But your work's over for the day."

"No. I have to…"

"Don't argue." He scooped her into his arms and headed toward her room.

"But the work…"

He made no reply.

In the bathroom he turned on the shower, then undressed her and held her under the warm spray. He shampooed her hair, then washed away all the blood that had seeped through her shirt. And as he gently dried her, he saw the bruises around her wrist and felt the bitter bile of fury. With an effort, he was able to swallow it back. Right now, Maggie didn't need any display of temper. What she needed was tenderness. And so he tenderly wrapped her in a bath sheet, and carried her to bed, settling her under a warm down quilt. Then he lay beside her and gathered her into his arms.

As if in a trance she whispered, "They're going to exhume Eve's body."

"I know." He stroked her back, her hair, and felt the way she held herself, stiff and rigid.

"But they…" she struggled to get the words out. It was important that she keep talking. To hold all the strange, terrifying feelings at bay. "They said they believe me. They had proof that Ray had preyed on other women. And that this young socialite would have been his next victim, if I hadn't…" She stopped. Swallowed.

"Let it out, Maggie." Chance pressed his mouth to her forehead. "Let it all out."

"I can't. I'm afraid if I do…" She took a deep breath and felt the tears burning the back of her throat. "Oh, Chance. What did I do?"

"You did what you had to, in order to survive."

"But I killed him. That makes me no better than him."

"It isn't the same, Maggie. If you hadn't shot him, he'd have killed us both. I don't know about you, but I'm so glad to be here beside you. Warm and safe."

"Warm and safe." She repeated the words, needing the reassurance. "We are, aren't we? Warm and safe." She touched a hand to his face, as though seeing him for the first time. "You're really here, aren't you, Chance?"

"I'm here, Maggie. I'm not leaving you. I'm never leaving you."

In the end, it was the tenderness that was her undoing. Overwhelmed by it, she gave in to the feelings of shock, of grief, of unbelievable sadness. And finally, after holding it all inside for so long, she wept bitter, cleansing tears, until there were none left.

"What do you mean, Maggie's leaving?" The following morning Ace stood in the doorway of the kitchen.

It looked as it always did. Glasses of fresh juice lined up on the gleaming countertop. A pot of freshly ground, freshly brewed coffee filling the room with the most amazing fragrance. But Maggie wasn't standing at the stove, making something wonderful for their breakfast. The day had gone suddenly flat.

"She has to go back to Chicago and make an official police report on Ray, so she can be done with that chapter of her life."

"And then?" Hazard stood beside Ace, voicing the question that troubled all of them.

Both brothers saw the way Chance's jaw tightened.

"I don't know. Maggie doesn't want to commit to anything until she can put the past behind her. My guess is, without Collier around, her restaurant will prove to be a success."

"You mean, you think she'll stay in Chicago? You don't think she'll come back here?"

Chance's tone was bleak. "I don't know what to think."

He'd been up since dawn, pacing. And watching her sleep.

"Where does that leave us?" Ace blurted.

"Us?"

At Chance's cold look, he tucked his hands in his pockets and shrugged. "It was pretty easy to get accustomed to all that good food. I don't think I could go back to Cody's chili or Hazard's overcooked burgers. And especially not to Agnes's coffee.''

Hazard punched him hard enough to rattle a few bones. "Why don't you go dig a few new mines or something?"

"Hey." Ace returned the punch, sending Hazard backward against the counter. "All I'm saying is, I got used to Maggie's cooking, and I don't want to lose her."

"You think Chance does?" Hazard reared back, ready to send his little brother into next week.

Ace looked over at Chance. "If you don't want to lose Maggie, you'd better do something about it fast, pal."

"What would you suggest? You think I should tie her up and hold her against her will?"

"That's a start." Ace shot him a grin that had him gritting his teeth. "Or you could start with a little honesty."

"Such as?" Chance could feel his temper heating up. When it reached the boiling point, he'd be happy to unleash it on whichever brother happened to be the closest to his fist.

Ace saw Maggie just stepping into the room. He dropped his hands to his sides and grinned. "I'll leave that to you to figure out, bro."

He ambled out of the room with Hazard right behind him. When the door closed, he halted, then leaned his ear against the door. When he felt a big hand close over his shoulder, he looked up with a frown.

"Hey. You can't blame a guy for trying to eavesdrop."

Instead of yanking him away, Hazard surprised him

by crowding in beside him. "Try to zip that lip, Ace. I don't want to miss a single word. This ought to be good."

Maggie stood across the room, staring around as if memorizing every detail. When she finally turned to Chance, she felt her heart do a series of somersaults. Even though she'd tried to prepare herself for this, she was afraid she wouldn't get through it without tears. She squared her shoulders, determined not to embarrass herself.

"I want you to know how sorry I am, Chance."

"Sorry?" He stood where he was, afraid to get too close. If he did, he'd have to touch her. And if he touched her, there was no way he'd ever stop.

"For bringing my troubles to your doorstep. You and your brothers deserved better."

"We're big boys, Maggie. We can take care of ourselves."

"I know." She took a deep breath and stared down at her hands. "I'll…think of you and the Double W often in the years to come."

"How comforting. We'll get the crumbs of your thoughts after you've spent the day making fancy dinners at that fancy restaurant?"

At his sharp tone, she looked up.

"You're angry!"

"You're damned right I am."

"But you just said…"

"Not about that. About the fact that you'd consider leaving without a thought to my feelings."

"But I have to go. You heard the detectives. They need the truth about Ray. And they're going to have to exhume…" She couldn't bring herself to say it.

"And you think I'm going to just let you walk out the door and go through all that alone?"

She blinked. "I won't ask you to leave all this. Your home. Your brothers. The demands of your job. You can't turn your back on all this just so you can hold my hand."

"And why not? Isn't that what people do when they love each other?" He took a step closer and saw the wary confusion in her eyes.

"Love? You never said anything about love."

"Maybe I...maybe I forgot to mention that. There just never seemed to be the right time."

Time, he thought with a frown. It was time to put into words all the things that were in his heart. If he didn't say them now, there wouldn't be a next time.

His tone deepened. "We're a team now, Maggie. When you hurt, I bleed. I'm not letting you go to Chicago without me."

"But this could take weeks."

"I don't care if it takes months. Years."

"You'd..." she stared up into his eyes and felt a jolt at the look of steely determination, "...you'd do that for me?"

"I'd like to do a whole lot more." He reached out a hand and caught a wisp of dark hair between his fingers. "Ace suggested I hog-tie you and keep you here by force. I'd try it if I thought it would work. But I know you have to see this through, so we'll see it together. But when it's over, if you're willing, I'd like you to come back to the Double W with me and live here as my wife."

"Wife?" She knew she sounded like a parrot, but she couldn't help herself. She simply couldn't think of a thing to say. This wasn't at all what she'd been expecting. She'd been steeling herself for a stilted good-bye. And now... "You're...proposing?"

"I know for a city girl life in Wyoming must seem pretty tame. You'll miss the excitement of the big city. And the challenge of a successful restaurant. Out here we're hemmed in by snow and ice half the year. But whenever it gets to be too much for you, I promise you, I'll fly you to some tropical island, and we'll play in the sun and surf until you've had enough."

"You'd do that for me?" He was so solemn, so serious. She tried not to laugh. "I guess I could get used to that."

"And don't worry about the isolation. Even though we're miles from our nearest neighbor, we can be anywhere in the world in a matter of hours. All you need to do is say the word and I'll call up the jet or the chopper."

"Isolation isn't so bad, Chance. It could make for some...interesting evenings."

He saw the smile in her eyes and felt the sudden quickening of his pulse. Maybe, just maybe, she could be persuaded.

He allowed himself to touch her. Just the curve of her shoulder. At the first touch, he felt her tremble. "You won't mind giving up the restaurant?"

She shook her head.

"I know it won't be easy, Maggie. I'm sure you'll miss the challenge of preparing exotic meals for hundreds of people."

"I don't know. Cooking for you and your brothers has become something of a challenge. And I suppose, when the spirit moves me, I could always start catering to the cowboys in the bunkhouse."

"So." He stared down into her eyes, trying to read her thoughts. "Is that a yes?"

She was too overcome for words. All she could do was nod her head.

As he bent to claim her lips, the door was shoved open.

"Was that a yes?" Ace demanded.

"I don't know." Hazard was grinning from ear to ear. "I didn't hear what Maggie said. But I think, by the smile on our big brother's face, that she's agreed."

Chance's smile faded. He shot them both withering looks. "Do you want to die?"

"No. What we want is a wedding. The sooner the better." Hazard hurried across the room to pat Maggie's shoulder. "You won't be sorry, Maggie. We've never had a sister. But I promise you, we'll be the best brothers in the world."

"We're not just gaining a sister," Ace said with a yelp of enthusiasm. "We're gaining a cook."

Chance grabbed him by the front of the shirt and dragged him close. "If you're not out of here by the count of ten, you won't be alive to enjoy her cooking."

Ace threw up his hands. "I'm going. I'm going."

As he backed away, his grin returned. He and Hazard dropped their arms around each other's shoulders and sauntered away.

Over his shoulder Ace added, "I never thought I'd be saying this, Maggie. To you or any woman. The way Chance felt about committing to marriage, we figured he'd be an old man before some woman snagged his heart. Anyway, welcome to the family, Maggie. I mean that from the bottom of my heart."

"That goes double for me, Maggie," Hazard called.

Chance was still frowning when the door closed behind them. Then he turned back to Maggie and burst into a roar of laughter.

"He's right, you know. I never thought I'd be saying this either. And I do mean it from the bottom of my heart." He dragged her close and muttered against her lips, "Welcome to the family, Margaret Mary Trainor. And be warned. I never intend to let you go."

"Promise?"

"Cross my heart." With a solemn look he made a cross over his heart, then drew her into the circle of his arms.

And then there was no need for words. As they came together, Maggie felt the familiar rush of heat and thrilled to it. The press of his lips on hers told her everything she'd ever wanted to know.

Epilogue

"Hold still." Ace, already dressed in a tuxedo, stood beside Chance and fumbled with his French cuffs. "Why do they make these cuff links too big for the buttonholes?"

"To test a man's patience." Chance scowled at his reflection in the mirror. "I don't know why we couldn't have been married in jeans and boots."

"No sense fighting it." Hazard finished tying his brother's tie, then stood back to admire his handiwork. "It's a female thing. You say wedding, they think fairy tale. And you, Prince Charming, just have to go along."

Chance stalked to the window to watch the parade of cars and trucks rolling up the drive. A dozen wranglers had been pressed into service to act as valets. "Look out there. Half the town of Prosperous."

"Not half the town, bro." Ace grinned. "The whole town. And half the state of Wyoming is invited to watch you tie the knot."

After a quick rap on the door, it swung open to admit Cody. "Well, don't you three look spiffy?"

Chance snarled, "We look like—"

Hazard interrupted. "How's the bride-to-be holding up?"

"That lady's absolutely amazing. Agnes and Thelma had to drag her into her room to get dressed. She was still arranging those trays of fancy canapés and telling the girls from town just how she wanted them served." He shook his head. "And the wedding cake she fixed— it looks like some kind of fairy castle, with white-frosted towers."

Ace turned to Chance. "See? I told you. A fairy tale. And you're her knight in shining armor."

"A knight? I look like a damned—"

Cody dropped a hand to his shoulder. "Getting cold feet?"

Chance shook his head. "Not about marrying Maggie. Hell, I'd walk through the town of Prosperous buck naked, if that's what she wanted. But I just want this over with."

"Yeah." Ace shot a look at Hazard. "Then comes the good part. So, what island paradise did you two decide on for the honeymoon?"

"You don't think I'm going to tell you. After two beers at Clancy's, you'd blab it to the whole town. And with my luck, I'd find some reporter from the *Wyoming Report* outside my room with a camera and a microphone." Chance began to pace. "How much longer?"

Ace glanced at his watch. "Reverend Young said he'd be here promptly at noon."

"That's another thing." Chance stopped his pacing. "Maggie insisted on inviting him to offer the service. I tried to warn her about how long-winded he can be.

Always in that same monotone. But she wants tradition. When she found out he officiated at Dad's wedding and his funeral, she became hell-bent on having him officiate at ours, too.''

''Let's hope your funeral can wait a few years.'' Hazard opened a box of cigars on his brother's desk and passed them around. ''As long as we have to kill time in here, why not enjoy ourselves?''

While he flipped open a lighter, Ace took down a dusty bottle of whiskey and filled four tumblers.

''Since we're drinking from Dad's stash, let's drink the first one to him.''

The four men lifted their glasses.

''To Dad,'' Chance said solemnly. ''And to his legacy.''

Cody watched as the three brothers downed their drinks in one long swallow. Then he followed suit. He waited until they refilled the tumblers, then said, ''And now I'd like to offer a toast. I've watched the three of you grow into fine men that your dad would be proud of. I know you always thought this land was the legacy he left you. Maybe that was part of it. But the real legacy is what the three of you share. The best thing your father could have given you is each other. So here's to the Wildes of Wyoming. Long may you live.''

They tilted their heads back and drank.

Suddenly Chance set his glass down with a clatter and headed toward the door.

''Hey. Where are you going?'' Hazard demanded. ''We're not finished yet.''

''Yes, we are. I'm not waiting another minute. I want to see Maggie right now.''

As he stormed away, Ace turned to Hazard.

''Ten dollars says Agnes and Thelma don't let him

get so much as a glimpse of his bride before the ceremony.''

Hazard shrugged. ''I don't know. He looks pretty determined.'' He turned to Cody. ''What do you think?''

The old cowboy threw back his head and laughed. ''I'm putting my money on Chance. There isn't a locked door that can hold that man back when he's set his mind to something.''

Hazard took some money from his pocket and slapped it into his brother's hand. ''I'm with Cody. I'm putting my money on Chance.''

''What's keeping you two?'' Thelma stopped her pacing long enough to pound on Maggie's bedroom door. ''I'm on my third cigarette. You should have been ready long ago. Why won't you let me help?''

''Keep your shirt on,'' came Agnes's muffled voice from the other room. ''We're just about done.''

A minute later the old woman opened the door with a flourish, then stepped aside to reveal the bride.

''Oh.'' Thelma stubbed out her cigarette, then stared at the vision in white. The gown was a simple column of white silk, with a softly rounded neck and long, tapered sleeves. A small crown of white pearls was nestled in Maggie's dark hair. Fastened to the crown was a veil that spilled around her shoulders. ''Oh, honey. You look so…'' Without warning, Thelma burst into tears.

''Thelma.'' Alarmed, Maggie rushed forward.

Before she could wrap her arms around the older woman, Thelma stepped back. ''No. Don't wrinkle your dress. I'm just being silly. But I can't help it. You look so beautiful. Just the way a bride should look on her wedding day.''

"Thanks, Thelma." Maggie held out a small wrapped box. "This is for you."

"For me?" The older woman tore aside the wrappings, and opened a small jeweler's box. Inside she found a string of pearls and matching earrings. "What's this for?"

Maggie smiled. "It's traditional for the bride to give her attendant a gift."

"Attendant?" Thelma's already painted brows shot up. "Me? You want me to stand up with you?"

"Who else? You're the first person I met when I arrived in Prosperous. You gave me a job and a place to stay. But even more important, you're the reason for today. If you hadn't encouraged me to take this job, I'd never have met Chance."

"Oh, honey." Thelma was crying again. Big wet tears that caused her makeup to smear until she resembled a raccoon.

Maggie turned to Agnes. "And this is for you."

The woman's eyes grew round as she opened the gift to find a similar pearl necklace and earrings. "But why?"

"You're the closest thing Chance has to a mother, Agnes. And that makes you my mother, too."

Agnes blinked hard, but failed to stop the moisture that burned her eyes. "You know, city-girl, I never thought I'd be saying this. But I sure am glad you're staying. I'd hate to think how I'd handle all those hostile cowboys if I had to go back to cooking for them."

Maggie chuckled. "Is that the only reason you're glad I'm marrying Chance?"

The old woman shook her head, fighting the lump in her throat. "There's another reason. I'm not sure I can say it out loud." She sniffed. "Here goes. I never had a daughter. But if I did, I'd want her to be just like you.''

Minutes later, when Chance stormed into Maggie's room, he found himself facing three weeping women who looked like they were about to attend a funeral.

As always, he leaped to Maggie's defense. ''What's going on here? Maggie, if somebody's hurt you…?''

''It's all right.'' She started forward, but Thelma put a hand on her arm to stop her.

''Now just a minute.'' She stepped in front of Maggie, as though shielding her from Chance's view. ''You can't see the bride before the ceremony.''

''The hell I can't.''

''Thelma's right.'' Agnes placed her considerable bulk between Chance and Maggie. ''Now you wait outside with your brothers until the music starts.''

''Maggie.'' Chance's eyes were narrowed with frustration. ''Tell these two mother hens to give us some privacy. Right this minute.'' When she looked as though she might refuse, his eyes darkened with misery. ''Please.'' The word nearly stuck in his throat.

Maggie patted the two women's shoulders, and leaned close to kiss their cheeks. ''Wait outside. We need a minute alone.''

Thelma nodded, then shot a look at Chance. ''One minute. But that's all.''

As she and Agnes stepped from the room, Chance slammed the door and locked it, then leaned against it and stared at the vision that stood before him.

''Losing your nerve, cowboy?''

''Never.'' He shook his head. ''How about you?''

She stepped closer. ''Not a chance. You're stuck with me.''

"Promise?" He caught her hand, and lifted it to his lips.

At once she felt the jolt, and had to press a hand to his chest to steady herself. "Oh, yes. I promise. I'm going to love you until you're tired of me, Chance Wilde."

"That wouldn't happen in three lifetimes." He stared at their linked fingers. "I feel like the luckiest man in the world. To have almost lost you, and then to be given another opportunity…" He shook his head. "I hope you won't feel smothered by the attention I intend to lavish on you."

She laughed. "Go ahead. Lavish all you want."

He drew her close and kissed her, long and slow and deep. As they stepped apart, he rested his forehead on hers. "How am I going to wait for this interminable day to be over?"

"You'll survive." She brushed her lips over his cheek. "Did you tell your brothers where we decided to spend our honeymoon?"

"Are you crazy? If they knew, they'd make pests of themselves. You know how they are. Especially Ace."

She couldn't help laughing at the annoyance she could hear in his tone. "All right. We'll keep it our secret. Did you already take up the supplies?"

He nodded. "Just what I thought was necessary. A case of Dom Perignon. Some steaks to grill on the fire. And I laid in enough firewood that I may not have to leave that range shack for a week." He looked suddenly contrite. "You haven't changed your mind? Are you sure you wouldn't rather go to some island paradise?"

She shook her head. "I can't think of any place I'd rather be with you than in a secluded cabin for two whole weeks."

He paused a beat, then cleared his throat. "I have a confession to make."

"A confession? Sounds ominous." She waited.

"About that trip to San Francisco…"

"What about it?"

He looked genuinely embarrassed. "I took you there because I wanted to impress you."

"I know."

His head came up. "You do?"

She couldn't help laughing at the look of astonishment on his face. "Don't worry. It worked. I was suitably impressed."

"Good." He bent to kiss her, but she put a hand to his chest to hold him at bay. "Now I have a confession of my own."

He arched a brow.

"I made every exotic dish I could think of, just to impress you with my skills."

"You did?"

"Yes."

He threw back his head and roared. "Why, Maggie. You devious woman. It had even more of an impact than my San Francisco trip. But the truth is, even if you couldn't cook a lick, I'd still be hooked. The minute I laid eyes on you, Maggie, I knew you were different from any woman I'd ever known."

As he bent to kiss her again, there was a furious pounding on the door, and the sound of Cody's muffled voice. "Better get a move on, you two lovebirds. Reverend Young is here. And if you don't get this show started soon, he's liable to keep us all afternoon."

That was enough of a threat to have Chance fumbling to unlock the door. As he opened it, he glanced at the flowers he'd set on a hall table. "I almost forgot. These are for you." He handed her a nosegay of white violets.

"Oh, Chance." She buried her face in their fragrance, then lifted shining eyes to him.

Minutes later she placed her hand on his arm and they walked together toward the waiting preacher.

As the guests murmured and whispered about the beautiful woman who had captured the heart of Chance Wilde, his two brothers merely smiled.

Ace turned to Hazard and whispered, "I'll lay another twenty that they won't stay away more than a week."

"Are you crazy? Why would they rush home in a week?"

"Because that's when Simmons expects to have the new contracts ready for the Saudi deal."

Hazard accepted his handshake. "You're on. I say even the Saudi deal won't pry Chance away from his honeymoon with Maggie."

The preacher glared at the two brothers, then launched into one of his long-winded monologues.

Halfway through, Thelma leaned close and whispered, "Reverend Young, I think I smell fire. Maybe you'd better get to the vows."

With a look of confusion the reverend thumbed through the pages until he came to the words he'd been seeking.

Chance breathed a sigh of relief and tightened his grasp on Maggie's hand. His. His woman. His wife. At long last.

He spoke his vows in loud, clear tones, suddenly grateful that so many friends had gathered to share his joy. He caught sight of his brothers standing proudly beside him and winked, before turning to stare into those loving eyes that would forever remind him of warm honey.

As Maggie repeated the words pledging her love, she thought again about how far she'd come. She'd lost her sister, her job and her direction in life. She'd bought a one-way ticket to Wyoming, fearing for her safety. And now, in just a matter of weeks, she'd found everything she'd ever longed for. Her good name had been restored. She'd been given a family, in the form of two brothers, who had already accepted her as one of their own. She had the opportunity to be part of an exciting, vital adventure at the Double W, unlike anything she'd ever known before. And most of all, she'd discovered this wonderful man. A man who would love her, without condition, for all time.

She had the feeling that life with Chance Wilde was about to become the most amazing adventure of all.

*   *   *   *   *

*Read about the irresistible lady
who ropes Hazard Wilde into marriage in*

THE WILDES OF WYOMING—HAZARD

*on sale April 2000
in Intimate Moments.*

INTIMATE MOMENTS®
Silhouette®

Those Marrying McBrides!

THOSE MARRYING McBRIDES!:
The four *single* McBride siblings have always been unlucky in love. But it looks as if their luck is about to change....

Rancher Joe McBride was a man who'd sworn off big-city women. But his vow was about to be sorely tested when he met Angel Wiley. Don't miss A RANCHING MAN (IM #992), Linda Turner's next installment in her *Those Marrying McBrides!* miniseries—on sale in March 2000

And coming in June 2000, *Those Marrying McBrides!* continues with Merry's story in THE BEST MAN (IM #1010).
Available at your favorite retail outlet.

Silhouette®
Where love comes alive™

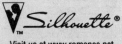

MONTANA
MAVERICKS
Big Sky Brides

Legendary love comes to Whitehorn, Montana,
once more as beloved authors

Christine Rimmer, Jennifer Greene and Cheryl St.John

present three brand-new stories in this exciting anthology!

Meet the Brennan women:
SUZANNA, DIANA and ISABELLE

Strong-willed beauties who find unexpected
love in these irresistible marriage of
covnenience stories.

Don't miss
MONTANA MAVERICKS: BIG SKY BRIDES
On sale in February 2000,
only from Silhouette Books!

Available at your favorite retail outlet.

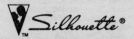

SILHOUETTE'S 20ᵀᴴ ANNIVERSARY CONTEST
OFFICIAL RULES
NO PURCHASE NECESSARY TO ENTER

1. To enter, follow directions published in the offer to which you are responding. Contest begins 1/1/00 and ends on 8/24/00 (the "Promotion Period"). Method of entry may vary. Mailed entries must be postmarked by 8/24/00, and received by 8/31/00.

2. During the Promotion Period, the Contest may be presented via the Internet. Entry via the Internet may be restricted to residents of certain geographic areas that are disclosed on the Web site. To enter via the Internet, if you are a resident of a geographic area in which Internet entry is permissible, follow the directions displayed on-line, including typing your essay of 100 words or fewer telling us "Where In The World Your Love Will Come Alive." On-line entries must be received by 11:59 p.m. Eastern Standard time on 8/24/00. Limit one e-mail entry per person, household and e-mail address per day, per presentation. If you are a resident of a geographic area in which entry via the Internet is permissible, you may, in lieu of submitting an entry on-line, enter by mail, by hand-printing your name, address, telephone number and contest number/name on an 8"x 11" plain piece of paper and telling us in 100 words or fewer "Where In The World Your Love Will Come Alive," and mailing via first-class mail to: Silhouette 20ᵗʰ Anniversary Contest, (in the U.S.) P.O. Box 9069, Buffalo, NY 14269-9069; (In Canada) P.O. Box 637, Fort Erie, Ontario, Canada L2A 5X3. Limit one 8"x 11" mailed entry per person, household and e-mail address per day. On-line and/or 8"x 11" mailed entries received from persons residing in geographic areas in which Internet entry is not permissible will be disqualified. No liability is assumed for lost, late, incomplete, inaccurate, nondelivered or misdirected mail, or misdirected e-mail, for technical, hardware or software failures of any kind, lost or unavailable network connection, or failed, incomplete, garbled or delayed computer transmission or any human error which may occur in the receipt or processing of the entries in the contest.

3. Essays will be judged by a panel of members of the Silhouette editorial and marketing staff based on the following criteria:

   > Sincerity (believability, credibility)—50%
   > Originality (freshness, creativity)—30%
   > Aptness (appropriateness to contest ideas)—20%

   Purchase or acceptance of a product offer does not improve your chances of winning. In the event of a tie, duplicate prizes will be awarded.

4. All entries become the property of Harlequin Enterprises Ltd., and will not be returned. Winner will be determined no later than 10/31/00 and will be notified by mail. Grand Prize winner will be required to sign and return Affidavit of Eligibility within 15 days of receipt of notification. Noncompliance within the time period may result in disqualification and an alternative winner may be selected. All municipal, provincial, federal, state and local laws and regulations apply. Contest open only to residents of the U.S. and Canada who are 18 years of age or older, and is void wherever prohibited by law. Internet entry is restricted solely to residents of those geographical areas in which Internet entry is permissible. Employees of Torstar Corp., their affiliates, agents and members of their immediate families are not eligible. Taxes on the prizes are the sole responsibility of winners. Entry and acceptance of any prize offered constitutes permission to use winner's name, photograph or other likeness for the purposes of advertising, trade and promotion on behalf of Torstar Corp. without further compensation to the winner, unless prohibited by law. Torstar Corp and D.L. Blair, Inc., their parents, affiliates and subsidiaries, are not responsible for errors in printing or electronic presentation of contest or entries. In the event of printing or other errors which may result in unintended prize values or duplication of prizes, all affected contest materials or entries shall be null and void. If for any reason the Internet portion of the contest is not capable of running as planned, including infection by computer virus, bugs, tampering, unauthorized intervention, fraud, technical failures, or any other causes beyond the control of Torstar Corp. which corrupt or affect the administration, secrecy, fairness, integrity or proper conduct of the contest, Torstar Corp. reserves the right, at its sole discretion, to disqualify any individual who tampers with the entry process and to cancel, terminate, modify or suspend the contest or the Internet portion thereof. In the event of a dispute regarding an on-line entry, the entry will be deemed submitted by the authorized holder of the e-mail account submitted at the time of entry. Authorized account holder is defined as the natural person who is assigned to an e-mail address by an Internet access provider, on-line service provider or other organization that is responsible for arranging e-mail address for the domain associated with the submitted e-mail address.

5. Prizes: Grand Prize—a $10,000 vacation to anywhere in the world. Travelers (at least one must be 18 years of age or older) or parent or guardian if one traveler is a minor, must sign and return a Release of Liability prior to departure. Travel must be completed by December 31, 2001, and is subject to space and accommodations availability. Two hundred (200) Second Prizes—a two-book limited edition autographed collector set from one of the Silhouette Anniversary authors: Nora Roberts, Diana Palmer, Linda Howard or Annette Broadrick (value $10.00 each set). All prizes are valued in U.S. dollars.

6. For a list of winners (available after 10/31/00), send a self-addressed, stamped envelope to: Harlequin Silhouette 20ᵗʰ Anniversary Winners, P.O. Box 4200, Blair, NE 68009-4200.

Contest sponsored by Torstar Corp., P.O. Box 9042, Buffalo, NY 14269-9042.

ENTER FOR
A CHANCE TO WIN*

Silhouette's 20th Anniversary Contest

Tell Us Where in the World
You Would Like *Your* Love To Come Alive...
And We'll Send the Lucky Winner There!

Silhouette wants to take you wherever
your happy ending can come true.

Here's how to enter: Tell us, in 100 words or less,
where you want to go to make your love come alive!

In addition to the grand prize, there will be 200
runner-up prizes, collector's-edition book sets
autographed by one of the Silhouette anniversary
authors: **Nora Roberts, Diana Palmer,
Linda Howard** or **Annette Broadrick**.

DON'T MISS YOUR CHANCE TO WIN!
ENTER NOW! No Purchase Necessary

Silhouette®
Where love comes alive™

Name:

Address:

City: State/Province:

Zip/Postal Code:

Mail to Harlequin Books: **In the U.S.**: P.O. Box 9069, Buffalo, NY
14269-9069; **In Canada**: P.O. Box 637, Fort Erie, Ontario, L4A 5X3

*No purchase necessary—for contest details send a self-addressed stamped envelope to:
Silhouette's 20th Anniversary Contest, P.O. Box 9069, Buffalo, NY, 14269-9069 (include
contest name on self-addressed envelope). Residents of Washington and Vermont may
omit postage. Open to Cdn. (excluding Quebec) and U.S. residents who are 18 or over.
Void where prohibited. Contest ends August 31, 2000.

PS20CON_R